THE WORST PART WAS I DIDN'T EVEN *remember* who killed me. There were whole chunks of my life missing, and I was left wondering who I'd been, what I'd done, and who I'd pissed off so much that they'd murdered me and then tricked my sister into assuming my identity.

There were so many suspects, but one lingered in my mind: Thayer Vega, Madeline's estranged brother, who'd skipped town last spring. His name kept popping up and rumors swirled that he and I were somehow involved. Naturally, I couldn't remember a thing about Thayer himself, but I knew that whatever he had meant to me in life was wrapped up in mystery—and danger.

But no matter how hard I tried, I couldn't remember what that danger was.

BOOKS BY SARA SHEPARD

Pretty Little Liars
Flawless
Perfect
Unbelievable
Wicked
Killer
Heartless
Wanted
Twisted
Ruthless
Stunning
Burned

Pretty Little Secrets
Ali's Pretty Little Lies

The Lying Game
Never Have I Ever
Two Truths and a Lie
Hide and Seek
Cross My Heart, Hope to Die

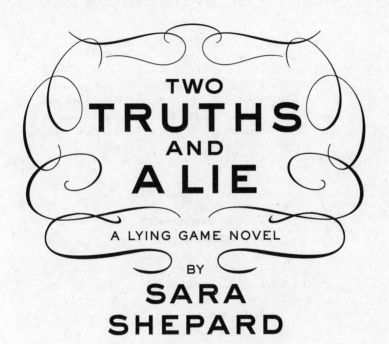

TWO
TRUTHS
AND
A LIE

A LYING GAME NOVEL

BY

SARA
SHEPARD

HARPER TEEN
An Imprint of HarperCollinsPublishers

HarperTeen is an imprint of HarperCollins Publishers.

Two Truths and a Lie

Produced by Alloy Entertainment
151 West 26th Street, New York, NY 10001

Library of Congress Cataloging-in-Publication Data
Shepard, Sara, 1977-
    Two truths and a lie / Sara Shepard. — 1st ed.
        p.   cm. — (A lying game novel ; #3)
    Summary: Now that troubled Thayer Vega is back in town, Emma
Paxton must struggle to figure out the relationship her twin has with
him . . . and whether he may have been the one to kill her.
    ISBN 978-0-06-186975-4 (pbk.)
    [1.   Twins—Fiction.   2.   Sisters—Fiction.   3.   Murder—Fiction.
4. Dead—Fiction.   5. Impersonation—Fiction.   6. Mystery and detective
stories.]   I. Title.
PZ7.S54324Two   2012   2011052411
[Fic]—dc23   CIP
                                                                    AC

Design by Liz Dresner

13 14 15 16   LP/RRDH   10 9 8 7 6 5 4 3 2 1
❖
First paperback edition, 2013

A half-truth is a whole lie.

—YIDDISH PROVERB

PROLOGUE

AN UNWANTED VISITOR

If anyone had peeked through my window, they would have thought it was just a normal slumber party, a festive night that involved popcorn, manicures, and six gorgeous girls from the most exclusive clique at Hollier High giving each other makeovers, sharing juicy gossip, and plotting their next prank for the Lying Game. My iPhone had dozens of photos of past sleepovers that looked exactly like it: a shot of my best friend, Madeline, holding up a picture of a model with fringe bangs and asking if the look would flatter her heart-shaped face; one of my other besties, Charlotte, sucking in her cheeks to apply the new shade of blush she'd bought at Sephora; one of my adoptive sister, Laurel, snickering at a D-list celeb in *Us Weekly*; and plenty of photos of me, Sutton Mercer, looking like the glamorous, powerful "It girl" I was.

But on this particular night, something was different . . . and five out of the six girls didn't even know it. The girl my best friends were laughing with, the girl they thought was me . . . *wasn't*. Because I was dead. My BFFs were talking to my long-lost twin, Emma, who'd taken my place.

I'd died a month ago and was now perched somewhere between the land of the living and the great beyond, watching my life continue, but with Emma as the star. Everywhere she went, I went, like we were still sharing the same womb. Bizarre, right? I didn't think the afterlife would be like this either.

That night, I watched as my twin sister sat among my friends. Her legs were curled beneath her on the plush white sofa in the exact same way I used to sit. Her heavy-lidded eyes sparkled with my favorite silver MAC shadow. She even laughed the same way I did—loud, staccato, and a bit sarcastic. Over the past month she had perfected my mannerisms, answered to my name, and worn my clothes, all with the aim of being me until my murderer was exposed.

The worst part? I didn't even *remember* who killed me. There were whole chunks of my life that had been wiped clean from my mind, and I was left wondering who I'd been, what I'd done, and who I'd pissed off so much that they'd murdered me and then tricked my sister into assuming my identity. Every once in a while I would get a sudden flash of lucidity and a whole scene would snap into brilliant clarity, but the moments before and after it? Complete blanks. It was like getting a few random screen-grabs from a ninety-minute movie and trying to make sense of the entire plot. If I wanted to find out what had happened to me, I would have to rely on Emma . . . and hope that she caught my killer before my killer caught her.

There were some things Emma and I had figured out: My friends all had alibis for the night I died. As did Laurel, meaning they were all cleared. But there were so many suspects left. A particular one lingered in both our minds: Thayer Vega, Madeline's estranged brother, who'd skipped town last spring. His name kept popping up, and rumors swirled that he and I were somehow involved. Naturally, I couldn't remember a thing about Thayer himself, but I could tell *something* had happened between us. But what?

I watched as my best friends giggled and gossiped and began to wind down. By 2:46 A.M., the lights were low, and each girl's breathing was slow and deep. The iPhone I'd sent hundreds of texts on before I'd died suddenly chimed, and Emma's eyes sprang open as though she were expecting the message. I watched as she checked the screen, frowned, and tiptoed out of the house and across the yard. Ethan Landry, the only person who knew Emma's true identity—apart from my killer, of course—stood waiting for her by the curb. And there, in the moonlit driveway, I watched as they talked, hugged, and shared their very first kiss. Even though I no longer had a body, a heart, I still ached all the same. I would never kiss anyone again.

But then footsteps crunched nearby. Emma and Ethan flew apart worriedly. I was yanked behind Emma as she rushed back inside. I glanced over my shoulder just before she slammed the door, and I saw Ethan running into the night. Then, a shadow passed across the front porch. I could hear Emma's shallow, nervous breathing. I could tell she was scared. With another jolt, I was tugged along as she ran toward the stairs to make sure my bedroom window was locked.

When she and I reached the landing, we both caught a glimpse of the inside of my old bedroom. The window was indeed open, and standing in front of it was a familiar-looking boy. The blood drained from my sister's face as she took in his features. I let out a scream, but it faded noiselessly into the ether.

It was Thayer Vega. He leveled a smirk at Emma that said he knew all of her secrets—including exactly who she *wasn't.* And I could tell, in an instant, that whatever it was he had meant to me in life was wrapped up in mystery— and danger.

But no matter how hard I tried, I couldn't remember what that danger was.

1

SHE'S SEEN HIM

"Thayer," Emma Paxton said, staring at the teenage boy in front of her. His mussed hair looked black in the darkness of Sutton's bedroom. His cheekbones were prominent above his full lips. His deep-set, hazel eyes narrowed sinisterly.

"Hey, Sutton," Thayer said, drawing the name out.

A nervous chill ran down Emma's spine. She recognized Thayer Vega from his missing person posters—he'd vanished from Tucson, Arizona, in June. But that was long before Emma had made the trek to Tucson to reunite with her long-lost twin sister, Sutton. Long before she'd received an anonymous note saying that Sutton was dead and that Emma had to take her place, and tell no one . . . or else.

Emma had scrambled to figure everything out about Sutton on the spot—who her friends were, who her enemies were, what she liked to wear, what she liked to do, who she was dating. She'd come to Tucson simply to find a family member—a foster child, she was *desperate* for family, *any* family—but now she was mired in solving her sister's murder. It had been a relief to rule out Sutton's closest friends and sister, but Sutton had made a lot of enemies . . . and any number of people could have been her killer.

And Thayer was one of them. Like so many other people in Sutton's life, what Emma knew about him she'd cobbled together from Facebook posts, gossip, and the Help Us Find Thayer website his family had created after he'd skipped town. There was something dangerous about him—everyone said he'd been mixed up in some kind of trouble and had a horrible temper. And according to the rumors, Sutton had something to do with his disappearance.

Or maybe, I wondered, staring at the wild-eyed boy in my room, *Thayer had something to do with mine.* A memory popped into my head. I saw myself standing in Thayer's bedroom, the two of us locked in a bitter stare-off. "Do what you want," I spat, wheeling toward the door. Thayer looked hurt, then his eyes flashed with anger. "Fine," he snapped. "I *will*." I had no idea what the fight was about, but it was obvious I'd really pissed him off.

"What's the matter?" Thayer assessed Emma now, crossing his arms over his toned, soccer-player chest. His knowing expression was identical to the one in his MISSING poster. "Scared of me?"

Emma swallowed hard. "W-why would I be afraid of *you*?" she asked in the toughest voice she could muster, the one she used to reserve for butt-grabbing foster brothers, borderline-personality foster moms, and creepy guys loitering in the dodgy neighborhoods she'd grown up in after our biological mother, Becky, ditched her. But it was all a front. It was almost 3 A.M. on Saturday. Sutton's friends, who were downstairs for a post-Homecoming sleepover, were fast asleep. So were the Mercer parents. Even the family's huge Great Dane, Drake, was snoring away in the master bedroom. In the eerie calm, Emma couldn't help but think of the note she'd received on Laurel's car her first morning in Arizona: *Sutton's dead. Tell no one. Keep playing along . . . or you're next.* And the strong, terrifying hands that had strangled her with Sutton's locket at Charlotte's house a week later, threatening her once again to keep quiet. And the imposing, shadowy figure she'd seen in the high school auditorium just after an overhead light fell inches from her head. What if Thayer was behind all that?

Thayer smirked as though he was reading her mind. "I'm sure you have your reasons." And then he leaned back and stared at her like he could see right through her—like he was why she was here, pretending to be her dead sister.

Emma looked around, assessing her options for escape, but Thayer grabbed her arm before she could put any distance between them. His grip was hard, and she let out an instinctive, piercing scream. Thayer clamped a hand over her mouth. "Are you insane?" he growled.

"Mmm!" Emma moaned, struggling to breathe through Thayer's suffocating hold. He was standing so close that Emma could smell his cinnamon gum and see the tiny freckles that dotted the bridge of his nose. She struggled against him, panic welling in her chest. She bit down hard on his hand, tasting earthy, salty sweat.

Thayer swore and stepped back, letting Emma go. She spun away from him. His elbow crashed into a sea-green vase on Sutton's bookshelf. It tipped over, plummeted to the ground, and shattered into dozens of tiny pieces.

A light flipped on in the hall. "What the hell was that?" a voice called. Footsteps sounded and, seconds later, Sutton's parents burst into the room.

They moved to Emma's side. Mrs. Mercer's hair was mussed and she wore a baggy yellow nightshirt under a robe. Mr. Mercer's white undershirt was messily tucked into blue flannel pajama bottoms and his hair stood out straight from his head in silver-flecked spikes.

As soon as the parents noticed the intruder, their eyes widened. Mr. Mercer inserted himself between Emma and Thayer. Mrs. Mercer wrapped a protective arm around Emma's shoulders and pulled her close. Emma sank gratefully into Sutton's adoptive mother's embrace, rubbing the five angry marks that had popped up on her skin where Thayer had gripped her.

I had mixed feelings about my parents protecting Emma from Thayer. Were they simply worried because she'd screamed . . . or was it because of something more sinister about Thayer himself, something they knew about him from a past run-in?

"You!" Mr. Mercer bellowed at Thayer. "How dare you? How did you get in?"

Thayer just stared at him, a hint of a smirk on his face. Mr. Mercer's nostrils flared. His square jaw was set menacingly, his blue eyes blazed, and a vein stuck out on his temple, visibly throbbing. For a second, Emma wondered if Mr. Mercer assumed Sutton had invited Thayer into her room and was mad that his daughter let a boy in at three in the morning. But then she noticed the way Mr. Mercer and Thayer were crouched, as if ready to fight. It felt like something dark and hate-filled hung in the air between them, something that had nothing to do with Sutton at all.

More footsteps pounded up the stairs. Laurel and Madeline appeared in the doorway, having come from the den where the sleepover was taking place. "What's going on?" Laurel grumbled, rubbing her eyes. Then she caught sight of Thayer. Her light eyes opened wide and she covered her mouth with trembling fingers.

Madeline was dressed in a black camisole and her black hair was pulled back in a perfect bun even though it was the middle of the night. She elbowed her way between Laurel and Mrs. Mercer. Her mouth fell open. She reached out for Laurel's arm as if she might fall to the ground in shock.

"Thayer!" Madeline's voice was shrill, her expression an odd mixture of anger, confusion, and relief. "What are you doing here? Where have you been? Are you okay?"

The muscles in Thayer's arms flexed as he balled his fists. He glanced around at Laurel, Madeline, Emma, and the Mercer parents like he was a wounded animal wanting to flee his attackers. After a beat, he spun on his heel and bolted in the opposite direction. He shot across Sutton's bedroom, hoisting himself out the window and shimmying down the oak tree that served as an escape hatch from Sutton's room. Emma, Laurel, and Madeline flew to the window and watched Thayer scramble through the darkness. His gait was uneven—he favored his left leg with a pronounced limp as he moved across the grass.

"Get back here!" Mr. Mercer screamed, racing from

Sutton's bedroom and banging down the stairs. Emma scampered after him, with Mrs. Mercer, Laurel, and Madeline following behind. Charlotte and the Twitter Twins staggered out from the den, looking sleepy and confused.

Everyone gathered around the open doorway. Mr. Mercer had run halfway across the yard. "I'm calling the cops!" he shouted. "Get back here, damn it!"

No answer came. Tires screeched around the corner. Just like that, Thayer was gone.

Madeline whirled around to stare at Emma. Tears welled in her blue eyes and her face was red and blotchy. "Did you invite him here?"

Emma gasped. "What? No!"

But Madeline sprinted out the door. A few sharp *bleep*s pierced through the air, and Madeline's SUV lights illuminated the darkness.

Laurel shot Emma a pissed-off look. "Now look what you've done."

"I didn't *do* anything," Emma protested.

Laurel looked at the other girls for support. Charlotte cleared her throat. The Twitter Twins fingered the iPhones in their hands, surely itching to post an update about this to their many social-networking sites. Laurel's glare was icy and incredulous, and Emma could guess why. Laurel and Thayer had been best friends before his disappearance, and Laurel had a major crush on him. But Thayer had barely registered Laurel's existence in Sutton's bedroom. From what Emma had gathered over the past few weeks in Tucson, something big had gone on between Sutton and Thayer before he went missing.

"Didn't *do* anything?" Laurel whipped back to face Emma. "You got him in trouble! *Again.*"

Mrs. Mercer ran her hands over her face. "Please, Laurel. Not now." She stepped toward Emma, cinching the belt of the pink terry-cloth bathrobe she'd stopped to grab on her way downstairs. "Sutton, are you alright?"

Laurel rolled her eyes. "Look at her. She's *fine.*"

Finally, Drake, the Great Dane, trotted down the stairs and nudged Mrs. Mercer's hand with his slobbery nose. "Some guard dog you are," Mrs. Mercer muttered. Then she turned back to Emma, Laurel, and the three remaining girls in the foyer. "I think you girls should go home now," she said wearily.

Without a word, Charlotte and the Twitter Twins turned back to the den, presumably to gather up their stuff. Emma's head felt too foggy to follow them, so she trudged back upstairs and took refuge in Sutton's bedroom to get her bearings. The room looked exactly as she'd left it: Old issues of *Vogue* lay neatly stacked on Sutton's bookshelf, necklaces were twined together on her dresser, school notebooks were piled on her white oak desk, and the computer cycled through images of Madeline, Charlotte, Laurel, and Sutton with their arms wrapped around each other—probably celebrating some perfectly pulled-off Lying Game prank. Nothing was missing. Whatever reason Thayer had to break in, it wasn't theft.

Emma sank to the floor, Madeline's hurt look flashing through her mind once more. One thing Thayer definitely *had* stolen was the tenuous peace she'd finally made with Sutton's friends and Laurel. Sutton had ruffled a lot of feathers while she was alive, and it had taken a fair amount of work to repair her relationships.

I bristled at Emma's thoughts. These were *my* friends she was talking about. People *I* had known forever and loved, and who loved *me* back. But even I couldn't deny that I'd made some questionable decisions. I'd stolen Charlotte's boyfriend, Garrett. I'd clearly had some sort of rocky relationship with Madeline's brother. I'd given Gabby a seizure during a Lying Game prank—and then told her sister that if she told anyone what I'd done, I'd make her life in high school a living hell. And I'd been dismissive of Laurel's feelings in too many ways to count. One thing I'd learned being dead was that I'd made a lot of mistakes when I was alive. Mistakes I could never set right. But maybe Emma could.

After a few minutes of deep breathing, Emma slipped out of Sutton's room and slowly went down the stairs.

The scent of roasted hazelnuts greeted her in the kitchen. Sutton's father was staring into a cup of black coffee, his face still twisted into an angry, almost unrecognizable mask. Mrs. Mercer traced circles between his shoulder blades with the tips of her fingers and whispered something into his ear. Laurel stared listlessly out the window, spinning a pineapple suncatcher around.

When Mrs. Mercer noticed Emma, she looked up and gave her a small smile. "The police will be here any minute, Sutton," she said softly.

Emma blinked, wondering how to react. Would Sutton's parents expect her to be relieved by this detail . . . or start vehemently defending Thayer? She settled on an expressionless face, crossing her arms over her chest and staring at Sutton's dad.

"Do you understand how dangerous that boy is?" Mr. Mercer asked, shaking his head.

Emma opened her mouth to speak, but Laurel was faster. She pushed past Emma and gripped the back of one of the wooden chairs that circled the round oak table. "That *boy* is one of my best friends, Dad," she growled. "And did it ever enter your mind that Sutton—not Thayer—is the one causing all the trouble?"

"Excuse me?" Emma squeaked indignantly. "How is this *my* fault?"

They were interrupted by the distant wail of sirens. Mr.

Mercer headed for the hall, and Mrs. Mercer followed. The sirens grew louder and louder until they were right outside of the house. Emma heard a car pull up the drive and saw red and blue lights flashing on the front porch. She was about to follow the Mercer parents into the foyer when Laurel caught her arm.

"You're going to throw Thayer under the bus, aren't you?" Laurel hissed, her eyes blazing.

Emma stared at her. "What are you talking about?"

"I don't know why he always comes to you first," Laurel continued, as if she hadn't heard Emma's question. "You just make his life worse. And you're never there to pick up the pieces. You leave that to me, don't you?"

Emma fiddled with Sutton's locket that hung from her neck, silently begging Laurel to explain herself, but Laurel just glared accusingly. Clearly whatever she was talking about was something Sutton was supposed to know already.

Except . . . I didn't.

"We've got coffee on," Mrs. Mercer's voice echoed from the foyer. Emma turned just in time to see Sutton's parents leading two officers into the kitchen. One of them had red hair and freckles and didn't look much older than Emma. The other was more weathered, with oversized ears and a woodsy cologne. Emma instantly recognized him.

"Hello again, Miss Mercer," the second cop said,

TWO TRUTHS AND A LIE

shooting Emma a weary look. It was Detective Quinlan, the officer who hadn't believed Emma when she had told him her real identity the day she'd arrived in Tucson. He'd assumed the long-lost-twin routine was another one of Sutton's hoaxes—the Tucson police had an entire case file dedicated to Sutton's wrongdoings as part of the Lying Game, a cruel club Sutton and her friends had invented over five years ago, which involved playing pranks on unwitting victims. One of the most horrific pranks involved Sutton pretending that her car had stalled on the train tracks as a commuter train barreled toward her and her friends. It had ended in Gabby's hospitalization for a seizure. Emma had only learned about it last week, after she'd purposely gotten caught shoplifting to get a peek at Sutton's rap sheet. She'd snooped, and she'd scored, but she wasn't exactly looking for more quality moments with the Tucson police force.

Quinlan sank into one of the kitchen chairs. "Why is it that whenever there's a call on my beat you have something to do with it, Miss Mercer?" he said in a tired voice. "Did you organize this meeting with Mr. Vega? Do you know where he's been all this time?"

Emma leaned against the table and glared at Quinlan. He'd had it in for her—er, Sutton—since the day she'd met him. "I didn't do anything wrong," she said quickly, flicking a strand of chestnut brown hair from her shoulder.

Mr. Mercer threw up his hands. "Sutton, *please*," he said. "Cooperate with the police. I want this kid out of our lives for good."

"I told you, I don't *know* anything," Emma argued.

Quinlan turned to Sutton's dad. "We've got three squad cars patrolling the area for Mr. Vega. We'll find him sooner or later. You can be sure of that."

There was something about his threat that made Emma shiver. I shivered right along with her, the same question on both our minds: *But what if Thayer found Emma again first?*

2

A BOY NAMED TROUBLE

"Sutton?" Mrs. Mercer's voice floated upstairs. "Breakfast!"

Emma's eyes slowly opened. It was Saturday morning, and she was lying in Sutton's bed, which was a zillion times more luxurious than any bed she'd ever slept on in her foster homes. She would have thought the plush mattress, thousand-thread-count sheets, down pillows, and satin comforter could ensure a perfect eight hours of sleep every night, but she'd slept fitfully ever since she arrived here. Last night, she'd woken up every thirty minutes to make sure Sutton's window was still locked. Each time she stood at the window ledge, looking out on the perfectly manicured lawn that Thayer had scurried across just hours before, the same thoughts ran through her head, over and over. What if she hadn't screamed? What if the vase hadn't broken? What if Mr. and Mrs. Mercer hadn't barged into Sutton's room when they had? Would Thayer have threatened Emma to her face at last? Would he have told her to stop snooping, or else . . . ?

Long-lost Twin Encounters Crazed, Possibly Murderous Runaway, Emma thought to herself. During her years as a foster kid, she'd gotten into the habit of titling her daily activities with a punchy headline as training for becoming an investigative journalist. She'd recorded the headlines in a notebook and named her newspaper *The Daily Emma*. Since moving to Tucson and taking over Sutton's life, her adventures really *were* newsworthy—not that she could tell anyone about them.

She rolled over, the events from last night flooding into her brain once more. *Could* Thayer be Sutton's killer? His behavior certainly wasn't dispelling her suspicions.

"Sutton?" Mrs. Mercer called again.

The sugary smell of maple syrup and waffles wafted up to Sutton's bedroom, and Emma's stomach rumbled with hunger. "Coming!" she yelled back.

With a groggy yawn, Emma climbed from the bed and pulled an Arizona Cardinals sweatshirt from the top drawer of Sutton's white wooden dresser. She yanked the $34.99 price tag from the collar and slid it over her neck.

The shirt was probably a present from Cardinals über-fan Garrett, who'd been Sutton's boyfriend when she died—now her *ex*-boyfriend after Emma turned down his naked and willing body at Sutton's eighteenth birthday party. There were some things sisters weren't meant to share.

Uh, yeah—like each other's lives. But I guess it was a little too late for that.

Sutton's iPhone buzzed, and Emma checked the screen. A small photo of Ethan Landry appeared in the upper right-hand corner, which made Emma's heart do a flip. ARE YOU OKAY? he wrote. I HEARD THERE WERE COPS AT YOUR HOUSE LAST NIGHT AFTER I LEFT. WHAT HAPPENED?

Emma shut her eyes and tapped her fingers on the keys. LONG STORY. THAYER BROKE IN. SUPER SCARY. MAYBE HE'S A SUSPECT. MEET UP LATER AT THE USUAL PLACE?

AREN'T YOU GROUNDED? Ethan wrote back.

Emma ran her tongue over her teeth. She'd forgotten that the Mercers had grounded her for stealing the purse from Clique last week. They'd only let her go to Homecoming because she'd done well in school—a first for Sutton, apparently. I'LL FIGURE OUT A WAY TO GET OUT, she typed back. SEE YOU AFTER DINNER.

Damn right she'd figure out a way. Other than my murderer, Ethan was the only person who knew who Emma really was, and the two of them had joined forces to try to identify Sutton's killer. He'd definitely want to know about Thayer.

But that wasn't the only reason Emma wanted to see Ethan. After the hubbub of last night, she'd almost forgotten that they'd reconciled . . . and kissed. She was dying to see him and take things to the next level. Ethan was the first real almost-boyfriend Emma had ever had—she'd always been too shy and moved around too much to make an impression on guys—and she wanted it to work out.

I was hoping that it would work out, too. At least *one* of us should find love.

Emma descended the stairs for breakfast, pausing for a moment to stare at the family photographs in the Mercers' hallway. Black-framed photos showed Laurel and Sutton with their arms wrapped around each other at Disneyland, sporting matching neon pink–trimmed ski goggles on a ski trip, and making a sand castle on a beautiful white-sand beach. A more recent one showed Sutton and her dad in front of a British racing-green Volvo, Sutton holding up the key gleefully.

She looked so happy. Carefree. She had a life Emma had always wanted. It was a question that plagued her constantly: Why had Sutton gotten such a wonderful family and friends, while Emma had spent thirteen years in foster homes? Sutton had been adopted into the Mercer family when she was a baby, while Emma had remained with their birth mother, Becky, until she

if their roles had been reversed, and Emm

to live with the Mercers? Would she be de

would she have lived Sutton's life differently,

her privileges?

I gazed at the photos, zeroing in on a recent snapshot of the four of us on the front porch. My mom, my dad, Laurel, and I looked like the picture-perfect family, all of us dressed in white tees and blue jeans, the Tucson sun brilliant in the background. I blended so well with them, my blue eyes almost the same as those of my adoptive mother. I hated when Emma assumed that I'd been a huge, ungrateful brat my whole life. Okay, so maybe I hadn't appreciated my parents as much as I should have. And maybe I'd hurt some people with Lying Game pranks. But did I really deserve to die because of it?

In the kitchen, Mrs. Mercer poured golden batter into a waffle iron. Drake sat patiently beneath her, waiting for the batter to ooze over the sides and drip onto the floor. When Emma appeared in the doorway, Mrs. Mercer glanced up with a pinched, worried expression. The lines around her eyes stood out prominently, and there was just a hint of gray at her temples. The Mercer parents were a little older than most parents she knew, possibly in their late forties or early fifties.

"Are you all right?" Mrs. Mercer asked, shutting the

top to the waffle iron and dropping the whisk back into the batter.

"Uh, fine," Emma murmured, even though she would have felt a lot better if she knew where Thayer was.

A loud *thwack* sounded across the room, and Emma turned to see Laurel sitting at the kitchen table bringing a long silver knife down hard over a ripe, juicy pineapple. Sutton's sister caught her eye and grinned mockingly, holding out a dripping slice. "Some vitamin C?" she asked coldly. The knife glinted menacingly in her other hand.

If it had been a week or so ago, Emma would have been afraid of that knife—Laurel had been in her top-ten suspect list. But Laurel's name had been cleared; she'd been at Nisha Banerjee's sleepover the whole night of Sutton's murder. There was no way she could have done it.

Emma looked at the pineapple and made a face. "No thanks. Pineapple makes me gag."

Mr. Mercer, who was standing by the espresso machine, turned around and gave her a surprised look. "I thought you loved pineapple, Sutton."

A fist inside Emma tightened. Emma hadn't been able to eat pineapple ever since she was ten, when her then foster mother, Shaina, had won a lifetime supply of canned pineapple after submitting a pineapple upside-down cake recipe to a cooking magazine. Emma had been forced to eat the slippery yellow chunks at every meal for six months. Of *course* it would be Sutton's favorite fruit.

It was the little details about Sutton, things she couldn't possibly know, that always tripped her up. Sutton's dad seemed hyper-aware of her gaffes, too—he was the only one who'd questioned Emma about a tiny scar when she'd first arrived in Tucson, one that her twin didn't have. And he always seemed to weigh whatever he had to say to her carefully, as though he were holding back, hiding something. It was like he knew something about his daughter was off, but couldn't quite put his finger on it.

"That was before I found out it was really high in bad-for-you carbs," Emma said quickly, thinking on her feet. It sounded like something Sutton would say.

Steam erupted from the espresso maker on the soap-stone countertop before anyone could respond. Mr. Mercer poured milk into four porcelain mugs printed with pictures of Great Danes much like Drake and then turned to Emma. "The police found Thayer last night. Picked him up trying to hitchhike on the on-ramp to Route 10."

"He's been arrested for unlawful entry," Mrs. Mercer added, adding a stack of waffles to a plate. "But that's not all. Apparently, he had a knife on him—a concealed weapon."

Emma flinched. One wrong move last night and Thayer might have slashed her.

"Quinlan says he resisted arrest," Mr. Mercer went on. "It sounds like he's really in trouble. They're holding him at the precinct for questioning about some other things, too. Like where he's been all this time and why he'd worried his family for so long."

Emma kept her expression neutral, but relief coursed through her body. At least Thayer was in jail, not roaming Tucson. She was safe—for now. With Thayer behind bars, she had time to get to the bottom of his mysterious relationship with Sutton . . . and to figure out if she really needed to be afraid of him.

"Can we visit him in jail?" Laurel asked as she stuffed the spiky stem of the pineapple into the garbage.

Mr. Mercer looked horrified. "Absolutely not." He pointed at both his daughters. "I don't want *either* of you visiting him. I know he was your friend, Laurel, but think about all the fights he got into on the soccer field. And if half those rumors about alcohol and drugs are true, then he's a walking pharmacy. And what was he doing carrying a knife? Trouble follows that kid wherever he goes. I don't want you mixed up with someone like that."

Laurel opened her mouth to protest, but Mrs. Mercer quickly interrupted. "Set the table, will you, sweetie?" There was a wobbly quality to her voice, as if she were trying to smooth everything over and sweep the mess under the rug.

Mrs. Mercer set a heaping mound of Belgian waffles on the kitchen table and filled everyone's glass with orange juice. Mr. Mercer strolled over from the coffee machine and sat down at his regular seat. He sliced a piece of waffle and popped it into his mouth. His eyes were on Emma the whole time. "So. Is there a reason Thayer snuck into your bedroom?" he asked.

Nerves darted through Emma's insides. *Because he might have killed your real daughter? Because he wanted to make sure I wasn't going around telling people about it?*

"You weren't expecting him, were you?" Mr. Mercer continued, his voice sharpening.

Emma lowered her eyes and grabbed for a bottle of Mrs. Butterworth's. "If I was expecting him, I wouldn't have screamed."

"When did you last see him?"

"Last night."

Mr. Mercer sighed exaggeratedly. "*Before* that."

These were questions Emma couldn't answer. She looked around at the table. All three Mercers were staring at her, waiting for her response. Mr. Mercer looked irritated. Mrs. Mercer was nervous. And Laurel's face was a murderous bright red.

"June," Emma blurted. It was the month that all the flyers in the police station and Facebook pages said Thayer went missing. "Just like everyone else."

Mr. Mercer sighed heavily, like he didn't believe her. But before he could say anything else, Mrs. Mercer cleared her throat. "Let's not worry about Thayer Vega anymore," she chirped. "He's in jail—that's what matters."

Mr. Mercer's brow wrinkled. "But—"

"Let's talk about happy things instead, like your birthday party," Mrs. Mercer interrupted. She touched her husband's arm. "It's only a few weeks away. Almost all the plans are complete." Even Emma knew about the plans for Mr. Mercer's birthday party. Mrs. Mercer had been planning the festivities at the Loews Ventana Canyon resort for weeks. Her party to-do lists were scattered around the house on bright yellow Post-its.

Mr. Mercer's face was still a stony grimace. "I told you I didn't want a party."

Mrs. Mercer scoffed. "Everyone wants a party."

"Grandma's coming, right?" Laurel asked after swallowing a slug of orange juice.

Mrs. Mercer nodded. "And you girls know you're welcome to invite your friends," she said. "I've already sent invitations to the Chamberlains and Mr. and Mrs. Vega. And I just ordered the cake from Gianni's, that gourmet baker who did the cake for Mr. Chamberlain's party," Mrs. Mercer went on. "Apparently they're the *best*. It's carrot with a cream cheese frosting. Your favorite!"

Her voice lifted higher and higher. *After Teenage Murder*

Suspect Breaks Into Home, Dutiful Wife Tries to Lighten Mood with Talk of Dessert, Emma thought with a smirk.

"May I be excused?" Laurel asked, even though a whole waffle remained on her plate.

"Sure," Mrs. Mercer said distractedly, her eyes still on her husband's face.

Emma jumped up, too. "I have German homework," she said. "Might as well get an early start on it." This was something Sutton clearly *wouldn't* say, but she was eager for the escape. She carried her dish to the sink and kept her head pointedly down as Laurel brushed past. Laurel muttered something under her breath. Emma was almost positive it was *bitch*.

When she passed by the table again, on her way toward the hall, she felt Mr. Mercer's eyes on her. He was giving her such a suspicious stare that a sharp pain shot through Emma's stomach. Suddenly, her mind flashed back to the look Mr. Mercer and Thayer had exchanged the previous night. Was it just her imagination, or did something big happen between them? Did they have some sort of . . . *history* together? Did Mr. Mercer know something about Thayer—something potentially dangerous—that he wasn't letting on about?

I had to agree—my dad definitely knew something about Thayer. As I followed Emma up the stairs, I caught a glimpse of the mountains outside the window, and two puzzle pieces connected for a brief moment in my mind. I saw spidery branches casting shadows across the packed earth while sticky, late summer air clung to my bare legs. I saw Thayer keeping pace at my side, sliding his arm through mine as we navigated a rocky path in the twilight. I saw him opening his mouth to speak, but the memory scattered before I could hear what he'd been about to say.

But maybe, just maybe, it had been something I hadn't wanted to hear.

3

EVERYONE LOVES A POET

Later that evening, Emma made her way to the local park. Even though it was dusk, there were still lots of people jogging on the dirt paths that wound up toward the mountains, cooking burgers on the public grills, and roughhousing with their dogs on the grass. A radio was playing a Bruno Mars song, and a bunch of kids were splashing each other with water from a fountain.

Just seeing that park made me ache. It was only a few blocks away from my house, and even though I couldn't remember specifics, I knew I'd spent lots of time here. What I wouldn't give to dip my fingers into the cool water of that fountain or bite into a juicy burger hot off the grill—even if it did go straight to my thighs.

There was still a basketball game raging, but all of the tennis courts were dark. Emma walked to the very last one and pushed open the creaky gate. She could just make out a figure lying on the ground near the net. Her heart swelled. It was Ethan.

"Hello?" Emma whispered.

Ethan jumped to his feet and walked toward her, his stride even and calm. His hands were shoved deep into the pockets of his worn Levi's. A tissue-thin T-shirt clung to his strong arms. "Hey," he said. Even in the dark she could tell he was grinning. "Did you sneak out?"

Emma shook her head. "I didn't have to. The Mercers lifted my punishment—I guess all the homework I've been doing changed their minds. But Mr. Mercer asked me a million questions about where I was going." She glanced over her shoulder at the dark trees beyond. "It's a wonder he didn't follow me. Then again, I guess I should be grateful. Nobody's ever cared enough to know where I was at all times." She laughed halfheartedly.

"Not even Becky?" Ethan asked, raising an eyebrow.

Emma gazed out at the twisted trees beyond the court. "Becky left me at a convenience store once, remember? She wasn't exactly a model parent." She felt guilty for trashing her mother. She had some good memories of

Becky—like the time she had let Emma dress up in a silky slip and play Snow White around their hotel room, or the many nights Becky had set up treasure hunts for her—but they'd never make up for how she had abandoned Emma when she needed her most.

"Well, I'm glad you made it," Ethan said, changing the subject.

"Me too," Emma answered.

She met his eyes for a brief moment. There was a long pause, and they both looked down. Emma kicked a loose tennis ball near the net. Ethan jingled change in his pockets. Then he reached out and took her hand. She caught the scent of his spicy aftershave as he leaned in close. "Lights on or off?" he asked. The tennis courts had manual lights—seventy-five cents for every thirty minutes.

"Off," Emma answered, excitement flooding her body.

Ethan tugged her down until they were both lying on the cement. The ground was still warm from the day's heat, and it smelled vaguely of tar and rubber sneakers. Above them, a silvery moon shone. An owl flapped to a high tree branch.

"I can't believe Thayer broke into your house," Ethan said after a beat, holding her close. "Are you okay?"

Emma rested her cheek against his chest, feeling suddenly exhausted. "I'm better now."

"So did Thayer sneak in to see Sutton?"

Emma pulled back and sighed. "I guess so. Unless . . . "

"Unless what?"

"Unless Thayer knows who I really am and came to remind me to stay in line." Just saying the words aloud made Emma shiver.

Ethan hugged his knees to his chest. "You think Thayer killed Sutton?"

"It's definitely possible. He's the only one of her friends we haven't been able to investigate. What do you think was going on between Sutton and Thayer before he ran away?" Emma placed her palm flat on the asphalt, feeling its heat. She needed to touch something solid, something she understood.

An expression of regret crossed Ethan's face. "I don't know," he admitted. "I wish I did, but they weren't my crowd."

"A couple of people hinted that he might've been fooling around with Sutton," Emma said. One of them was Garrett, Sutton's ex—he'd more or less accused Sutton of it at Homecoming on Friday. And Nisha Banerjee had pretty much spelled out how Sutton had stolen Laurel's crush. Then there were the icy glances Laurel had been shooting Emma ever since Thayer had turned up in Sutton's bedroom, and the cryptic thing she'd said. *You just make his life worse.* What was *that* about?

"Then again, other people have made it sound like

Sutton did something that caused Thayer to leave town,"
Emma said slowly.

"I heard something about that." Ethan kicked at a crack
in the court with the heel of his sneaker. "But who knows
if it's true? People only started whispering that recently.
When Thayer first went missing, everyone assumed he'd
just run away to escape his dad. He was always screaming at Thayer during soccer matches and putting a ton of
pressure on him."

Emma winced, remembering something else from the
night of the dance. At Homecoming, Emma had noticed
purple bruises on Madeline's arms. She said they'd come
from her father. She'd also said he was hard on Thayer, too.
The moment had been heart-wrenching, but it also felt
special. It was the first time Emma had had a real, honest
conversation with one of Sutton's friends. She craved that
connection: Other than her best friend, Alex, who lived
in Henderson, Nevada, it had been hard to make many
lasting friends because she'd moved around so much.

I had to admit it made me sort of sad that Emma was
bonding with my bestie. In some ways, Emma was a *better*
version of me, Sutton 2.0, which really stung. Madeline
had never shared her secret about her dad with me—she'd
more or less implied that she thought I didn't care. I'd definitely sensed something was up with Mr. Vega, though.
One night, Charlotte, Laurel, and I had sat in Madeline's

bedroom as Mr. Vega flung pots and pans around the kitchen, screaming at Mads and Thayer about God knows what. When Madeline returned to her room, eyes wide and bloodshot, we'd all pretended nothing had happened. If only I'd taken the time to ask Mads if she was okay. She'd probably given me plenty of clues. My twin was turning out to be a better friend to Mads and Char than I'd ever been—and now there wasn't a thing I could do about it.

Ethan leaned back on his elbows, exposing a taut line of tanned stomach muscles. "Thayer could have left for a reason other than his dad or Sutton. I've heard people say that he was mixed up in some really dangerous stuff."

"Like what? Alcohol? Drugs?" Emma asked, recalling what Mr. Mercer had said.

Ethan shrugged. "It was all just vague gossip. I can try to ask around. Now that he's back, people will definitely be talking about him. It'll just be a matter of separating rumor from fact."

Emma flopped down on the hard court. "Have I mentioned how frustrating this is? I have no idea how to find out exactly what happened between Thayer and Sutton without giving away who I really am."

Ethan linked his fingers through hers. "We'll figure this out. I promise. We're so much closer than we were a month ago."

Gratitude washed over Emma like a wave. "I don't know what I'd do without you."

Ethan waved his free hand. "Stop that. We're in this together." Then he shifted his weight and pulled out a crinkled piece of paper from his back pocket. "Hey . . . so I wanted to ask you . . . Do you have any interest in going to this with me?"

Emma smoothed the creases from the paper. 10TH ANNUAL POETRY SLAM CONTEST, a typewriter font read. The event was in early November. She glanced up at him questioningly.

"I've read my poems at Club Congress the last couple of weeks," Ethan explained. "I just thought it might be nice to have some moral support in the audience for once."

Emma couldn't stop the grin that spread across her face. "You're going to let me hear your poetry?" The very first night she'd met Ethan—which was also the very first night she'd been in Tucson—she'd seen him scribbling poems in a notebook. She'd been dying to read his work but was afraid to ask.

"As long as you don't make fun of it." Ethan ducked his head.

"Of course I won't!" Emma clasped his hand. "I'll absolutely be there."

Ethan's eyes shone. "Seriously?"

Emma nodded, moved by how vulnerable he seemed. Her fingertips touched the inside of his palm. Fireflies sparked in the distance, flitting back and forth between cacti and madrone trees. The wind gusted through the dark pieces of Ethan's hair as he put his arm around Emma's shoulders. Emma inched closer, her knees brushing against the denim of Ethan's jeans. She thought of their kiss last night, of how soft his lips had been on hers. It felt selfish to indulge her feelings for Ethan while her sister's murder remained unsolved, but Ethan was the only thing keeping her sane right now.

And weirdly, watching my sister do something that made her feel so happy made *me* feel sane, too.

Emma leaned forward and tilted her chin. Ethan moved close. But suddenly, a metallic clinking noise rang out from the other side of the fence. Emma whipped around and squinted. A long-legged figure slithered between two oak trees.

"Hello?" she called, her pulse inching up a notch. "Who's there?"

Ethan jumped to his feet, jammed a few quarters into the machine, and turned on the lights. They were so bright that Emma had to shade her eyes for a moment. They both scanned the court, the silence deafening. The basketball game had stopped, and there wasn't even any traffic on the road. How long had it been quiet like this? How loudly had she and Ethan been talking? Had someone heard?

When the figure emerged from the trees, Emma grabbed Ethan's arm and stifled a scream. Then her eyes adjusted. She saw a girl in black leggings, a metallic sports bra, and white sneakers. Her blonde hair was in a high ponytail, and she jogged in place as though she'd just arrived. Emma's mouth dropped open. It was Laurel.

Laurel's eyes widened at Emma and Ethan. After a moment, she raised her hand and gave a four-finger wave. "Oh, hey, guys!" She said it as though she hadn't been eavesdropping on them, but Emma knew better.

I did, too. Especially when Laurel mouthed *Caught ya!*, before popping her iPod earbuds back into her ears. Then, ponytail swinging, she darted through the trees and disappeared.

4

HOMECOMING HANGOVER

On Monday morning, the Hollier High campus looked like it was still recovering from Friday night's Homecoming festivities. The school had a tradition of throwing a Halloween-themed dance, and remnants of the raucous evening were everywhere. A lone strand of bright-orange crepe paper fluttered from a windowsill outside the gym. A set of discarded fangs lay in a patch of grass. The remains of a burst black balloon were splattered on the cement sidewalk. And a wad of pink gum was stuck to the loincloth of the granite statue of a Native American that trickled water in the courtyard.

"This place looks hungover," Emma murmured.

Laurel, who was sitting next to her in the driver's seat of the VW Jetta, didn't even snicker. She was Emma's ride to school until Emma figured out where Sutton's car had disappeared to—it had been impounded for unpaid tickets sometime before Sutton went missing, but Sutton had allegedly retrieved it from the impound the night she died. The car had been missing ever since.

Emma had tried to make small talk with Laurel on the ride over—she didn't dare confront Laurel about spying on her and Ethan in the park on Saturday, even though she was dying to know what she'd heard. But Laurel had just stared stiffly ahead, her jaw set and her eyes narrowed, not wanting to talk about the new Beyoncé single or how Maybelline Great Lash mascara didn't hold a candle to DiorShow.

Sighing, Emma stepped out of the car and veered around a forgotten Mardi Gras mask. She was so sick of Laurel's hot-and-cold moods. Last week, she and Laurel had gotten along swimmingly, and it seemed that whatever bitter rivalry there'd been between Sutton and Laurel was beginning to dissolve, but Thayer's appearance had set them back ten paces. Emma missed smiling at Laurel at breakfast, doing their makeup side-by-side at the bathroom mirror in the morning, and singing along to the radio on the drive to school. Laurel had given her a taste of what having a sister could be like, something she'd never had.

As she crossed to the front lawn, she noticed everyone was buzzing excitedly. One name cropped up over and over: *Thayer Vega.*

"Did you hear Thayer was arrested for breaking into the Mercer house?" a girl in a faux-fur vest whispered. Emma froze and ducked behind a column, wanting to hear the conversation.

The girl's friend, a guy with a pronounced widow's peak, nodded excitedly. "I heard it was a huge set-up. Sutton knew he was coming all along."

"Where do you think he's been?" Faux Fur asked.

Widow's Peak shrugged. "I heard he went to L.A. to make it as a male model."

"No way." A junior girl with frizzy blonde hair had joined Widow's Peak and Faux Fur. "He was mixed up in a Mexican drug cartel and got shot in the leg. That totally explains the limp."

"That makes sense." Widow's Peak nodded sagely. "Thayer probably broke into Sutton's bedroom to steal her laptop to pay off his drug-lord debt."

Faux Fur rolled her eyes. "You guys are lame. He broke into Sutton's room because they had unfinished business. She was the reason he left."

"Sutton?"

Emma whirled around and saw Charlotte advancing toward her. The three kids who had been talking about

Sutton flinched as they spotted Emma behind a column. Other kids passing by stared at her curiously. A couple of guys chuckled.

I had a feeling this wasn't the response I used to get when I walked through the halls of Hollier. People might have whispered about me, but no one would have dared laugh.

"News travels fast, doesn't it?" Emma said as Charlotte fell in step beside her. Emma tugged at the hem of Sutton's gray pinstriped short shorts. If she'd known she would be so ogled today, she wouldn't have worn an outfit quite so revealing.

"News like this does." Charlotte adjusted a wave of silky red hair over her shoulder and handed Emma a Starbucks latte. Then she glared at a goth girl who was gaping at Emma. "Is there a problem?" she asked in a pinched tone.

The goth girl shrugged and slunk away. Emma shot Charlotte a grateful smile as the girls settled on a bench. It was times like this when Emma appreciated Charlotte's flinty bitchiness. She was the loudest and most controlling of their clique, the kind of girl who you desperately wanted on your side and didn't dare cross. In Emma's old life, she'd known plenty of girls like Charlotte, but only from afar. Mostly, the Charlottes of the world looked at Emma like she was some kind of foster-girl freak.

Charlotte sipped from her own cup of coffee and looked around the lawn. "What a mess," she murmured. Then her green eyes widened. Emma followed her gaze and saw Madeline stepping from her SUV. She straightened to her full height as she walked through a mob of gaping students.

"Mads!" Charlotte called, waving.

Madeline turned her head and froze at the sight of Charlotte and Emma. For a split second, Emma thought she was going to spin and run in the opposite direction. But then she strode toward them with all of her ballet-dancer grace and settled next to Charlotte on the bench.

Charlotte squeezed her hand. "How are you doing?"

"How do you think?" Madeline snapped. She was impeccably dressed in a tight-fitting cashmere sweater and navy shorts ironed within an inch of their life, but her alabaster skin looked even paler than usual. Then Emma noticed a pair of Chanel sunglasses propped on top of her head. They were new shades, even though Emma and Madeline had picked out a vintage pair last week, a very *un*-Sutton move. Had Mads deliberately chosen not to wear the sunglasses today to show she was pissed at Emma, or was Emma reading too much into things?

"Thayer's arraignment hearing was this morning," Madeline explained, looking at Charlotte but not at

Emma. "His bail is set at fifteen thousand dollars. My mom won't stop crying. She's begging my dad to pay his bail, but he refuses—he says he's not going to waste his money bailing Thayer out because he's just going to bolt again. I'd bail him out myself, but where am I going to get fifteen grand?"

Charlotte draped an arm around Madeline and squeezed her shoulder. "I'm so sorry, Mads."

"At the hearing he just sat there, staring at us." Madeline's lower lip trembled. "It's like he's become this complete stranger. He has a tattoo he won't explain, and that crazy limp. He'll never be able to play soccer again. It was his biggest love—the thing he was best at—and now his future is ruined."

Emma reached out her hand to rest it on Madeline's. "That's awful."

Madeline tensed her shoulders and pulled away. "Worst of all, Thayer won't tell us where he was all this time."

"At least you know where he is now, and that he's safe," Emma offered.

Madeline whipped around and stared at her. Her blue eyes were puffy, and her mouth was a straight line. "What was he doing in your bedroom?" she asked bluntly.

Emma flinched. Charlotte fidgeted with a heart-shaped keychain that hung on her leather Coach purse, avoiding eye contact with both of them.

"I already told you I don't know," Emma stammered, feeling her stomach muscles bunch up into a tight knot.

"Did you know he was coming to your house that night?" Madeline's eyes narrowed.

Emma shook her head. "I had no idea. I swear."

Madeline raised an eyebrow like she wanted to believe her, but couldn't. "Come on, Sutton. You knew when he was going to take off. You've been talking to him while he was gone, right? You knew where he was all along."

"Mads," Charlotte said. "Sutton wouldn't—"

"Mads, if I had known where he was or was communicating with him, I would have told you," Emma interrupted. She could only guess at the truth of this. Yes, *she* hadn't been talking to Thayer. But had Sutton?

I had the sinking suspicion that Emma was right, even if I didn't want it to be possible that I could have kept that from Mads. I had hurt so many people and kept so many secrets. If only I could remember what they were.

Madeline chipped a fleck of gold nail polish from her index finger. "I know what was going on with you guys before he left."

A sharp, bitter taste filled Emma's mouth. She breathed in to speak, but couldn't find the words. What was she supposed to say? *Maybe you could fill me in?*

Just then a shrill bell blared across the courtyard. Charlotte shot up. "We should go."

But Madeline just sat there, glaring.

Charlotte rested a hand gently on the sleeve of Madeline's sweater. "The last thing we need is your dad getting a phone call about you being late to class."

Finally, Madeline sighed and slung her bag over her shoulder. Charlotte murmured something about seeing Emma at lunch, then looped her arm through Madeline's and guided her toward their first class. Even though Emma's class was in the same direction, she got the distinct impression that she wasn't invited.

A hand clamped down on Emma's shoulder, and she flinched. When she turned, Ethan smiled sheepishly behind her. "I didn't mean to scare you," he said. "I just wanted to know if you're okay."

Emma reached out for Ethan's hand, then pulled back. Her eyes swept furtively around the yard. A couple of drama kids were rehearsing a scene near the parking lot. There was a small line for coffee at the kiosk just inside the school doors. No one was looking at them, but she still felt paranoid. Ethan wasn't part of Sutton's clique, nor did he want to be.

She sighed. "I've only been here for ten minutes and already it's been a long day," she moaned. "And from the way Madeline's acting, something was definitely going on between Sutton and Thayer before he skipped town."

Ethan nodded. "Sounds like Sutton was playing Garrett, then."

"I guess," Emma said. She didn't want to assume her sister was cheating, but it was really looking like she had been.

"So how are you going to find out more?" Ethan asked.

Emma took a long sip of the coffee Charlotte had brought for her. "Continue eavesdropping on all the gossip, maybe?" she said with a shrug.

Ethan looked like he was going to say something else, but he was cut off by the final bell. Both of them snapped to attention. "We'll talk about this later, okay?"

"Okay," Ethan said. He stepped forward just as Emma did. They bumped feet and stepped back.

"Sorry," Emma murmured.

"It's cool," Ethan said gruffly, shifting his backpack higher on his shoulder. Their eyes met for a moment, but then Ethan lowered his head again and scuttled toward the doors. "I'll see you," he mumbled.

"Okay," Emma said to his disappearing shape. She swung around and began to walk in the opposite direction.

Suddenly, a rustling in the bushes made her stop short. Someone snickered behind a podium. Emma squinted, trying to make out who it was. Was someone watching her? Was it Laurel again, spying on her and Ethan? Before she could get a glimpse, whoever it was ducked into the school and darted up the stairs.

5

GAME, SET, OUTMATCHED

After school that day, Emma walked off the tennis court at Wheeler High, Hollier's main rival, shading her eyes from the bright glare and smiling bashfully at the smattering of applause. All of Hollier's sports teams were playing Wheeler that week, and Emma had just finished a grueling match against a petite redhead. Well, it wasn't *supposed* to be grueling—Coach Maggie had basically said that the girl was so subpar she could be beaten with an ankle strain and a badminton racket. Before Emma had arrived in Tucson, the most tennis she'd ever played was on a Ping-Pong table in a dingy basement with Stephan, her Russian foster brother. She *did* use some of the Russian curse words he had taught her when she wanted to swear during a match without getting in trouble, though.

For me, it was yet another reminder of how different our childhoods had been.

"Good game, Sutton," several people Emma didn't recognize said as she passed. She collapsed into a chair on the sidelines, kicked off the state-of-the-art tennis sneakers she'd found in Sutton's closet—not that they helped her game any—and let out a groan.

"Someone still out of shape?" a voice lilted.

Emma looked up and saw Nisha Banerjee leaning against the fence, a smirk on her face. Nisha's long, slender fingers rested on her trim waist, her überwhite tennis uniform gleamed—she probably bleached it after every match—and there wasn't even a hint of sweat on the terrycloth band that circled her head of sleek, dark hair. She was Sutton's tennis co-captain, and she never missed a chance to tell Emma how undeserving she was of the title. Emma bit her lip and tried to tell herself that Nisha was being mean because she was hurting inside—she'd lost her mother this past summer and was dealing with a lot of pain. In a parallel universe, maybe she and Emma would even bond over their absent mothers.

But not in this *universe*, I wanted to tell her. Nisha Banerjee and Sutton Mercer were sworn enemies and always would be. If Nisha hadn't had a solid alibi for the night of my murder—she'd had the entire tennis team over at her house for a sleepover—she would have been at the top of my suspect list.

Emma grabbed her gym bag and made her way inside the school. Wheeler's locker room smelled like old socks and strawberry-scented body spray. A shower head dripped in the corner, and a flyer for intramural water polo hung limply on the cinderblock wall. Emma crumpled her sweaty white socks into her gym bag, pulled her tennis uniform over her head, and changed into Sutton's pink ballet flats, denim shorts, and V-neck tee. As she walked toward the sinks, the muscles along the backs of her thighs protested loudly, and she winced. She had eight more tennis matches to go before the end of the season. She'd probably have to get thigh replacements after that.

As she turned the corner, she saw girls in swim caps printed with HOLLIER SWIM TEAM. The room was filled with steam, and shower taps whooshed. Emma caught snippets of conversation: about someone's butterfly splits, and then about some hot Wheeler swimmer named Devon. When she heard the name *Thayer Vega*, the hair rose on the back of her neck. She inched toward the showers.

"And you just know Sutton Mercer had something to do with it," a girl chirped.

"Doesn't she always?" said another, her voice raspier than the first.

"It's unreal how Thayer went to her house after everyone says she put his life in danger. I mean, what's that guy *thinking* getting involved with her again?"

A prickly feeling crawled along Emma's body. Sutton had put Thayer's life in danger? Suddenly, she remembered something Ethan had told her on Friday, right before they kissed: There was a rumor that Sutton had almost killed someone with her car. She pictured Thayer's exaggerated limp as he ran from the Mercers' house. Was it possible?

Sutton's iPhone buzzed, and Emma scrambled to answer it. She ducked into a bathroom stall so that the swimmers wouldn't see her spying and checked the screen. It was an unknown number with a 520 area code. "Hello?" she whispered.

"Sutton?" a low voice grumbled. "This is Detective Quinlan."

She clenched the phone tighter, her heart lurching. Emma had grown up fearing the police. Becky had had some run-ins with them, and Emma had always worried the cops would throw her in jail, too, by association. "Yes?" she squeaked.

"I need you to come to the station to answer some questions," Quinlan barked.

"About . . . what?"

"Just come."

Emma couldn't exactly say no to the police. Sighing,

she said she'd be there soon. Then she pocketed the phone and pushed out of the changing room into Wheeler's marble halls. There was a long line of lockers on the far wall, many of them decorated with stickers, miniature pom-poms, and graffiti that said things like GO WHEELER or ENGLISH SUCKS or JANE IS A HO. Late afternoon sunlight streamed through an open window and cast rectangles of gold onto the cornflower-blue walls.

Emma looked at her phone again. The police station was right next to Hollier High, five miles away. How was she going to get there? Laurel still wasn't talking to her, and she'd no doubt report back to the Mercers that Sutton was in trouble again. The questioning could have something to do with Thayer, which meant she couldn't call Madeline. Charlotte was still finishing up her tennis match, and Ethan was taking his mom to the doctor. The Twitter Twins were the only option left.

Emma scrolled through Sutton's iPhone and found Lili's number.

"Of *course* I'll drive you," Lili said when she answered and Emma explained her plight. "What are friends for? Gabby and I are on our way!"

In minutes, the Twitter Twins' shiny white SUV pulled up to the curb. Lili sat in the driver's seat, wearing a Green Day T-shirt and ripped jeans, while Gabby lounged in überpreppy rugby stripes on the passenger side. Both girls had their iPhones in their laps. As Emma hopped into the back seat, she could feel the twins' eyes on her.

"So," Gabby started as they pulled away, her voice dripping with hunger. "You're going to visit Thayer in jail, aren't you?"

"We knew it," Lili said before Emma could answer. Her blue eyes widened as she glanced in the rearview mirror, clumps of mascara dotting her lashes. "We knew you couldn't stay away."

"But we won't tweet about it if you don't want us to," Gabby said quickly. "We can keep a secret." The Twitter Twins, true to their name, were the school's biggest gossip hounds, airing everyone's dirty laundry on their Twitter pages.

"I heard his trial is set for a month from now and his dad's going to let him rot in jail until then," Lili said. "Do you think he'll go to prison?"

"I bet he looks good in orange," Gabby trilled.

"I'm not going to see Thayer," Emma said as lightly as she could, leaning against the leather backseat. "I, um, just need to sign something about the shoplifting fiasco. The shopkeeper is dropping all charges." That piece, at least, was true. Ethan knew the salesgirl at Clique and had gotten her to back down.

Gabby frowned, looking disappointed. "Well, since you're there, you could stop in to see him just for a second, couldn't you? I'm dying to know where he's been all this time."

"You know, don't you?" Lili jumped in, waving her finger in the air. "Naughty, naughty, Sutton! You knew where he was this whole time and you didn't tell anyone! So how did you guys communicate? I heard it was secret email accounts."

Gabby nudged her sister. "Where'd you hear that?"

"Caroline's sister is friends with a girl whose friend hooked up with the goalie on Thayer's traveling soccer team," Lili explained. "Apparently, Thayer told him lots of stuff before he took off."

Emma glared at the Twitter Twins in the front seat. "I think I feel a migraine coming on," she said icily, summoning up her best I'm-Sutton-Mercer-and-you-will-do-anything-I-ask voice. "How about we ride the rest of the way in silence?"

The twins looked deflated, but turned down the radio and drove the final stretch in utter silence. Emma glanced out the window at the sand-colored buildings of the University of Arizona whizzing past. Could Sutton have communicated with Thayer through a secret email account? She hadn't come across anything on Sutton's computer or in her bedroom, but Sutton was nothing if not sneaky and smart. They could have communicated any number of ways—disposable cells, fake email addresses or Twitter accounts, regular old mail . . .

I racked my memory for any kind of correspondence with Thayer—secretive or not. I saw myself sitting at my desk with a blank computer screen in front me, a familiar feeling of restlessness in my body, like there was something I needed to tell someone, anyone. Maybe Thayer. But the computer screen stayed as white and untouched as fresh snow, the blinking cursor mocking me with its steady beat.

The car passed a ranch called the Lone Range, where three palomino horses grazed in a rectangular pasture. A woman dressed in a flowing white skirt and a raisin-colored tube top sold turquoise jewelry next to a handwritten sign advertising HIGH QUALITY, LOW PRICE. The sun blazed just above the horizon.

When they pulled into the parking lot of the police station, Lili caught Emma's eye in the rearview mirror. "Do you want us to wait for you?"

"Yeah, we could even come in with you, you know, for moral support," Gabby added.

"I'll be fine." Emma slid out of the backseat and slammed the door. "Thanks for the ride!"

Emma and I didn't need to turn back around to know that Gabby and Lili were watching her as she walked through the glass doors marked TUCSON POLICE DEPARTMENT.

6

LITTLE EMMA IN THE BIG WOODS

The inside of the station was the same as the past two times Emma had been there: first to report that Sutton was missing, then after she'd stolen the bag from Clique. It still had that rancid smell of old takeout. The telephones bleated loudly and jarringly. An old HAVE YOU SEEN HIM? flyer with Thayer Vega's face and information hung on a bulletin board in the corner, next to a document listing Tucson's most wanted. Emma stepped forward and gave her name to an emaciated woman with a helmet-perm who sat at the front desk.

"S-U-T-T-O-N M-E-R-C-E-R," the woman repeated, her purple acrylic nails tapping each letter on an ancient-looking keyboard. "Have a seat and Detective Quinlan will be right with you."

Emma sat on a hard yellow plastic chair and looked at the bulletin board again. The calendar was still on August. Emma guessed it was the receptionist who had chosen the picture of a kitten chasing a tattered ball of red yarn. Next she scanned the MOST WANTED poster. It looked like the majority of the guys on it had outstanding warrants for drug possession. Finally, she let her eyes graze the MISSING poster. Thayer's hazel eyes stared directly at her, the hint of a smile playing across his lips. For a moment, Emma swore the boy in the photo actually *winked* at her, but that was impossible. She ran her hands over the back of her neck, trying to get a grip. But Thayer was somewhere *in* this building. Just his proximity made her shudder.

"Miss Mercer." Quinlan appeared in the doorway wearing dark brown pants and a tan button-down. At six feet tall, he cut an imposing figure. "C'mon back."

Emma stood and followed him down the tiled hallway. Quinlan opened the door to the same cinderblock interrogation room he'd stuck Emma in the week before, when he'd questioned her about shoplifting from Clique. As soon as the door whooshed open, Emma was enveloped in lavender Febreze. She pressed her hand to her nose and tried to breathe through her mouth.

Quinlan scraped back a chair and gestured for Emma

to sit. She lowered herself into it slowly, and Quinlan sat across from her. He leveled a look at her over the table, as if he expected her to just start talking. Emma studied the gun at his waist. How many times had he used it?

"I called you in about your car," Quinlan finally said. He steepled his hands and stared at Emma over his fingertips. "We found it. But first—is there anything you want to tell me about?"

Emma tensed, her mind drawing a blank. She knew very little about Sutton's car—that she had used it in a cruel prank against her friends a few months ago, pretending to stall the vehicle on the train tracks when an Amtrak commuter was barreling down on them. That she had signed it out of the impound lot the night she died. That it had since vanished, along with Sutton.

I wished I remembered what I'd done with the car that day. But I didn't.

Still, Emma's heart quickened with excitement, too. Sutton was driving that car the day she died. Maybe the car held a clue inside of it. Maybe there was some sort of evidence in there. Or maybe—she cringed—maybe it contained Sutton's body.

I hoped not. But suddenly, a flash of memory sparked in my mind. I felt my feet pounding over rocks and my ankles scratching against tree branches and cactus needles as I sprinted across a dark path. Fear pulsed through me as

I ran. Then I heard footsteps hammering the earth behind me, but I didn't stop to turn around to see who was following me. In the distance, I was able to make out the outline of my car waiting in a clearing beyond the brush. But just before I could reach it, the memory popped like a soap bubble.

Quinlan cleared his throat. "Sutton? Can you answer my question?"

Emma swallowed hard, wrenched from her spinning thoughts. "Um, no. I don't have anything to tell you about the car."

The detective sighed loudly, raking his hands through his dark hair. "Fine. Well, the car was abandoned in the desert a few miles away from Sabino Canyon." He sat back, crossed his arms over his chest, and looked at Emma meaningfully, as if waiting for some sort of reaction. "Want to explain how it got there?"

Emma blinked, her nerve endings firing rapidly. "Um . . . it was stolen?"

Quinlan smirked. "Of *course* it was." The corners of his mouth lifted. "So then I'm guessing you don't know anything about the blood we found on it?"

Emma's entire body shot to life. "*Blood?* Whose?"

"We don't know yet. We're still testing the evidence."

Emma pushed her hands to her lap so Quinlan wouldn't see them shake. The blood had to be Sutton's.

60

Had someone run down her sister then stashed the car and Sutton's body in the desert? Who?

Quinlan leaned forward, perhaps sensing Emma's fear. "I know you're hiding something. Something big."

Emma shook her head slowly, not trusting her voice to work.

Then Quinlan reached behind him and pulled a plastic bag from a rusted metal shelf. He emptied the contents onto the table in front of Emma. An ikat-print silk scarf fluttered across the table, along with a stainless-steel water bottle, a duplicate of the sign-out sheet from the impound lot with Sutton's signature on it in big, bold letters, and a copy of *Little House in the Big Woods*.

"We found these items inside the car," he explained, pushing them across the table.

Emma's fingers traced a line across the silk scarf. It smelled exactly like Sutton's room—like fresh flowers, chocolate mint, and that organic, Suttony essence she couldn't quite put her finger on.

"And as for the car, we're holding it—along with these items—until we figure out whose blood is on the hood." Quinlan leaned forward and eyed Emma sternly. "Unless you're going to change your mind and enlighten us."

Emma stared at the detective, the air heavy and stale between them. For a moment, she considered telling him that it was Sutton's blood. That someone had killed her twin sister and was after her, too. But Quinlan wouldn't believe her any more now than he had a month ago. If he *did* believe her, he might presume what Ethan had warned her about—that *Emma* had killed Sutton, all because she wanted to ditch her foster-kid persona and take over Sutton's charmed life.

"I don't know anything," Emma whispered.

Quinlan shook his head and slapped his hand on the table. "You're just making this more difficult for all of us," he grumbled. Then he turned as the door to the interrogation room opened. Another cop stuck his head in and mouthed something Emma didn't catch. Quinlan stood and moved for the door. "Don't go anywhere," he warned Emma. "I'll be right back."

He slammed the door hard. Emma waited until he padded down the hall, then gazed down at the items he'd left on the table. The scarf, heavily perfumed with eau de Sutton. The sign-out sheet, Sutton's signature in loopy swirls at the bottom. Then she stared hard at the cover of *Little House in the Big Woods.* A young girl in a red dress clutched a brunette doll. Emma had loved the books when she was younger, spending hours getting lost in the hardships of Laura Ingalls Wilder's characters—for all of Emma's shitty home situations, at least she didn't have to live in a mud hut like the pioneers. But what was Sutton doing with a copy of this book in her car? Emma doubted it was something she would read at eighteen—if at all.

I had to agree. Just looking at the cover made me want to yawn.

Emma picked up the book and rifled through the pages. It smelled musty, as if it hadn't been opened in a while. When she reached the middle, a postcard fell to the floor. She bent down and turned it over. The front was printed with a generic image of a sun setting over two multiarmed saguaro cacti. WELCOME TO TUCSON, it said in hot-pink bubble letters on the top.

Emma flipped it over to read the black ink printed on the back: *Downtown bus station. 9:30 PM. 8/31. Meet me. —T.*

Her heart began to pound. August thirty-first. That was the night Sutton died. And . . . *T.* There was only one person in Sutton's life with that initial: Thayer. So was Thayer with Sutton the night she died? Wasn't he supposed to be out of town?

Emma ran her fingers along the card. There was no postage stamp on it, meaning no date to signify when the postcard had been mailed—or from where. Perhaps Thayer had sent it in an envelope. Perhaps he'd slipped it under Sutton's bedroom door or under her windshield wiper.

Footsteps pounded down the hallway. Emma froze, looking at the postcard in her hands. At first, she considered

SARA SHEPARD

shoving it back into the book—it was probably wrong to tamper with evidence—but at the last minute she dropped it into her bag instead.

Quinlan walked through the door, and a second person followed. At first, Emma thought it was just going to be another cop, but then her eyes widened. It was Thayer. She gasped. His hazel eyes were lowered to the ground. His high cheekbones jutted as though he'd lost weight rapidly. Handcuffs circled his wrists, clasping his hands together like he was praying. A dingy rope bracelet was pushed up his forearm. It was so tight that it cut into his skin.

I stared at him, too. Just seeing him again made a strange tingle shoot through me. Those deep-set eyes. That dark, messy hair. That permanent smirk. There was something sexy and dangerous about him. Maybe I *had* fallen for him.

Quinlan made a grunting noise from behind Thayer and pushed him toward the table. "Sit," he commanded.

But Thayer just stood there. Even though he wasn't looking at Emma, she scooted her chair away, afraid he might lunge for her.

"I suppose you both are wondering why I brought you in here for a little reunion," Quinlan said in an oily voice. "I thought that if I spoke to you both at the same time, we could clear some things up."

He pulled another plastic bag from his pocket and

64

held it in front of Thayer's face. A long rectangular piece of paper was lodged within the plastic. "I believe this is yours, Thayer," he said, shaking the bag under Thayer's nose. "I found it in Miss Mercer's car. Care to explain?"

Thayer glanced at it. He didn't flinch—didn't even blink.

Quinlan yanked the paper from the bag. "Don't play dumb, kid. There's your name, right there."

He slammed the plastic bag on the table and pointed to the piece of paper. Emma leaned forward. It was a bus ticket with a Greyhound logo in the corner. The point of departure was Seattle, WA, and the destination was Tucson, AZ. The date was August thirty-first. And there, printed in small, neat letters at the bottom, was the passenger's name: THAYER VEGA.

I drew in a breath the same time Emma did. So Thayer *was* in my car the night I died.

Quinlan eyed Thayer. A blue vein at his temple pulsed. "You were back in Tucson in August? Do you know what you put your parents through? What you put this *community* through? I spent a lot of time and money searching for you, and it turns out you were right here, under our noses!"

"That's not quite true," Thayer said in a quiet, steady, discomfiting voice.

Quinlan crossed his arms over his chest. "Then how about you tell me what *is* true?" When Thayer didn't answer, he sighed. "Is there anything *you* can tell us about the blood on the hood of Ms. Mercer's car? Or how your ticket ended up in her car?"

Thayer limped over to where Emma sat. He put both palms on the table, glancing from Emma to Quinlan. He opened his mouth like he was about to give a long speech, but then just shrugged. "Sorry," he said, his voice creaking as though he hadn't spoken for days. "But no. There's nothing I can tell you."

Quinlan shook his head. "So much for being cooperative," he grumbled, then shot to his feet, grabbed Thayer by his muscular forearm, and dragged him from the room. Just before Thayer slipped out the door, he turned his head and gave Emma a long, eerie look. Emma stared back, her lips slightly parted. Her gaze fell from Thayer's face to his shackled hands, and then to the rope bracelet around his wrist.

I looked at the bracelet, too, and was overcome with a strange snapping feeling. I'd seen that bracelet somewhere. All of a sudden, the pieces fell into place. I saw the bracelet, and then Thayer's arm, and then his face . . . and then a setting. More and more dominoes fell over, more and more images flashed into my mind. And before I knew it, I was falling headlong into a full-blown memory . . .

7

NIGHT HIKING

I pull up to the Greyhound station in Tucson just as a silver bus chugs into the parking lot. I roll down my window and the pungent smells of a hot-dog vendor's cart waft into my British racing-green 1965 Volvo 122. Earlier this afternoon I rescued my car, my baby, from the impound. The paperwork flutters on the dash, my signature prominent at the bottom, a big, red-stamped AUGUST 31 at the top. It had taken me weeks to save up the money to pay cash to get the car off the impound lot—there was no way I was going to charge it on a credit card, since my parents always saw the statement.

The bus door sighs open, and I crane my neck to scan the

exiting passengers. An overweight man with a fanny pack, a teenage girl bopping her head to an iPod, a family who looks shell-shocked from the long journey, all of them holding pillows. Finally, a boy tumbles down the stairs, black hair disheveled, shoelaces untied. My heart leaps. Thayer looks different, slightly scruffier and skinnier. There's a tear in the knee of the Tsubi jeans I bought him before he left, and his face looks more angular, maybe even wiser. I watch as he scans the parking lot, looking for me. As soon as he spots my car he breaks into his trademark, soccer-star sprint.

"You came," he cries as he wrenches open the door of my car.

"Of course I did."

He climbs inside the car. My arms reach out and wrap around his neck. I kiss him hungrily, not caring who might see us—even Garrett, my so-called boyfriend. "Thayer," I whisper, feeling the layer of stubble along his jaw rough against my cheek.

"I missed you so much," Thayer answers, pulling me close. His hands are low on the small of my back and his fingers graze the top of my yellow cotton shorts. "Thanks for meeting me."

"Nothing could keep me away," I say, making myself pull back slightly. I check the plastic alligator-print watch on my wrist. Most of the time, I wear the Cartier tank watch my parents got me for my Sweet Sixteen, but what they don't know is that I love this cheap thing more. Thayer won it for me at the Tucson County Fair the last day he was in town.

"So how much time do we have?" I whisper.

Thayer's green eyes shine. "Until tomorrow night."

"And then do you turn into a pumpkin?" I tease. This is a longer visit than usual, but I feel greedy. "Stay another day. I'll make it worth your while." I toss my hair over my shoulder. "I bet I'm more fun than wherever it is you run off to."

Thayer runs his finger along my jaw line. "Sutton . . ."

"Fine." I turn away, squeezing the steering wheel. "Don't tell me where you've been. I don't care." I reach for the radio dial and turn up the sports channel. Loud.

"Don't be like that." Thayer's hand covers mine. His fingers trail along my bare arm until they pause at my neck and uncurl. My skin warms beneath his hands. He leans closer until I can feel his breath against my shoulder. It's minty, like he chewed a whole pack of gum on the ride here. "I don't want to fight with you the only day we're together."

I face him, hating the lump that forms at the back of my throat. "It's just hard here without you. It's been months. And you said you'd come back for good this time."

"I will, Sutton, you have to trust me. But not quite yet. It's not right."

Why? I want to ask. But I've promised not to ask questions. I should be happy that he has left wherever he's been staying to see me, even if it's only for twenty-four hours. Coming back here under such secrecy is a risk. So many people are looking for him. So many people would be furious if they knew he was here and hadn't reached out.

"Let's go somewhere special," Thayer says, tracing a pattern on my leg. "Want me to drive?"

"You wish!" I tease, checking my rearview mirror and revving the engine. And just like that, I feel better. There's no use in dwelling on what I don't know and what the future might hold for us. Thayer and I have twenty-four blissful hours, and that's what matters.

I peel from the station's lot and turn onto a main road. Two kids wearing cut-off jean shorts and clutching duffel bags who look our age are trying to hitchhike from next to a patch of desert broom. The Catalina Mountains tower in the distance. "How about a night hike?" I ask. "No one else will be out right now— we'll have the whole mountain to ourselves."

Thayer nods and I switch the radio to a scratchy jazz station. Saxophone music filters through the car. I reach to change it, but Thayer stops me.

"Leave it," he says. "It puts me in the mood."

"In the mood for what?" I ask, giving him a sly sideways look. I put my index finger to my lips and tap them like I'm thinking hard. "I bet I can guess."

"You wish, Sutton," he says with a smirk.

I laugh and reach across the seat to punch his arm.

We're quiet on the rest of the drive to Sabino Canyon. I roll both windows down and wind rushes across our faces. We pass a coffee shop called the Congress Club that advertises a book reading and open-mic night, a dog groomer's named Mangy Mutts, and an ice cream shop with a neon sign for make-your-own sundaes. Thayer takes my free hand as we drive along a quiet stretch of the highway. Cacti appear in the distance. The scent of wildflowers wafts into the car.

Finally, we ascend the dirt road leading to the canyon and park in a secluded spot by a bunch of metal trash barrels. The night sky is black, the moon a shining orb floating high above our heads. The air is still warm and heavy as we climb from the car and find the entrance to the winding path that leads to the overlook. As we walk, Thayer's hand brushes my shoulder, trails down my spine and lands on the small of my back. His touch feels hot on my skin. I bite my lip to keep from turning and kissing him—even though I want to, it's more delicious to resist for as long as possible.

We walk a few more yards in silence up the gravelly path. Technically, the park is closed at night, and there's not a soul in sight. A slight breeze makes me shiver. The boulders stand out in sharp relief against the moonlight. And then, after another minute, I hear it: a crackle of a branch followed by what sounds like a sigh. I freeze. "What was that?"

Thayer stops and squints in the darkness. "Probably an animal."

I take another step, checking cautiously over my shoulder once more. There's no one there. No one is following us. No one knows Thayer is here . . . or that I'm with him.

It's not long before we reach the overlook. All of Tucson spills *out below us, a sea of glittering lights. "Whoa," Thayer breathes. "How did you find this?"*

"I used to come here with my dad years ago." I point to the precarious ground below. "We used to put a little blanket there and camp out with a picnic lunch. Dad's a big bird-watcher, and he got me into it, too."

"Sounds fun," Thayer says sarcastically.

I cuff him on the arm. "It was." Sadness fills me, suddenly. I remember how my dad would perch me on top of one of the huge rocks up here and hand me my purple water canteen—the only one I'd use during grade school. We'd clink our glasses and make up fake toasts. To Sutton, *my dad would say,* the most agile trailblazer to cross Sabino Canyon since 1962. *I'd tap my purple canteen against his, and say,* To Dad, your hair is getting kinda gray, but you're still the fastest climber these parts have ever seen! *We'd laugh and laugh as each toast became sillier than the one before.*

It feels like ages have passed since my dad and I were close like that, and I know it's my fault as much as his. I stare up at the stars that dot the dark sky and resolve to try a little harder with him. Maybe I can get our relationship back to the way it used to be.

I step carefully to the edge. "Dad had just one rule," I go on. "I had to stay away from this ledge. There were all kinds of rumors that people fell right over the side. No one could rappel down to get their bodies—the drop is too steep—so there are a bunch of skeletons down there."

"Don't worry," Thayer says, wrapping his arms around me. "I won't let you fall."

My heart suddenly melts. I lean forward and press my lips to his. His arms wrap around my waist, pulling my body into his. His hands are in my hair as he returns my kiss.

"Don't leave me again," I plead. I can't help myself. "Don't go back to wherever it is you're hiding."

He kisses my cheek and pulls away to look at me. "I can't explain right now," he says. "But I can't be here—not now. I promise, though, that I won't be gone forever."

His hands cup my chin. I want to understand. I want to be strong. But it's so hard. Then I notice a white woven rope bracelet on his wrist. "Where'd you get that?" I ask, pinching the rough twine between my fingers.

Thayer shrugs and avoids my glance. "Maria made it for me."

"Maria?" I stiffen. "Is she cute?"

"She's just a friend," Thayer says, his tone gruff and hard.

"What kind of friend?" I press. "Where did you meet her?"

I feel his muscles tense beneath his gray T-shirt. "It doesn't matter. Anyway, how's Garrett doing?" He says the name Garrett like it's a flesh-eating disease.

I turn away, filled with guilt. I love Garrett—in a way. He's a good boyfriend. And he's here, in Tucson, not God-knows-where like Thayer. But there's something I can't explain that pulls me to Thayer and makes me want to sneak around with him like this. It's like every reason I give myself to stop doesn't matter.

Thayer shifts closer to me. "When I come back, will things be different between us?" he asks in a low voice. He curls his palms around my hip bones, gripping me tight.

Our bodies are so close. I focus on his full bottom lip, wishing I knew how to answer him. When I'm with him, all I want is him. But I can't deny that part of what makes our relationship work is that we've kept it a secret.

"I want to, but I don't know," I whisper. "There's Laurel. And God knows how Madeline would deal. It's so . . . complicated, don't you think?"

Thayer disentangles himself from me, kicking at a fallen tree branch. "You're the one who keeps begging me to come back." The cold, closed-off tone is back.

"Thayer," I protest. "Remember that no-fighting thing?"

But he won't look at me. He mutters something beneath his breath. Suddenly, his foot flies out. There's a crack as his toes make contact with one of the big boulders in the clearing.

"Are you trying to break all your bones?" I cry. Thayer doesn't answer. I take a step closer and put what I hope is a soothing hand on his shoulder. "Thayer, listen. I do want you here. I miss you like crazy. But maybe right now isn't the best time for us to tell everyone how we feel."

Thayer whirls around. "Really, Sutton?" he spits. "Well, I'm sorry our relationship is less important than you maintaining appearances."

I grab for his hand. "I don't mean that. I was just saying—"

"*Enough.*" *His mouth tightens.* "*Maybe it was a mistake to come back. I've had enough.*"

His eyes darken as he rips his hand from mine. I spin away from him, my heart suddenly in my throat. I've never seen Thayer like this. In many ways, he's reminding me of his father. Explosive. Mercurial. Volatile.

Crickets chirp in the distance. A bunch of little pebbles cascade over the side of the cliff. All at once, I realize how alone and vulnerable I am, here on the edge of this mountain with a boy who ran off to some mysterious place he won't tell me about. How much do I really know about what Thayer's been up to lately, anyway? I've heard all the rumors about him—especially the ones about the trouble he's mixed up in here, the dangerous things he's done. What if some of them are true?

But then I realize how crazy my fear is. Of course Thayer won't hurt me. What we have is special—he would never harm me. I close my eyes and spread my fingers wide, feeling the cool mountain air. If I can gather my thoughts, maybe I can explain what I'm feeling, why I think it isn't the right time for Thayer and I to go public. I let go of a breath and open my eyes, but Thayer is gone.

I look right and left, but all I see is darkness. "*Thayer?*" *I call out.*

A scratching noise sounds a few feet away. "*Thayer?*" *I call again. No answer.* "*Ha, ha. Very funny!*"

A shadow slides across the trees and something skitters in the distance. Leaves rustle and whisper. A shiver runs the length of my body. "Thayer?"

Suddenly all I want is to be off this mountain. I whirl around once more, ready to take off down the path toward my car, but a hand clutches my arm, hard. Terror shoots through me. I feel breath on my neck. But before I can cry out, before I can whirl around and see who it is, the memory cracks down the middle and fades to absolute whiteness.

8

WHAT NOW?

Emma sat alone in the interrogation room, waiting for Quinlan to return. She inhaled deeply, forcing herself to remain calm. The weight of what she'd just discovered washed over her anew. Thayer had been in Sutton's car the night she died. That blood on the car had to be Sutton's. Had she finally learned how her twin had died?

I couldn't help but wonder if she had. The memory I'd just seen flickered and snapped in my mind like a neon sign. The tumultuous look that had crossed Thayer's face. The fear I'd felt on the trail. The cops *had* found my bloodstained car at Sabino Canyon, exactly where Thayer and I had gone for our night hike. I thought about the heated fight we'd had. And then there was that hand on my shoulder, just before the memory faded out . . .

Emma barely had any time to catch her breath before Quinlan returned, a frown marring his face. With a quick jerk of his hand, he motioned for Emma to stand. "I give up. If the two of you can't be bothered to tell the truth, you're wasting my time. Get out of here."

He kicked the door open with his boot and gestured into the hall. Emma followed the detective numbly toward reception. The lights in the front room were bright, making her head ache. Emma wanted to ask Quinlan when she could get Sutton's car back—or if the cops were going to tell her whose blood was on it—but Quinlan slammed the door to the waiting area loudly and firmly before she could. She watched through the little window as he sauntered back down the hall, hands in his pockets, handcuffs jingling on his belt.

Okay. So was she free to go, then? Swallowing hard, Emma made her way across the lobby and pushed through the glass doors into the parking lot. Almost an hour had passed since she'd gone inside the station. The sun had set, and the air had a cool snap to it. Emma hugged her arms over her camisole and tried to warm up, although she doubted that even the coziest sweater would be able to chase away the chill that had settled in her bones after seeing Thayer.

She pulled out Sutton's iPhone and composed a text to Ethan. CAN YOU PICK ME UP? She typed quickly, praying he was finished taking his mom to the doctor.

Blessedly, a reply text appeared in minutes. WHERE ARE YOU? Ethan asked.

POLICE STATION. Emma wrote back.

That got his attention—Ethan's response was immediate. WHAT? I'M ON MY WAY.

Emma sat back and waited. Two black-and-white police cars sped from the lot with sirens blaring. A door to the station swung open, and two cops strolled out for a smoke break. They looked at her suspiciously, perhaps recognizing her. One of them said something to the other that sounded a lot like *Thayer.*

She thought about Thayer's hardened expression in the interrogation room. When Quinlan had asked him to explain himself, he hadn't offered a word. Was it because he was guilty of something awful? Had he killed Sutton? Had he made the trip back to Tucson on the thirty-first for exactly that reason? Or had he come to spend time with her . . . and lost control? Maybe they'd had a fight. Maybe Sutton had said something to hurt him. Perhaps Thayer had grabbed Sutton's car keys and run her down, then hid the car in Sabino Canyon. But where had he put Sutton's body? Quinlan would have said something if it had been in the car.

With every fiber of my nonexistent being, I didn't want Thayer to be my killer. In the brief memory I'd been given, I could tell Thayer and I shared something very, very special. I wasn't the type of girl to beg a guy to stay—*or* to get jealous when another girl made him a stupid bracelet. If Thayer planned to kill me, I had been blindsided by it. I had loved him, deeply and truly.

But then something occurred to me: In my memory, when Thayer had run from the bus station to my car, his gait had been strong and graceful. There had been no visible limp whatsoever. Whatever had happened to his leg had happened afterward. Maybe he'd gotten hurt running from the cops. Or maybe from dragging a body into a deep, dark hiding place.

Ethan's beat-up bloodred Honda pulled up in front of the police station and sputtered to a stop. Emma raced toward him, flinging the car door open and sliding into the leather seat. The radio was turned up, blaring a Ramones song. The inside of the car smelled slightly of cigarettes, even though Emma didn't think Ethan smoked. She turned to face him, taking in his light blue eyes and the smooth, tan skin that stretched over his high cheekbones. "I don't think I've ever been so happy to see you," she blurted.

Ethan grasped her hands. "What happened?"

"Just get me out of here." Emma pulled her seat belt

over her lap and pressed her back against the worn cushion.

As Ethan pulled out of the lot, Emma explained her visit to the police station. "The postcard and ticket prove he was with her in her car the night Sutton died," she concluded. "I've made a decision. I really need to talk to Thayer alone and find out exactly what happened. It's the only way I'll get to the bottom of this."

Ethan paused at a stop sign and pulled up a side road. Two preteen girls rode Appaloosa horses along the shoulder. Reflective stripes covered the Western saddles and Ethan swerved to give them more room. "Are you crazy?" he asked. "You're just going to serve yourself up to Sutton's killer?"

Emma shrugged defensively. "It's the best way to get answers. I'm not going to tell him I'm on to him. I'll just act like Sutton, pretend I don't know he's behind this."

"Do you hear yourself?" Ethan slammed his palm hard on the steering wheel. "That doesn't even make any sense. It's too dangerous. You don't know who you're dealing with. Thayer is conniving—he can twist things around just as deftly as Sutton could. He could expose you to the cops. You know what would happen then." His voice was urgent. "You've been living Sutton's life—everyone will think *you* killed Sutton so you could steal her identity."

"Thayer already had the chance to do that today and he didn't," Emma reminded him.

"Well, he could do much worse than that," Ethan said,

running a hand through his dark, inky hair. "If he ever gets out, he could hurt you."

Emma stared out the window at the streetlamps illuminating the way for the car along the deserted road. She didn't want to think about that possibility. She hoped that Thayer would just stay locked up forever. And she didn't like Ethan's tone. Maybe he was just being protective of her, but having lived thirteen years with *no one* looking out for her, it felt strangely unwelcome to have someone telling her what she could and couldn't do—especially a boyfriend, who was supposed to be on her side.

"You don't know Thayer," Ethan urged. "He has a temper, just like his dad."

Emma shot him a look. "You don't think I can handle tempers? I'm not Sutton, Ethan. I didn't grow up in a happy bubble of a delusion. I was a foster kid. I've been screamed at all my life. I was *abandoned* by my real mom. I'm tougher than you think."

"You don't have to get angry," Ethan protested.

"I just don't understand why you aren't backing me up on this. I thought you wanted to find Sutton's killer just as badly as I do."

"I don't want you to get hurt," Ethan argued, his expression hard.

"Yeah, well, spare me your fatherly lectures," Emma said darkly.

Ethan let out a small, incredulous sniff. They were silent for a little while, driving down the dark streets past the adobe houses and gravel lawns. A boy on a bicycle with a flashing light on the back wobbled on the shoulder.

"I just want you to be safe," Ethan said finally. "Just hold off visiting him for now—for me? Maybe there's another way we can figure out what happened that night. A way that gives you solid proof to bring to the police."

Emma let out a sigh. Ethan was right about the risks involved in a jailhouse visit. And she had to admit that the thought of facing Thayer again terrified her. "Fine. I'll give it a couple more days. After that, if we haven't made any progress, I'll have no choice but to talk to Thayer."

Emma may have been reluctant, but I, for one, couldn't wait to hear what he had to say.

9

STARSTRUCK

"Sutton?" Mrs. Mercer called out as Emma flew into the Mercer house after Ethan dropped her off. "You missed dinner!"

"Uh, yeah, I had some stuff to do after the tennis match," Emma called vaguely on her way up the stairs.

She heard Mrs. Mercer's footsteps in the hall. "I'll leave a plate for you in the warming drawer, okay?"

"Got it," Emma said, escaping into Sutton's room like a fugitive. Not that she had any idea what a warming drawer was. And she wasn't about to have a conversation with Mrs. Mercer right now. One look at Emma's stricken, freaked-out expression and she'd know something was up.

She shut the door to Sutton's bedroom and peered around, trying to get her bearings. *Get a grip, Emma,* she told herself, too keyed up to even make up a headline for what was happening right now. What she needed to do was figure out more about Thayer and his relationship with Sutton. Was it an intense friendship? A romantic tryst? Why had they secretly met the night Sutton died? If Thayer had arrived in Tucson the night of the thirty-first, then he was either the last person to see her alive—or he was her killer. But where had he been hiding since then? Why had he come back now? And how was she going to find out the answers to those questions without asking him point-blank—or revealing that she wasn't Sutton?

Emma wished there were clues in Sutton's room, but she'd already ransacked the place several times over since she arrived. She'd found information about what the Lying Game was, including pranks Sutton and the others had played and people they'd hurt. She'd scoured Sutton's Facebook page and emails. She'd even read Sutton's diary— not that it told her much at all, most of it vague snippets and inside jokes. New evidence wasn't going to fall into her lap just because she wanted it to.

If only it would. I wished I could beam my thoughts into Emma's mind and let her know that I'd been in love with Thayer and that we'd gone hiking together the night

I died. This one-way-communication thing was a serious flaw in the whole being-dead thing.

Emma booted up Sutton's MacBook Air laptop and navigated to the Greyhound website, researching the pick-up and drop-off points for Greyhound buses in Seattle and Tucson. It was a long trip, over a day, with a driver change halfway, in Sacramento.

She dialed the customer service number on the site and waited almost ten minutes on hold, listening to a Muzak version of a Britney Spears song. Finally, a sweet-sounding woman with a Southern accent answered. Emma cleared her throat, steeled her nerves, and started to speak.

"I'm really hoping you can help me." Emma tried to sound as though she were distraught. "My brother ran away and I have reason to believe that he took one of your buses out of Tucson. Is there any way you can tell me if he bought a ticket? It would have been in early September." She couldn't believe the story had just spilled from her lips. She hadn't rehearsed it beforehand, but she was surprised at how natural it sounded. It was an old trick she remembered Becky doing quite a bit: sobbing when she needed to get her way. Once, when they were at an IHOP and were pre-sented with a bill they couldn't pay, Becky told the waitress a long, drawn-out tale of woe about how her deadbeat husband must have cleaned out her wallet without telling her. Emma had sat next to her in the booth, gaping at her mother, but whenever she breathed in to correct Becky, her mother kicked her sharply under the table.

The woman on the other end of the phone coughed. "Well, I'm not really supposed to do something like that, honey."

"I'm really sorry to ask." Emma let out a loud sob. "I'm just so, so desperate. My brother and I were really close. I'm devastated he's gone, and I'm worried he's in danger."

The woman hesitated for a moment, and Emma knew she had her. Finally, she sighed. "What's your brother's name?"

Score. Emma bit back a smile. "Thayer. Thayer Vega."

She heard a series of clicks on the other end. "Ma'am, I see a Thayer Vega on a Seattle-to-Tucson bus that left at 9 A.M. on the morning of August thirtieth, but that's the only entry I have with his name in the system."

Emma switched the phone to the other ear, feeling deflated. "Are you sure? Maybe it's out of a different city? What about Phoenix? Flagstaff?"

"Anything is possible," the woman answered. "I only have his name on the original trip because he booked online. He could have paid cash at any station—there's no way for us to track that."

Emma jumped at this piece of information. "Is there any way to look at where he booked that ticket online? Maybe an IP address?"

There was a long pause. "No, I don't have that ability. And I've really told you more than I should . . ."

Figuring she'd gotten everything she could, Emma thanked the woman for her time and hung up. *Shit.* She knew calling Greyhound was a long shot—she was lucky they had released any information at all.

She closed the laptop and ran her hands along its smooth, shiny surface. Suddenly, the four walls seemed to be closing in on her. Putting the computer back on Sutton's desk, she slipped on Sutton's ballet flats and started down the stairs.

Dusk had fallen outside, and the house was cool, dark, and silent. Emma didn't know where the family had gone—it was too early to go to bed. She walked down the empty hall, her footsteps ringing out on the terra-cotta-tiled floor, and entered the kitchen. The pungent scents of roasted potatoes and grilled beef filled the air. The oven was still on, and Emma could just make out a plate waiting for her in a little lower compartment. She couldn't help but feel touched. No foster mom had ever made her a plate of leftovers. Mostly she'd had to fend for herself.

But she wasn't hungry right now. Emma walked through the kitchen and let herself out onto the red-tiled patio behind the Mercer's house. The night had a cool edge to it and after the warmth of the day, it felt like plunging into a swimming pool after a soak in a hot tub. She dragged one of the wooden chaise lounges to the darkest corner of the lawn, then stretched out on it. She'd always done her best thinking outside.

The midnight blue sky was alive with stars. They twinkled like faraway Christmas lights, bright and clear. It had been ages since Emma had sat out and just stared up at the sky. One of the last times she'd done it was the night she discovered the strange snuff video of Sutton online, back when she was living in Vegas. She'd gazed up at the cosmos, picking out her favorite stars, the ones she'd named the Mom Star, the Dad Star, and the Emma Star shortly after Becky had abandoned her, holding on to the hope that one day her true family would unite on Earth just like in the sky. Little did she know that a few moments after that, her whole life would change. She *would* find a family member, a *sister*, something she wanted more than anything in the entire world. In a roundabout way, she'd get a family, too. She had even gotten a boyfriend. But none of it was in the way she wanted.

"What are you doing out here?"

Emma jumped and turned. Mrs. Mercer slid the glass door shut behind her and joined Emma out in the yard. She was barefoot, and her raven hair was down around her shoulders. She tugged a magenta cashmere scarf around her long, slender neck.

Emma pushed herself up into a seated position. "Just looking at the stars."

Mrs. Mercer smiled. "That used to be your favorite thing when you were little. Remember how you gave the stars your own names? You said it wasn't fair that other people got to name them just because they happened to be born thousands of years before you were."

"I named stars?" Emma sat up, startled. "What did I call them?"

"Nothing that original. I think there was the Mom Star. The Dad Star. The Laurel Star. The Sutton Star. And the E Constellation, for your favorite doll." Mrs. Mercer pointed to a patch of stars just to the west. "Actually, I think that cluster up there might be it. See? It forms an *E*. You used to love that."

Emma stared into the sky, dumbfounded. Sure enough, six stars formed a wide capital *E*.

A chill ran down her spine. It was the same cluster of stars she'd chosen, too. She knew Sutton had an old doll that she called E—maybe even for Emma—but it was uncanny that Sutton had fixated on those same stars, had even given them names. Was it a cosmic twin connection? Did Sutton know of Emma's presence, and vice versa, somewhere deep down inside?

For what felt like the millionth time, Emma wondered what her life would have been like if she and Sutton hadn't been separated. Would they have been friends? Would they have helped each other survive Becky's manic moods? Would they have been placed together in foster care, or separated?

I couldn't help but wonder, too. If I had grown up with Emma, with a twin to watch my back, would I still be alive?

Mrs. Mercer sank down into the other chaise and laced her hands behind her head. "Can I ask you something without you biting my head off?"

Emma stiffened. She wasn't really into prying questions. She got enough of those from Quinlan. "Uh, I guess."

"What's going on with you and your sister?" Mrs. Mercer scooted farther back in her chair. "Ever since . . . what happened on Friday night, things have been worse than usual between you two."

Emma lowered her gaze from the sky and stared at her fingernails. "I wish I knew," she said in a forlorn voice.

"You seemed to be getting along pretty well last week," Mrs. Mercer said softly. "You guys went to Homecoming together, talked during dinner, didn't get into the usual fights about the usual stupid things." She cleared her throat. "Is it me, or did things change because Thayer appeared in your bedroom?"

Emma's skin prickled just at the sound of Thayer's

name. "Maybe," she admitted. "I think she's . . . mad, somehow. But I didn't *ask* him to show up that night."

Mrs. Mercer pulled her lower lip into her mouth, thinking. "You know, Sutton, Laurel loves you, but you're not exactly the easiest sister to have."

"What do you mean?" Emma asked, crossing her legs and shifting closer toward Mrs. Mercer. A stiff wind tousled her hair and numbed her nose.

Yeah, I thought indignantly. *What* did *that mean, Mom?*

"Well, you're beautiful, you're smart, and everything seems to come so easily for you. Friends, boyfriends, tennis . . ." Mrs. Mercer leaned forward and pushed a lock of Emma's hair behind her ear. "Thayer may have been Laurel's best friend, but no one could deny the way he looked at you."

Emma's breath caught in her throat. Did Mrs. Mercer know something about Sutton and Thayer's relationship? "And . . . *how* did he look at me?"

Mrs. Mercer studied Emma for a second, her expression giving nothing away. "Like he'd do anything to be with you."

Emma waited, but her mother didn't continue. She wished she'd say something concrete. But she couldn't exactly ask, *Hey, by the way, did I ever secretly date Thayer? And do you think it's possible that he lost his temper and killed me?*

A wistful smile tugged at the edges of Mrs. Mercer's lips. "Your father used to look at me like that, you know."

"Mo-om, gross!" Emma made a face, knowing that would have been Sutton's reaction. But secretly she liked that Mrs. Mercer was telling her about her and Mr. Mercer's courtship. It was nice to hear about two adults in love, two parents who wanted children and did everything in their power to give them the best life. People like that didn't exist in her old life.

"What?" Mrs. Mercer pressed a hand innocently to her chest. "We were as young as you once, you know. Many, *many* years ago."

Emma looked at the fine lines around Mrs. Mercer's eyes and at her newly dyed hair. She'd found out that Sutton's parents hadn't adopted her until they were in their late thirties, after they'd been married for nearly twenty years. It was a stark contrast to Becky, who bragged to Emma that she was the "cool, young mom," only seventeen years older than Emma was. But she always seemed more like Emma's wayward older sister as a result.

"Are you glad you waited so long to have to kids?" Emma blurted before she could stop herself.

A tight expression passed over Mrs. Mercer's face. A woodpecker banged away at a nearby tree. A car sputtered to life down the street. A cloud passed over the moon, momentarily darkening the night. Finally, she breathed in. "Well, I don't know if *glad* is the right word. But I'm so thankful every day to have you and Laurel in our lives. I don't know what I'd do if something ever happened to one of you."

Emma shifted uncomfortably, the guilt gripping her like a vise. It was moments like these that she regretted having to keep a secret from Sutton's family—a *big* secret. Their daughter had been murdered, and every day that passed was a missed opportunity to find her killer. When Emma had been on the bus to Tucson, eager to meet Sutton, she'd carried a small torch of hope that maybe, just maybe, Sutton's adoptive family would take her in, too, let her live her senior year with them. Ironically, she'd gotten her wish. What would they do to her if they found out the truth? Throw her out for sure. Probably even have her arrested.

She wanted so badly to come clean to Mrs. Mercer. To tell her that something bad had already happened to one of her daughters. But she knew it was impossible. Ethan was right. She couldn't tell anyone who she was. Not yet.

The door opened again, and a second figure stepped onto the patio. Laurel's frizzy blonde hair was backlit against the floodlights on the roof. "What are you guys doing out here?"

"Stargazing," Mrs. Mercer called cheerfully. "Come join us!"

Laurel hesitated for a second, then padded across the grass toward them. Mrs. Mercer nudged Emma, as if to say, *Look! This is your chance to make things right!* Laurel kept her head down as she dropped into a seat next to her mother. Mrs. Mercer leaned over and began braiding Laurel's hair.

"You were looking at the stars?" Laurel asked incredulously.

"Uh-huh," Mrs. Mercer chirped. "And I was telling Sutton about how much I love you two. And how much I want you two to get along."

Even though it was dark out, Emma could tell Laurel was making a sour face.

Mrs. Mercer cleared her throat, obviously undeterred. "Now isn't this nice, all three of us spending time together?"

"Uh-huh," Laurel muttered unconvincingly, refusing to look at Emma.

"Maybe you two can even make up?" Mrs. Mercer pressed.

Laurel's shoulders visibly stiffened. After a beat, she rose to her feet and wrapped her arms around her torso. "I just remembered some homework I have to do," she mumbled, running for the door. It was like she couldn't get away from Emma fast enough.

The door slammed hard. Mrs. Mercer looked dejected,

as if she really thought her efforts would pay off. Emma sighed and stared up at her constellation once more. She picked out the two brightest stars near Mom Star, Dad Star, and Emma Star and named them Sutton Star and Laurel Star, hoping that their proximity up there could influence her and Laurel's relationship down here.

But by the disgusted, hateful look on Laurel's face, I had a feeling it would take a lot more than that. And Emma should know the truth about stars—even though it seems like they're close together, up there in the heavens, they're a zillion light-years apart.

10

GONNA GETCHA

The following day, the bell rang and Emma grabbed her English textbook and joined the stream of students in the hall. As soon as she rounded the corner for the art wing, she heard the whispers and felt the stares.

"Her and Thayer . . ."

"Did you know she sent him away?"

"His hearing is a month from now. Do you think he's going to rot in jail that whole time?"

A female basketball player with streaky highlights and a snub nose shot Emma a curious look, then leaned in to a boy with dreadlocks. Both of them started snickering. Emma winced and kept her head held high. She'd had plenty of experience with weird looks from kids at the many schools she'd attended. In fact, she'd even composed a list of nasty comebacks she could shoot at passersby if they commented about her thrift-store clothes and the fact that she was a foster kid. She'd written down the list on a pocket-size Moleskine notebook and kept it with her at all times, just like foreign tourists who carry around English translation handbooks. She'd never been brave enough to use any of the comebacks, though. Sutton probably would have been.

Suddenly, something at the far end of the lobby caught Emma's eye. A long table had been set up at the doors, and a line of students were standing in front of it, signing something. As the crowd parted, Emma saw Laurel and Madeline sitting on chairs, both wearing black T-shirts with words printed in white across the boobs. Emma squinted, not believing her eyes. The shirts said FREE THAYER.

Emma walked up to the table, curiosity getting the best of her. "Oh, hey, Sutton!" Madeline said in a saccharine voice. "We'll be ready for lunch in a sec."

"What's that?" Emma asked, pointing at a clipboard all the kids were signing.

"Nothing." Laurel pulled it away from a guy in a baseball jersey who'd just signed the paper and covered it with her hand. "You wouldn't be interested."

"She *should* be interested," Madeline said under her breath. "She's the reason he's in this mess."

Madeline pushed the clipboard toward Emma. PETITION TO FREE THAYER VEGA, it said at the top. Tons of student signatures were scrawled on lines down the page. There was also a jar marked BAIL FUND filled with ones, fives, tens, and even a twenty-dollar bill or two.

"Want to contribute, Sutton?" Madeline lilted, an edge to her voice. "Fifteen thousand is a lot of money, and we could use every dollar. There's no way Thayer can last in jail until next month. We need to get him out sooner."

Emma ran her tongue over her teeth. The only thing keeping her sane right now was the fact that Thayer was in jail until his hearing. But she couldn't exactly *tell* Mads and Laurel that. She wondered what would happen if she showed up tomorrow in a THAYER MAY HAVE KILLED MY LONG-LOST TWIN SISTER shirt.

She glanced up to catch Laurel glaring at her. She thought about what Mrs. Mercer had said—that Sutton was a hard sister for Laurel to have. Emma wished she knew exactly why Thayer's return had made Laurel so angry. Was it because Thayer went to Sutton's room and not Laurel's? Was Laurel jealous because of that, or did she know that Thayer had been in love with Sutton? Or maybe she thought that Sutton had stolen him away.

But maybe Laurel was upset about something else

entirely—something Emma and I couldn't even begin to imagine.

Luckily, Emma was saved from making an excuse to not sign the petition by Charlotte, who looped her arm around Emma's shoulder. "C'mon, girls. Even activists need to eat," she boomed loudly, beckoning for Madeline and Laurel. "I've scored our favorite lunch table."

Shrugging, Madeline and Laurel slipped the petitions and banners back into their purses and stood. Charlotte wordlessly led them to a wooden table in the big courtyard outside the cafeteria. Desert flowers bloomed all around them. Hummingbirds flitted to the little daisy-shaped feeders that hung around the perimeter. At the table next to them, a bunch of girls in band uniforms were giggling at a picture on an iPad. Freshman meathead guys blew straw wrappers at each other at another table. A bunch of überskinny girls sat on the stucco wall, eating minuscule bites of Greek yogurt.

A squeal of laughter rang through the tension and Emma turned to see the Twitter Twins approaching. Gabby wore capri pants piped in grosgrain ribbon with a matching headband. A tiny piece of peach coral on a delicate chain peeked out between the pearlized buttons of the lime green collared shirt she had on. Lili, on the other hand, looked like she'd raided Courtney Love's closet, wearing an übershort plaid skirt held together by a zillion safety pins, ripped black tights, and an off-the-shoulder black top that showed more than a bit of cleavage.

"Hello, ladies," Gabby said, twirling a long strand of blonde hair around her index finger.

"Hey," Madeline said unceremoniously.

"Don't look so excited to see us," Lili scolded.

Laurel rolled her eyes and drenched a piece of sushi in soy sauce.

The Twitter Twins plopped down and opened their lunch bags. Both had brought organic strawberry yogurt and a banana. "So, girls," Lili said as she peeled the fruit. "Now that we're card-carrying members of the"—she looked around and lowered her voice—"*Lying Game*, who are we going to prank next?" Her blue eyes sparkled with excitement.

Madeline shrugged a shoulder. She ran the back of her hand across the shimmery peach blush that dotted her porcelain skin. "I don't care," she said, casting a disinterested stare over Emma's head.

But then Laurel's face lit up. "Actually, I have an idea." She glanced around conspiratorially, then lowered her voice. "What about him?" She pointed at someone directly behind Emma. Everyone swiveled to follow her gaze. When Emma saw who it was, her heart sank. Ethan was facing away from them, his feet propped up against the brick wall, a book in his hand.

"Ethan Landry?" Gabby said, a surprised note in her voice.

"Why not?" Laurel asked. She looked up and met Emma's eyes, and Emma felt heat rise to her cheeks. She'd admitted that she liked Ethan when they'd bought Homecoming outfits together last week. And Laurel had seen them snuggling up at the tennis courts. This was an obvious screw-you, perhaps as revenge for Thayer showing up in Sutton's bedroom.

Charlotte twisted her mouth, looking unconvinced. "Ethan? Wouldn't that be a repeat?"

"Yeah, we said no repeats, Laur," Madeline reminded her.

Emma nearly choked on the dry turkey sandwich she'd pulled out of Sutton's lunch bag. What did *that* mean? Had they pranked Ethan before? She thought about the Lying Game videos she'd seen on Laurel's computer. Not a single one involved Ethan. When had this happened? Why hadn't Ethan told her about it?

"It's technically a repeat, I guess," Laurel acceded, tapping her lips thoughtfully. "But we never did get him back for ruining our prank on you, Sutton." She was referring to the night Ethan stumbled upon Charlotte, Madeline, and Laurel blindfolding Sutton and staging a fake strangulation snuff film, the same film that landed on the Internet and led Emma to search for Sutton in the first place. Ethan had thought something terrible was happening to Sutton and intervened to stop it. But he'd told Emma that Sutton had laughed it off and pretended like it was nothing. "And we'll make sure the prank itself is different."

Madeline popped a grape into her mouth. "You know, Ethan *is* a pretty good target. He's so sensitive and *emo*. He'll probably, like, cry or something."

"Boo hoo," Lili lilted. She tapped something into Twitter, her fingers flying.

"I think a planning session's in order," Madeline said. "My house, tomorrow?"

Emma swallowed hard. It felt like everything was racing forward too fast, out of her control. "Shouldn't we leave Ethan alone?" she blurted, her voice cracking.

Everyone turned and stared at her. "Why, Sutton?" Laurel asked, clearly enjoying herself. "Is someone keeping a secret we don't know about?"

Emma gazed around the table at Sutton's friends, feeling resentful that Laurel had forced her into this position. Laurel was the only person she'd confided in about Ethan—she wasn't sure if the other girls would understand. Dating Ethan had to be an extremely un-Sutton thing to do, a strange choice after popular Garrett. And *what* would she tell them? She wasn't exactly sure what was going on between her and Ethan. It wasn't like they were boyfriend and girlfriend . . . yet.

Emma snapped the top from her Diet Coke and felt a

tiny spray of soda bubbles against her fingertips. "I'm not keeping secrets," she said smoothly, summoning up her best snooty Sutton voice. "Especially not about *Ethan*." It hurt her heart just to say the words.

"Well, then, you'll have no problem pranking Ethan with us," Laurel said, clapping her hands together in a loud smack. She pointed across the courtyard at Ethan's straight back. "I do believe, girls, that Mr. Emo Boy is next."

11

PARTY OF FOUR

That night, strains of Laurel's latest hip-hop ballad obses-
sion filtered from her bedroom, down the hall, and into
Emma's ears. Emma pushed her index and middle fingers
into her temples. What she wouldn't give for an afternoon
with Alex, her best friend from Henderson, listening to
Vampire Weekend or any music that didn't involve "Baby,
baby, baby" in the lyrics. She wondered if her twin had
shared Laurel's awful taste in music.

For the record, my music taste has always been impeccable. Maybe I couldn't tick off all the amazing concerts
I went to—I'm sure I'd gone to more than a few—but
whenever Adele, Mumford & Sons, or Lykke Li came

on the radio, I knew they had to be on my most-played iTunes list. The lyrics came back in haunting chunks, siren voices from my past.

"I can't come, Caleb," Emma heard Laurel shout over the music. "I told you, we're going to dinner tonight as a *family*."

Sighing, Emma rose and made her way to Sutton's closet and sorted through a row of T-shirts stacked neater than the anally folded T-shirts at the Gap. Sutton had kept everything neatly ordered when it came to her clothes. Emma pulled a turquoise boat-neck tee from the pile, yanked it over her head, and selected a pair of dark denim leggings and metallic flats to go with it.

"Yeah, I know it sucks." Laurel's voice vibrated through the walls. "I so don't want to go. The less time I spend with her, the better."

Emma guessed she was the *her* to whom Laurel was referring. When she and Laurel had gotten home from tennis practice, Mrs. Mercer had announced that the family was in serious need of bonding time—in other words, Emma and Laurel needed to bury the hatchet—so they were going out for a nice meal at Arturo's, an expensive restaurant in one of the Tucson resorts. In her past life, Emma most likely would have worked at Arturo's as a hostess instead of dining there with a family. Emma wished she could tell Mrs. Mercer not to bother with a special let's-kiss-and-make-up dinner. After the whole let's-prank-Ethan announcement, she wasn't sure if she wanted to reconcile with Laurel, either.

Another peal of laughter sounded from Laurel's bedroom. Emma stared at her reflection in the mirror, running a round brush through her hair. Did Caleb know about Laurel's crush on Thayer? What did he think of her camping out at the Free Thayer petition table, wearing that stupid black T-shirt? Had he signed the petition? And what did Laurel know about Thayer and Sutton, anyway? Once again she thought about Laurel's vague comment: *You got him in trouble! Again.* What was she referring to? How could Emma find the answer?

"I'll call you when we get home," Laurel promised, interrupting Emma's thoughts. "Bye!" And then the music shut off abruptly, filling the second floor with silence. Emma heard a drawer open and shut, and then Laurel's door creaked. She saw a shadow pass under Sutton's door, and then heard Laurel's voice downstairs in the kitchen, calling out to Mrs. Mercer.

Suddenly, an idea came to her. She sprang up from Sutton's bed and padded into the hall. Laurel's bedroom door was ajar. Light from a bedside table spilled onto the carpet. Listening to make sure Laurel wasn't coming back up the stairs, she tiptoed toward the bedroom. Within seconds, she was inside. She pulled the door closed, listening to the lock catch.

Laurel's bedroom was eerily similar to Sutton's, down to the white bubble chair and the purple pillows on the bed. Emma stepped to the far wall where a recent collage of tennis team pictures hung next to a calendar of puppies. OCTOBER, the calendar heading read. Laurel had covered the days with notes about homework assignments, tennis matches, and parties.

Slowly, quietly, she pulled a lime-green tack from the wall and flipped the calendar pages back to August, which featured three tiny Boxer puppies. Laurel had written FAMILY VACAY in bold letters across the squares marking the first week of the month. Emma's eyes immediately zoomed toward August thirty-first, the day Sutton vanished. Laurel had drawn a blue heart in the upper right-hand corner of the day. She'd colored the heart in with thick, scrabbling lines, the ink pressed hard into the page.

Emma stared at the heart for a moment, unsure what it meant. She flipped to September, staring at the dates marking Nisha Banerjee's end-of-summer party, the first day of school, the first tennis invitational. Nothing was amiss. But then something on the back side of the August page caught her eye: Pressed into the paper, directly behind the box for the thirty-first, were the initials TV.

For Thayer Vega?

Emma's heart picked up speed. Laurel had obviously

written the initials first, then covered them up with the solid blue heart. But why?

I wish I knew.

"What are you doing in here?"

Emma let the calendar fall back to October and whipped around to see Laurel standing in the doorway. Her lips were pursed. Her hand was on her jutting hip. She shot across the room and pushed Emma away from her calendar.

Emma scrambled for an excuse. "The Haverford match," she said quickly, pointing to a Friday two weeks in the future. "I just wanted to check the date."

Laurel peered around her desk, as though to make sure nothing was missing or out of place. "With the *door closed*?"

A tiny beat passed, then Emma stood up straighter. "Paranoid much?" she snapped, channeling her inner Sutton. "The air conditioning must have pushed it closed."

Laurel looked like she was going to say something else, but then Mrs. Mercer's voice sounded at the bottom of the stairs. "Girls? We have to leave now!"

"Coming!" Emma trilled, as though she'd done nothing wrong. She swept past Laurel, trying to remain poised, blameless, and aloof. But she could feel Laurel's eyes searing into her back.

I could, too. It was obvious she hadn't bought Emma's lie.

Mrs. Mercer was standing at the bottom of the stairs, checking her BlackBerry. She smiled at the girls as they walked down the stairs. "You both look lovely," she said in an eager voice. Probably *too* eager. Emma knew she was going to be disappointed by tonight's outcome.

Mr. Mercer rounded the corner and jangled a set of keys in the air. He'd changed from hospital scrubs into a pair of wrinkle-free khakis and a salmon-colored button-down, but his eyes looked tired and his hair was mussed. "Ready?" he said a bit breathlessly.

"Ready," Mrs. Mercer echoed. Laurel crossed her arms over her chest sulkily. Emma just shrugged.

They walked to Mr. Mercer's SUV and climbed in. As Emma belted herself into the seat behind Sutton's mother, Mr. Mercer caught her eye in the rearview mirror. She quickly looked down. Aside from a few run-ins in the hall, she'd hardly spoken to Sutton's dad since Saturday morning—he'd been working around the clock at the hospital. Now he was staring at her like he knew she was hiding something.

As Mr. Mercer hit reverse and pulled into the street, Mrs. Mercer plucked a gold-tone compact from her purse and smoothed on a layer of mauve lipstick. "This weather is so odd for early October," she chattered. "I can't think of the last time we expected rain like this."

No one responded.

Mrs. Mercer cleared her throat, trying again. "I got that great mariachi band you love for your party, honey," she said, laying a hand on Mr. Mercer's arm. "Remember how brilliant they were at the Desert Museum benefit?"

"Great," Mr. Mercer answered in a tepid voice. It seemed like he didn't really feel like doing family dinner either.

Mrs. Mercer fell quiet, looking defeated.

I watched them all settle into stony silence. Something about this situation seemed familiar to me. I wondered how many other times my parents had tried whatever means necessary to force Laurel and me to be friends. We'd been close, once—I had glimmers of us spying on our parents together during family vacations, playing a game I'd made up called Runway Model in the basement, and even me teaching Laurel how to hold a tennis racket and hit a decent backhand. But something had happened over the years—I'd begun to push Laurel away. Part of it might have been jealousy—Laurel was my parents' real daughter, while I was their adopted child. I worried they loved her more. Maybe Laurel was just reacting to me. And things had just snowballed until we went through phases of barely speaking to each other.

Fifteen minutes and zero conversational topics later, Mr. Mercer eased the SUV over a speed bump and pulled into the resort parking lot. A little grotto with the name

ARTURO'S etched in a boulder was lit up with Christmas lights. Outside the front entrance, a man in a business suit with a briefcase talked on his BlackBerry. A woman stood next to him, fussing with her blonde hair. Two waiters dressed in dark pants and crisp white button-downs took a smoke break next to a spindly cactus.

Emma followed Sutton's family along stone steps that wove through a garden spotted with tiny yellow and violet flowers. Inside, thick, dark wood framed the windows in the adobe walls. Exposed beams hung overhead, and soft classical music floated from miniature speakers. The room was full of people, and waiters swirled with plates full of beautiful-looking racks of lamb, strip steaks, and lobster.

A maître d' with a pencil mustache and a dark gray suit checked their reservation, and then led them to their table. As they walked through the room, Emma stood up a little straighter, feeling out of place.

"This is lovely," Mrs. Mercer cooed as they sat, picking up a thick piece of cardboard and perusing the wines listed. "Isn't it, girls?"

Emma murmured in assent. But Laurel's gaze was on something—some*one*—across the room. "I think you're going to have a visitor, Sutton," she said nastily.

Emma looked up just in time to see a guy with an angular jaw and short blond hair advancing toward their table. Her stomach flipped uncomfortably. It was Garrett, Sutton's ex. And he didn't look happy.

"Hello, Garrett!" Mrs. Mercer said, her mouth wobbling, sending a worried glance at Emma. Emma shifted in her seat. She'd told Sutton's dad that she and Garrett were no longer an item, and no doubt he'd told her mom. What they didn't know was that he'd accosted her in the supply room at Homecoming on Friday. In fact, he'd been a little . . . *violent*.

"Hi, Mr. and Mrs. Mercer." Garrett nodded politely at Sutton's parents. Then he turned to Emma. "Can I talk to you for a minute?" He slid his eyes toward a little hallway at the back of the restaurant. Clearly he meant *alone*.

"Um, I'm here with my family," Emma said, scooting a little closer to Sutton's mom. "We were about to order."

"I just have a quick question," Garrett said. His voice was pleasant enough, but his eyes were cold and calculating. All at once, Emma knew what this was about: He'd no doubt heard that Thayer had broken into Sutton's bedroom. Garrett had been shocked that Emma had dumped him, and he was convinced that she had been cheating on him. No doubt he was going to accuse Emma of seeing Thayer behind his back—and maybe Sutton had been.

I took in Garrett's Abercrombie button-down and khaki pants, feeling a vague flicker of the fun times we'd spent together hiking, going for long bike rides, and having picnics in the park. I was sure there had been some point where I'd been thrilled that he was my boyfriend. But what had happened that made me choose Thayer instead? I thought again about the memory that had come back to me, the push-and-pull of guilt I felt for cheating on Garrett and the thrill of kissing Thayer. Garrett was right about me: I *was* a cheater. He had every right to be mad.

"I'm sorry," Emma said. "But I just sat down."

"Okay, I can ask you here if you'd prefer," Garrett said challengingly, placing his hands on his hips. He glanced at the Mercer parents. "I just wanted to see how your visit to the police station went yesterday, Sutton."

Emma bristled. How did he know *that*? The Mercers stiffened. "You were at the police station?" Mrs. Mercer blurted. "Why didn't you tell us?"

Garrett faked a look of surprise. "Oh!" he said. "I figured you would have said something. I'll leave you guys alone." Then he backed away, returning to his parents' table in the corner.

Emma faced Sutton's parents, feeling her cheeks flush. She'd kind of hoped that they wouldn't find out about her little trip to see Quinlan.

"Were you in trouble again?" Mrs. Mercer asked, looking heartbroken, no doubt thinking about how she'd visited the police station to reprimand her daughter for shoplifting the week before.

"I bet she was there to see Thayer," Laurel said, her voice dripping with hatred.

"I wasn't in trouble," Emma said, her voice rising. "And I wasn't there to see Thayer, either. I only went because Quinlan called me in. I didn't want to tell you because it wasn't important."

"Yeah, right," Laurel said under her breath. "Like you're *such* the good daughter. Like you tell them *everything*."

Emma shot her a look. "What about you? Have you told them about the Free Thayer campaign? How you're asking kids to contribute to his bail fund?"

Mr. Mercer turned to her for a moment, looking horrified. Laurel reddened. "It's a project for my government class," she said quickly. "We were learning how petitions impact laws, and we had to put it into practice."

"You could have petitioned for something *other* than freeing the boy who broke into your home and scared the hell out of your sister," Mr. Mercer said sternly. Then he held up a hand. "We'll get to that in a second. Why did you go to the police station, Sutton? *Was* it about Thayer?" He leaned forward, staring Emma down. Fear prickled along Emma's spine. Sutton's dad looked just as furious as he had the night he'd found Thayer in Sutton's bedroom.

"I . . ." Emma started. But she wasn't sure what to say.

A waitress appeared beside them, then noticed the family's expressions. She waved her hands deferentially, and backed away toward the kitchen. Mr. Mercer laid his palms on the table, his face softening. "Well, Sutton?" he said in a milder voice. "Please tell us. We won't be upset. We're just concerned. Thayer is troubled. No normal guy runs away and then sneaks into your bedroom. We're just trying to keep you safe."

Emma lowered her eyes, her heart slowing down. Sutton's dad was using the same gentle-but-protective voice he'd used in the garage last week when she'd helped him work on his motorcycle. He was just trying to be a good parent. Still, there was no way she could tell him about what had happened at the police station.

"I was just signing paperwork about the shoplifting incident," she said, thinking quickly. "Nothing else happened. I promise. Garrett was just trying to get me in trouble because he's pissed off because we're not together anymore. You're making too big a deal about this."

She hid her shaking hands under the table, hoping they bought her story. Mr. Mercer stared at her. Mrs. Mercer bit her mauve-lined lip. Laurel sniffed, clearly not believing a word of it. But finally, the Mercer parents sighed and shrugged. "Next time you're at the police station, maybe you could let us know," Mrs. Mercer suggested calmly.

"Let's hope there *isn't* a next time," Mr. Mercer said gruffly, a crinkle forming between his eyes.

Emma looked away uncomfortably, her gaze floating to where Garrett and his family were sitting. At that very moment, he glanced over and gave her a smirk. *Jerk*, she thought. She hadn't wanted to open the Thayer can of worms tonight. But when she turned back to her parents, they were discussing whether they should order a bottle of Shiraz or Malbec from the wine list. She was off the hook—for now.

Or was she? I couldn't help but notice Laurel glaring at Emma across the table. And I couldn't help but remember those tiny little initials scribbled on her calendar the night I died. *TV.*

Laurel knew something. I only hoped Emma found out what it was before it was too late.

12

I AM WOMAN, HEAR ME ROAR

The following day, Emma stood in the Hollier parking lot, baking beneath the brutal Tucson sun. The girls' soccer team ran laps around a dusty field in the distance. Emma had no idea how they weren't keeling over—it had to be almost 110 degrees outside. She'd played thirty minutes of tennis at practice and felt like she needed to be hooked up to an IV for rehydration.

I remembered hot tennis practices like that. But weirdly, floating next to Emma, I felt neither hot nor cold. Just . . . nothing. It sounds strange, but I'd love to be sweaty and short of breath one more time. It surprised me that I desperately missed even those parts of being alive.

TWO TRUTHS AND A LIE

A horn honked, and Charlotte pulled up in her silver Mercedes. "Get in, bitch," she called out the window.

"Thanks for the ride," Emma said, throwing her tennis gear and purse in the backseat. "My sister is so lame for abandoning me." They were all meeting at Madeline's house for a prank-planning session today, but after tennis, Laurel had vanished without waiting for Emma. Luckily, Charlotte hadn't left school yet, though Emma would have given anything to skip the meeting. The last thing she wanted to do was embarrass Ethan. When she'd seen him in the halls today she'd felt terrible, sure he knew that she was keeping something from him. She felt stuck: If she told Ethan what they were up to and blew the prank, Sutton's friends would never forgive her. But if she *didn't* tell him, she might lose him forever.

As soon as Emma was inside, Charlotte hit the gas and the car lurched out of the parking lot onto the highway. Within minutes they were passing a long stretch of desert, then a mini mall packed with local clothing boutiques, a 1950s-looking ice cream parlor, Starbucks, and a video store. Charlotte took a right into a familiar housing development. Emma was glad Charlotte was driving. She'd only been to the Vegas' house once, when she and the girls had been planning a prank on the Twitter Twins, and she didn't really remember where it was. It was one advantage of Sutton's car having been missing for all this

119

time—if Sutton's friends thought she couldn't find her way around Tucson, they'd probably check her into the mental hospital.

As they waited at a stoplight on Orange Grove, the local news came on. "Tucson is abuzz with the story about Thayer Vega, the missing boy from this summer," a woman reporter said. Emma sat up straighter and tried not to gasp.

"Mr. Vega broke into an alleged girlfriend's house early Saturday morning, and now he's being held on a fifteen-thousand-dollar bail for breaking and entering, resisting arrest, and carrying a concealed weapon," the reporter went on. "However, Geoffrey Rogers, the lawyer assigned to his case, is convinced he'll get it dismissed."

A man's voice boomed through the stereo speakers. "My client is a minor—he should not be tried as an adult," Thayer's lawyer said. "This is a matter of bad blood between him and a certain member of the Tucson police force."

"Bad blood?" Emma said aloud before she could stop herself.

Charlotte looked at her. "Yeah, between him and Quinlan. Remember how that guy spearheaded the Find Thayer campaign? Thayer was like his white whale. He was furious that he couldn't find him. Everyone's saying that's why his punishment is so harsh—and that Quinlan made up the part about how Thayer resisted arrest."

Emma raised her eyebrows. What if that was true? What if the lawyer could get Thayer out before his trial? She didn't want to think of what might happen then.

"So Laurel's pretty pissed at you, huh?" Charlotte asked.

Emma nodded. "She thinks it's my fault that Thayer's in jail."

"Right," Charlotte said noncommittally, her expression giving nothing away. Emma wondered where she stood on the Thayer debate. While Madeline and Laurel had been out-and-out accusatory of Emma, Charlotte had defended her. And yet, Emma had seen her signing the Free Thayer petition earlier today. Maybe she just wanted to straddle the two sides and not make any waves.

"So how do you think Mads is doing about this whole Thayer thing?" Emma asked casually, popping a strawberry Life Saver into her mouth. "It's not like she'll talk to *me* about it." Charlotte and Madeline had been hanging out more recently; maybe Madeline had revealed something to Charlotte about Thayer that could help Emma understand his relationship with Sutton.

Charlotte kept her eyes on the road. "She's not happy, that's for sure. Apparently her dad's being an even bigger jerk than usual. Things are tense at home."

"Do you think she's . . . *hiding* something?" Emma asked, cracking the candy between her teeth.

"About what?"

Good question, Emma thought. She was taking a blind stab in the dark here, trying to grasp at anything. "About Thayer, maybe. About where he was all this time."

Charlotte turned her gaze from the road and gave Emma a long, incredulous look. "I think Mads is wondering the same thing about *you*."

Emma swallowed hard, not sure how to answer. *Did* Sutton know where Thayer had gone?

I had a feeling I didn't. I wouldn't have asked Thayer all of those questions about the secrets he was keeping if I had known.

Out the window, two junior-high-age kids skateboarded off a homemade ramp in the driveway next to Madeline's. Their mom looked on with her arms crossed over her chest and a disgruntled expression on her face. Finally, Charlotte shrugged. "It wouldn't surprise me if Madeline was hiding something, though."

"How come?" Emma asked, trying not to sound too eager.

"Because." Charlotte put her car in park and rested her fingertips on the console between them. "Everyone in the Vega family has secrets."

Before Emma could ask more, Charlotte got out of the car, adjusted her denim miniskirt, and started up the front walk to the stucco house. Emma got out, too, and followed her to the Vegas' front door. When Emma raised her finger to press the doorbell, Charlotte said, "No need," and she rummaged through her black hobo bag. "I have the key." She tugged a keychain attached to a wonky-looking miniature doll from the bag and pinched a bronze key between her thumb and index finger.

"You have the Vegas' key?" Emma asked, stopping short.

Charlotte gave Emma a weird look. "Uh, yeah. I've had it since eighth grade. I have yours, too—and you have mine, amnesia patient." She frowned. "You haven't misplaced my key, have you? My dad will flip. He'll have to change all the locks."

"No, I still have it," Emma covered, even though she had no idea where Charlotte's key might be. A fault opened in her mind. She thought about the person who'd tried to strangle her in Charlotte's house a few weeks ago. At first, she'd thought it had been one of Sutton's friends— the alarm hadn't been tripped, so whoever had done it was either inside the house from the start or knew the code. Could Thayer have stolen Madeline's key to Charlotte's house? Could he know the alarm code somehow?

"But could you tell me your alarm code again?" Emma's heart thudded, wondering how far she could push this line of questioning. "It's something really easy, right? 1-2-3-4?" Maybe Thayer had just guessed at the code and gotten it right.

SARA SHEPARD

Charlotte snorted. "What planet are you living on? It's 2-9-3-7. Just put it in your phone and quit asking me every two weeks. Madeline did and now she never has to ask."

"Madeline has your alarm code in her phone?" Emma repeated. "That doesn't seem safe." Her heart pumped faster. This was huge. Not only could Thayer have stolen Madeline's key to Charlotte's house, he could have found Charlotte's alarm code in Madeline's phone, too. She thought about the strong hands around her neck in Charlotte's kitchen. The whisper in her ear that she needed to stop digging. Those hands felt like a guy's. And that voice might have been the same one that called out to Emma in Sutton's bedroom Saturday morning.

I wondered if it was true. I thought about the hike we'd taken, the way Thayer easily maneuvered the rockiest trails and steepest inclines, always waiting impatiently for me to catch up. Sneaking into Charlotte's house or climbing up the rafters at school to drop an overhead light dangerously close to Emma's head would have been no challenge for him. I thought about myself alone in Sabino Canyon with Thayer the night I died. What if he'd thrown me over the cliff that I'd been coming to with my father ever since I was a little girl?

Charlotte opened the door to Madeline's house, and they stepped through the foyer. The inside smelled like a mix of potpourri and Mexican cooking, and four pairs of shoes, ranging from Tory Burch flats to Boutique 9 heels, were lined up by the closet. A bunch of photographs sat on a small console table along the wall. One was Mr. and Mrs. Vega's wedding photo, another was of a much younger Madeline in a tutu and pointe shoes. Emma frowned, sensing something was missing. The last time she had been here, she'd sworn she'd seen a photo of Thayer on that table, too. Had the Vegas taken it down? Were they trying to remove all evidence of Thayer? Were they embarrassed that he was their son?

Lili appeared at the top of the stairs. "Finally," she trilled, adjusting the dozen strands of black leather that wrapped her left wrist. "We're up here."

Emma and Charlotte stomped up to Madeline's bedroom. Music was playing loudly, and the flat-screen TV blared an episode of *The Rachel Zoe Project*. Madeline, Gabby, and Laurel looked up from their magazines as Emma, Charlotte, and Lili settled in. Old issues of *Vogue* and *W* were stacked in mini towers on the wooden floor. Coffee-colored shades were drawn to expose the Catalina Mountains in the distance. Framed posters of ballerinas in various poses dotted the pale peach walls, along with a snapshot of Madeline and Thayer on a ski trip.

Emma couldn't tear her gaze away. His deep-set eyes stared out from the photograph, seemingly glaring at her and only her.

Laurel found an issue of *Cosmopolitan* beneath Madeline's bed and opened it to an article titled "How to Make Your Man Roar Like a Tiger." "Who writes these things?" she scoffed, rolling her eyes.

"Wait!" Charlotte leaned over to take a look. "I'm dying to know how to get my man to roar like a tiger!" She narrowed her eyes and pursed her lips in a mock-sexy pout.

Laurel shook a bottle of dark green Essie nail polish and stuffed hot pink foam dividers between her toes. "I wonder what makes Ethan Landry roar," she said mischievously.

Emma's stomach dropped an inch.

Lili sat up straighter and shot a look at Gabby. Gabby gave a small nod, her eyes widening. "So Gabs and I spent last night brainstorming ideas for our first official prank," Lili announced. She glanced at Emma deferentially. *Of course*, Emma thought. *She thinks I'm Sutton. She's about to pitch prank ideas and is waiting for my approval.*

It was interesting watching how powerful I was from afar. I remembered how many suggestions I'd shot down, how many get-togethers I canceled when I simply wasn't feeling up to it, and how many evenings were spent doing *exactly* what I'd planned. After all, my ideas were the best ones. And everyone knew it.

Emma gritted her teeth, then decided to use Sutton's power to her advantage. She let out a barking laugh and cocked her head to the side. "Nice try," she said icily. "But I don't think the Lying Game is taking suggestions from newbies just yet."

"Yeah, watch and learn, girls." Charlotte closed *Cosmo* and sat up straighter. "So. Does anyone know what Ethan's into?"

A smile rolled across Laurel's face. "Sutton knows what he's into, right, Sis?"

Emma's throat tightened.

The girls looked at her. "And why would you know what Ethan Landry's into?" Madeline asked incredulously.

"I *don't* know," Emma snapped, shooting a nasty look at Laurel.

"Sure you do," Laurel said cheerfully. She plucked a stuffed dog off of Madeline's bed and cradled it in her arms. "Don't be so modest, Sis. You know all the dirt." She turned to the girls. "Sutton just told me this past weekend that Ethan secretly does poetry slams at Club Congress downtown."

"I never told you that!" Emma cried, heat rising to her chest, racking her brain to remember when she and Ethan had discussed the poetry slam. And then . . . it hit her. At the park, on Saturday. So Laurel *had* been spying. But what else had she heard?

"Of course he does poetry." Charlotte rolled her eyes. "Every good emo boy does." She whipped out her phone and loaded up Google. After a moment, she let out a squeal. "Here he is! Ethan Landry, listed as contestant number four on the slam list. We can make an awesome prank out of this!"

Madeline scooted closer. "We could hire people to sit in the audience to boo him or throw tomatoes at him."

"Or what if we planted a fake editor in the audience?" Lili breathed. "He could say he's super into Ethan's work and wants to publish him—but only if Ethan flies out to New York to meet with the publisher. But when Ethan gets there, they'll say they've never heard of him!"

Gabby nodded, her eyes wide. "He would feel like *such* a loser."

"Or . . ." Laurel said leadingly, waggling his eyebrows, "We can sneak into his house, steal a couple of his poems and post them online under a fake name. Then when he goes to read them, we can hire someone to pretend to be the real author and accuse Ethan of plagiarism. And when he shows that he uploaded the poems two weeks prior to the reading, Ethan will be *so* humiliated."

"That's genius!" Charlotte cried. "We'll tape the whole thing and put it on YouTube!"

Madeline high-fived Laurel. "Totally brilliant."

Gabby gestured dramatically, like she was giving a Shakespearean monologue, and trilled, "Roses are red, violets are blue, Ethan Landry, prank's on you!"

Laurel turned and eyed Emma. "What do *you* think, Sutton?"

Emma's entire body flushed with heat like she was about to be sick. She turned away from the girls, pretending to examine one of the Degas prints on Madeline's wall so they wouldn't see the look on her face. Every fiber of her being wanted to derail this prank, but she couldn't figure out a way to stop it. Sutton probably would have. Sutton would've made a biting comment that would have put everyone in their places. It made her feel like Old Emma again—tongue-tied, acquiescent, and wimpy.

"I, um, have to go to the bathroom," she blurted, jumping to her feet and running into the hall. If she stayed in Madeline's room a moment longer, she might burst into tears.

She made her way down the beige-carpeted hallway, trailing her hand along the adobe walls. Where the hell *was* Madeline's bathroom, anyway? She peered into the first available door, but it was just a linen closet. Behind the second door was an office with a computer and an industrial-sized printer. She passed the third door, which hung slightly ajar, and peeked inside. It was a room done up in light blue carpeting, darker blue walls, and a black bedspread. Soccer posters were taped to the walls, and shiny trophies stood on a shelf by the window.

Thayer's room.

Her stomach lurched. *Of course.* Why hadn't she thought of this sooner? If Sutton and Thayer had a secret relationship, maybe there would be some sort of evidence of it in here.

She shot a quick glance over her shoulder, then nudged the door open and tiptoed inside. Books were stacked neatly on the desk. There wasn't a trace of dust or clutter anywhere. A swivel chair with leather padding was tucked beneath his dark wooden desk. No one had bothered flipping the months on the Arizona Diamondbacks calendar tacked to the wall—a photo of a uniformed player swinging a bat and about to make contact with a blurry white ball hung above block letters marking JUNE. It was clear that this room had already been thoroughly searched, probably by the cops—by Quinlan—when Thayer went missing. Emma ran her fingertips along the stereo. She picked up an iPod and put it back down.

Seeing the iPod and stereo made my mind expand. I saw myself in Thayer's room, listening to an Arcade Fire song on that iPod. Thayer lay next to me on the carpet, grazing his fingertips across my knee. Strands of carpet tickled the backs of my bare legs. I reached forward to toy with the edge of his light green T-shirt, lifting it just a sliver to touch the hard stomach muscles beneath. Thayer cupped my chin with his palms and leaned forward until his mouth was a breath away. His lips covered mine and I felt my entire body spark. And then a door creaked open. We froze for a split second before breaking apart, sneaking down the back staircase, and slipping into the den. Just as Mr. Vega crossed the foyer and stared at us with wide, suspicious eyes, the memory faded away.

Emma circled the room, running her hands under the pillows on Thayer's bed, peeking into the bureau and desk drawers, and poking her head into the nearly empty closet. It was as bare and impersonal as a hotel room. Nothing was out of the ordinary. There were no left-behind tubes of lipstick that might have been Sutton's. No pictures of her on his bulletin board. If Thayer had a relationship with Sutton, he'd kept it a secret.

But then, suddenly, she saw it. There, stacked along-side the crime novels on the bookshelf, was a tattered, pale yellow book. *Little House on the Prairie*, said the spine. Emma reached for it. If it was random that Sutton had a book from the Little House series, it was downright bizarre that soccer-star-jock-boy Thayer had one.

The book felt light in Emma's hands. When she turned it over, she realized the pages had been removed and the book was hollow. Shaking, she plunged her hand into the opening and felt her fingers close on a bunch of papers. As she pulled them out, she got a whiff of a flowery fragrance she instantly recognized. It was the same musky smell Emma had spritzed on herself from an expensive-looking bottle with a gold-trimmed label marked ANNICK on Sutton's dresser.

With trembling fingers, she unfolded the papers. Sutton's distinctly rounded handwriting stared back at her. *Dear Thayer,* it began. *I think about you all the time . . . I can't wait until we can meet up again . . . I am so in love with you . . .*

She turned to the next page, but it said more or less the same thing. So did the six letters after it. Every one was addressed to Thayer and signed with an oversized *S.* Sutton had written a date at the top of each page; the letters started in March and continued through June, just before Thayer disappeared.

I looked at the letters, too, trying to make a connection, but nothing came. I had to have written them. A secret tryst with Thayer must have been intoxicating for me. I was a girl who lived on the edge, after all.

Emma stuffed the letters into the front pocket of her hoodie, then slipped back out into the hallway, pulling the door nearly shut after her, the same way she'd found it.

"Sutton?"

Emma flew around with a gasp. Mr. Vega stood right behind her, seemingly nearly twice her size. His dark hair was slicked back with gel, exposing a pointed widow's peak and making him look like he should be playing cards in a dark, smoke-filled hall. The tanned skin on his forehead wrinkled as his eyebrows met in the center.

He glanced at Emma's hand on Thayer's doorknob. "What are you doing?" he demanded.

"Um, just going to the bathroom, sir," Emma squeaked.

Mr. Vega stared at her. Sutton's letters felt bulky in her pocket. She folded her arms in front of her chest, trying to hide the bulge.

Finally, Mr. Vega pointed to another door. "The guest bathroom is on the other side of the hall."

"Oh, right!" Emma smacked her forehead. "Just got a little turned around. It's been a long week."

Mr. Vega pursed his lips. "Yes. It's been a trying time for all of us." He shuffled his feet, looking uncomfortable. "Actually, since you're here, I wanted to apologize for my son's behavior. I am deeply embarrassed that he broke into your home. Trust me when I say that I'll make sure he learns his lesson."

Emma nodded grimly, thinking about the bruises on Madeline's arm. She could only imagine how Mr. Vega planned to hit that message home to his son. "Well, I should probably get back to the girls," she mumbled.

She started to inch around Mr. Vega, but he grabbed her arm. Emma inhaled sharply, her heart leaping to her throat. But Mr. Vega let go immediately.

"Please ask Madeline to come talk to me for a minute, will you?" he said in a low voice.

Emma let out a breath. "Oh. Sure."

She moved toward Madeline's room, but he caught her once more. "And Sutton?"

Emma turned around, raising her eyebrows.

"You never used to call me 'sir.'" His lips were pressed in a flat line and he openly studied Emma. "No need to start now."

"Oh. Okay. Sorry."

Mr. Vega held Emma's gaze for a moment longer, inspecting her thoroughly and carefully. Emma fought hard to keep her expression neutral. Finally, he turned and smoothly made his way down the stairs. She wilted against the wall and shut her eyes, feeling the lump of papers in her pocket. *So close.*

Maybe too *close*, I thought.

13

LOVE, S.

An hour later, Emma sat stiffly next to Laurel in the VW. Laurel might have abandoned her at school, but there was no way for her to get out of driving her home from Madeline's. She hadn't said a word to Emma the whole time, and was wrinkling her nose at Emma as though she smelled like raw sewage.

Spying a strip mall that contained a grocery store, a Big Lots, and a bunch of other random shops on the corner, Emma grabbed the wheel and veered the car into the right lane. Laurel slammed on the brakes. "What the hell are you doing?"

"Getting you to pull over," Emma said, gesturing to the parking lot. "We need to talk."

To Emma's surprise, Laurel signaled, turned into the lot, and shut off the engine. But then she got out of the car and stomped toward the strip mall without waiting for Emma to follow. By the time Emma caught up with her, Laurel had pushed into a shop called the Boot Barn. The place smelled like leather and air freshener. Cowboy hats lined the walls, and there were shelves and shelves of cowboy boots as far as the eye could see. A country singer crooned something about his Ford pickup truck in a twangy voice over the loudspeaker, and the only other customer in the store was a grizzly-looking guy with a wad of chewing tobacco in his mouth. The shopkeeper, an overweight woman wearing a vest with galloping palominos embroidered on the front, gazed at them menacingly from behind the counter. She looked like the type who knew her way around a shotgun.

Laurel walked over to a black western button-down that had silver stud accents around the shoulders. Emma snickered. "I don't think that's quite your style."

Laurel placed the shirt back on the rack and feigned interest in a display of ornate belt buckles. Most of them were in the shape of cattle horns.

"Seriously, this ignoring me thing is getting a little old," Emma said, following behind her.

"Not for me, it isn't," Laurel said.

Emma was grateful she'd at least said *something*. "Look, I don't know why Thayer came into my room, and—"

Laurel whipped around and stared at her. "Oh, really? You *really* don't know?" Her gaze fell to Emma's waist. Emma sucked in her stomach, feeling the folded letters she'd found in Thayer's bedroom press against her. It almost felt like Laurel knew they were there.

"I really don't know," Emma said. "And I don't know why you're so pissed about it, but I wish you would tell me what I can do to make it up to you so you aren't mad anymore."

Laurel narrowed her eyes and backed away. "Okay, now you're freaking me out. Sutton Mercer doesn't *repent*. Sutton Mercer doesn't *make it up to* anyone."

"People change."

Or sometimes they die and their nicer twin takes their place, I thought grimly.

A new country song blared over the loudspeakers, this one about loving the good old USA. Laurel absent-mindedly picked up a pair of pink cowboy boots and put them back down again. Her expression seemed to soften. "Fine. There is one thing you could do to make it up to me."

"What?"

Laurel leaned forward. "You could get Dad to drop the charges against Thayer. Or you could tell Quinlan that you invited Thayer over. That way the cops will be forced to let him go."

"But I didn't invite him over!" Emma protested. "And

I'm not going to go behind Dad's back and lie to the police."

Laurel blew air out of her mouth angrily. "Like that's ever stopped you before."

"Well, I'm trying to turn over a new leaf. Trying not to have Mom and Dad pissed at me every other day for once."

"Yeah, right." Laurel snorted.

Emma balled her fists in frustration, staring at the tobacco-colored carpet. The bells to the store jingled, and an incongruous-looking tall girl in a peasant skirt walked through. She was wearing a T-shirt that said CLUB CONGRESS POETRY SLAM. Laurel's expression shifted; she'd obviously noticed the shirt, too.

"Look," Emma said, eyeing the girl, "if you're mad at me, be mad at *me*. Don't drag Ethan into it. We shouldn't ruin his poetry reading."

For a second Laurel looked guilty. But then her features hardened again. "Sorry, Sis. No can do. The plan's already in motion."

"We could call it off," Emma tried.

Laurel smirked. "Sutton Mercer, calling off a prank? That's not your style." She leaned against a rack of what looked like burlap wizard cloaks. "I'll make a deal with you. You get Thayer out of jail, I stop the prank."

"That's not fair," Emma hissed.

"Well, then, no can do." Laurel turned on her heel perfunctorily. "I guess you don't care that much about your secret boyfriend, huh? Then again, that's not really a surprise. You treat *all* your secret boyfriends like shit." With that, she shot Emma a knowing look, pushed against the door, and walked out into the sun. The jingle bells on the handle mocked Emma as the door slammed shut.

A few hours later, Emma pedaled up to the curb of a familiar-looking ranch house across from Sabino Canyon. Her legs ached from the ten-mile uphill bike ride from Sutton's house, and her skin was slick with sweat, even though dusk had fallen and the air had cooled. She had no choice but to ride to Ethan's house tonight—it wasn't like Laurel would drop her off. She had to see him.

Ethan's house was next door to Nisha Banerjee's, where Emma had attended a party her first night as Sutton. The Landry property was situated on a small plot of land bordered by a white picket fence that needed painting. Sparrows sat on the thin branches of an oak tree at the edge of the yard and the setting sun cast long shadows onto the slightly overgrown lawn. Tiny purple flowers in clay pots lined the front porch, and a rocking chair with chipped yellow paint sat next to three days' worth of newspapers rolled in blue plastic bags. Even though the house was nicer than anything Emma had ever lived in, it seemed small compared to the Mercers' five-bedroom bungalow. It was weird how quickly one got used to luxury.

She knocked loudly. A few seconds later, Ethan's face appeared in the window. He gave Emma a surprised smile as he unlocked the door to his house.

"Sorry I didn't call first," Emma said.

Ethan lifted a shoulder. "It's cool. My parents aren't home." He stepped aside, making room for Emma. "Come on in."

She turned the letters over in her hand as she followed him down a long hallway wallpapered in a light pink–colored floral print. On the walls were the kinds of paintings Emma had only seen in funeral homes, various watercolors of roses and sunsets. There were no photos of Ethan. The house had a strange smell to it, too—kind of closed-up and musty. It definitely wasn't welcoming.

Ethan led Emma into a small, dark room. "This is my bedroom," he said, running a hand through his hair. "Obviously," he added, as though suddenly embarrassed.

Emma looked around. She'd imagined what Ethan's room looked like plenty of times since they'd become friends, figuring it was a little bit cluttered, full of star-gazing maps, telescope parts, old chemistry sets, dog-eared notebooks, and tons and tons of books of poetry. But this room was spotless. The tracks from a vacuum cleaner were visible on the carpet. A pair of black climbing gloves rested on the nightstand along with the leather journal Emma had noticed the first day she met Ethan. The only item on the desk was a beat-up-looking laptop—nothing else, not even a ball-point pen. The bed was made so neatly it could've passed a hotel's service inspection, the duvet pulled tight, the pillows stacked one in front of the other. Emma had once worked as a maid in a Holiday Inn, and her managers always yelled at her for not fluffing the pillows correctly.

She glanced at Ethan, wanting to ask him if this was really his room. It was almost completely devoid of character. But Ethan looked so awkward that she didn't want to make him feel worse. Instead, she sat down on the bed and reached for the packet of papers in her pocket.

"I found these in Thayer's room today," she said. She unfolded the letters onto the bedspread. "Sutton wrote them to him. It proves that they had a romantic relationship."

Ethan picked up each letter and scanned the contents. Emma felt a flicker of guilt, as though she was betraying her sister by unveiling her secret feelings.

Even though I understood why Emma was showing Ethan the letters, I felt a pang of protectiveness, too. These were my private thoughts.

"*I never thought I could be so into someone,*" Ethan read aloud. He flipped to the next page. "*I want to kiss you in the*

U of A football stadium, in the brush behind my parents' house, on the top of Mount Lemmon . . ." He stopped, clearing his throat.

Emma felt heat rise to her cheeks. "They obviously really liked each other."

"But she was still with Garrett," Ethan said, pointing to a line in one of the letters that said, *I want to break up with Garrett and be with you, I swear. But it's not the right time, and we both know it.* "Maybe Thayer was pissed that Sutton was still with her boyfriend during all this . . . and killed her."

A chill went through me. I thought about how quickly Thayer had changed when Garrett came up that night on our hike. His anger was intense—even he admitted it was his worst quality, the thing that reminded him most of his father. Could that have been enough to set him off?

Emma leaned back on the bed and stared at the popcorn ceiling. "That seems pretty extreme. Killing someone because they wouldn't break off a relationship?"

"People have killed for much less." Ethan stared at his hands. He looked distant, as though something was upsetting him. When he finally spoke, his words were slow and deliberate. "Maybe Sutton drove him mad. She was a master at manipulation."

"What's that supposed to mean?" Emma asked sharply. She didn't like the tone of Ethan's voice. Or what he'd said about her sister.

"One minute, she liked you," Ethan said. "And the next, she treated you like dirt. I saw her do it to a million guys." He frowned. "Maybe she was doing that to Thayer. Maybe it was driving him insane and he just . . . snapped."

Emma's palms felt clammy. Could her sister's fickle behavior be the thing that pushed Thayer to the brink? If she'd been hot and cold with him—all while dating Garrett—it could have sparked a rage inside of him. "Maybe," she whispered.

"So what do you think we should do about it?" Ethan asked.

"We could call the police," Emma suggested.

"Or we *couldn't*." Ethan shook his head. "If we do that, you'll have to out yourself as Sutton's twin. It's too risky." He crossed his leg over his knee and jiggled his navy Converse sneaker. "We're getting close, though. You need more solid proof. What about the blood on the car? That's definitely Sutton's, right?"

Emma rose from the bed and began pacing around the room. "Probably. Although the police aren't done testing it yet. I'm guessing they'll also be looking at the fingerprints on the steering wheel—maybe Thayer's will come back a match." Then she made a face. "But wouldn't the person have to be in the criminal system for them to find a DNA match?"

"Thayer's been in trouble before," Ethan offered. "And they would have fingerprinted him when they arrested him."

"And we already *know* he was in the car," Emma went on. "Even if his prints are on the steering wheel, what does that prove?"

"True," Ethan said, sounding deflated. "It just means we'll have to dig deeper. Find out what his motive was. Find out something to really nail him to the wall."

"Yeah," Emma murmured, but she felt exhausted. She was so close . . . but so far away.

She closed her eyes, suddenly overwhelmed at the task ahead of her. A teenage soccer star didn't become a murderer out of nowhere. Something made Thayer Vega break.

When she opened her eyes again, she noticed Ethan's glowing laptop screen. A Safari window was open to Sutton's Facebook page.

"You're on Facebook?" Emma smirked. "You don't seem like the type."

Ethan shot off the bed and closed the laptop. "I'm not, really. I mean, I have a page, but I don't really post on it or anything. I was just thinking about leaving you a message on your—well, Sutton's wall. But I don't know." He peeked at her cagily. "Would that be weird? Your friends don't really know about . . . how we talk."

Emma felt a rush of pleasure that they were even

discussing their potential relationship. But then a pit formed in her stomach. She recalled how the girls had giggled about the prank today. She considered telling Ethan about the plan to ruin his poetry reading, but the thought nauseated her. She would just have to thwart the plan, plain and simple.

"Actually, Laurel knows about us," Emma said instead. She flushed instantly. Was what she said okay? Calling them *us*? It wasn't like they were a couple yet.

"Does that bother you?" Ethan asked, a slight smile tugging the edge of his lips.

"Does it bother *you*?" Emma countered.

Ethan took small steps toward Emma and sat down on the bed beside her. "*I* don't care who knows. I think you're amazing. I've never met anyone like you."

Emma's heart squeezed. No one had ever said anything like that to her before.

Ethan leaned forward, running his fingers across the nape of her neck. He kissed her gently, his lips warm and soft, and Emma instantly forgot about everything that'd happened since she arrived in Tucson. She forgot about just how excited she'd been when she stepped off the bus to meet her sister. She forgot how quickly the hopes of her and Sutton's reunion were dashed. She forgot about the note threatening her to be Sutton—or else. She forgot about the investigation into Thayer, or whoever had killed

Sutton. In that moment, she was just Emma Paxton, a girl with a brand-new boyfriend.

And I was just her sister, happy that she had found someone she truly cared about.

14

IF THE KEY FITS

That night Emma's body tangled among Sutton's light blue bedsheets as she tossed from one side to the other. Sutton's smattering of ratty stuffed animals were lined up at the foot of the bed and stared at Emma, their eyes glassy in the moonlight. They were so unlike Sutton, one of the only sentimental things Emma could find that her sister had kept from her past. They reminded her of the toys Emma had kept—a hand-knitted monster toy a piano teacher had given her for mastering a hard piece of music, and Socktopus, which Becky had bought for her on a trip to Four Corners. Sutton's toys made Emma think of all of the time they'd missed, the memories they could have had of playing for hours together in a shared bedroom, making up secret worlds only the two of them understood. Hours they could never get back.

An owl called from the oak tree just outside Sutton's window. Emma stared at the branches, noting that it was the same tree she'd used the night she snuck out with Ethan, and the same tree Thayer had used to break into Sutton's bedroom. Suddenly, she jolted up with a start. The window was wide open. And a hulking figure stood in the corner of the room, his breath coming in jagged rasps.

"Did you really think it'd be that easy to get rid of me?" his voice said.

Even though he was in the shadows, Emma recognized him immediately. "Thayer?" she squeaked, the name barely escaping her mouth.

She scrambled back against the headboard, but it was too late. Thayer launched forward, his hands closing around her neck, his lips inches from hers. "You betrayed me, Emma," he whispered, his hands tightening around her throat. His bottom lip grazed hers. "And now it's time for your reunion with Sutton to become a reality."

Emma dug her nails into Thayer's skin as her oxygen supply dwindled and her life seeped slowly from her. "Please, no!"

"Goodbye, Emma," Thayer sneered. His hands squeezed

and squeezed . . . seemingly to the tune of Kelly Clarkson's "Mr. Know It All."

Emma shot up in bed. The same Kelly Clarkson song blared in her ears. She looked around. She was in Sutton's bedroom, Sutton's sheets clinging to her wet skin. Sunlight streamed through the window—it was, indeed, open. But the corner was empty. She touched her neck, and she didn't feel any evidence that she'd been strangled. Her skin felt smooth. Nothing hurt.

A dream. It was just a dream. But it had felt so real.

It felt all too real to me, too. I looked hard at the corner, startled that Thayer wasn't really there. It still shook me that I was carried along with Emma everywhere she went, even into her dreams.

Emma's fingers trembled as she tugged her light blue pajama top down over her stomach and glanced around Sutton's bedroom once more. The computer screen glowed with familiar images of Sutton and her best friends—this particular photo was taken after a tennis team victory. The girls had their arms slung around each other and flashed peace signs at the camera. A German textbook lay open on Sutton's desk along with a small book of poetry Ethan had given Emma the week before. There were no stuffed animals anywhere—the real Sutton had been too mature for toys.

But there was that open window again. Emma could

have sworn she shut and locked it the night before. She pushed back the covers, walked to it, and peered out. The Mercers' impeccable lawn stretched in waves of green before her, not a white wicker lawn chair or potted plant out of place. The Tucson sun was a ball of fire above the Catalina Mountains and the sound of birds chattering filtered into the bedroom.

Bzz.

Emma jumped and turned around. Something was sounding from underneath Sutton's bed. She realized almost immediately that it was her BlackBerry from her old life. She dove for it and checked the screen. It was Alex, her best friend from Henderson. Clearing her throat, she pressed the green answer button. "Hey."

"Hey. Everything okay? You sound weird."

Emma flinched. But Alex couldn't know what Emma had just dreamed about. She didn't even know Emma was in danger—as far as she was concerned, Sutton was still alive, and Emma was experiencing a foster-girl's dream life with her long-lost sister. "Of course everything's fine," she croaked. "I was just sleeping."

"Well, get up, sleepyhead," Alex giggled. "I haven't heard from you in ages. I wanted to see how things are going."

"Everything's fine," Emma said, forcing herself to sound upbeat. "Great, in fact. Sutton's family rocks."

"I can't believe you've been given this instant new life. You should be on *Oprah* or something. Want me to submit your story?"

"No!" Emma said, perhaps too forcefully. She padded into Sutton's closet, partly to select an outfit for the day, but partly because it was more private in there—there was less chance of Laurel hearing her.

"Okay, okay! How's school? Do you like Sutton's friends?" Alex asked.

Emma paused in front of a blue silk tank top. "Honestly, things with them are a little tense right now."

"How come? Can't they handle two of you?" Alex's voice was momentarily muffled, and Emma could picture her getting dressed for school, brushing her hair, and shoving a cinnamon bun in her mouth. Alex was the queen of multitasking and had a wicked sweet tooth.

"They're just a pretty tight-knit group," Emma said. "They have so much history that I can't even begin to understand."

Alex chewed and swallowed. "History is just that—history. Plan something fun and create your own stories with them, maybe even apart from Sutton."

"Yeah, maybe," Emma said, realizing that she barely ever hung out with any of Sutton's friends one-on-one.

Drake let out a low bark downstairs, and Emma heard Mrs. Mercer shush him. "Listen, I should go—I promised Sutton I'd help her with homework before classes start."

She disconnected the call after promising she'd keep in better touch, then wandered out of Sutton's closet and flopped back on her bed, her head suddenly throbbing. It was awful to lie to Alex. She thought of all the afternoons she'd spent in Alex's bedroom, finding new music on Pandora and predicting each other's futures. They'd shared a mauve-colored journal, taking turns updating it with new entries every few days. They'd stashed it in a trapdoor cut into the carpet below Alex's bed so no one would find it. They had secrets they kept from the world, but not from each other—until now.

Emma sat up. If Thayer had kept Sutton's notes, maybe she'd kept his, too. But where did she hide them?

Emma swung her legs over the side of Sutton's bed and ducked beneath the folds of the comforter. Two shoeboxes were shoved up against the wall, but she'd already gone through them weeks ago. She pulled them out anyway, dumping the contents onto the bed, in case she'd missed something. Old tests and graded papers scattered across the sheets along with a neon green rubber band and concert ticket stubs for Lady Gaga. A Barbie doll with vacant blue eyes stared back at Emma, her tangled blonde hair cascading over an elaborate silk prom dress. This wasn't E, the doll Sutton had perhaps named after Emma—she was in a hope chest in the Mercers' bedroom. But Emma had seen all this stuff before.

Emma moved to Sutton's dresser and yanked each drawer open one by one, tossing the contents onto the floor. There had to be something she was missing. She rifled through T-shirts and shorts and stuck her hands into tennis socks. She skimmed every page of three worn notebooks filled with history notes and algebra equations, and sorted through tubes of lip gloss, half a dozen chandelier earrings, and a small pot of moisturizer whose label promised to revitalize tired skin.

After she'd searched the drawers of Sutton's desk as well, she slumped against the wall, scanning old photos to make sure there wasn't something she had missed the first dozen times. But what would that be? A figure lurking in the background at a tennis match? Someone holding a sign saying I KILLED YOUR SISTER at her birthday party? Someone holding a knife to her back at prom?

Emma's spine straightened and her head snapped up. Prom Queen Barbie. She didn't fit with everything else Sutton had stashed under the bed and inside the drawers. Emma yanked the doll from where she'd dropped her in a tangle of light blue blankets and flipped her upside down.

The folds of fabric fell away, exposing a tiny pouch sewn into the innermost layer of the ball gown. *Bingo.*

Nice work. Even I wouldn't have thought to check the doll—and presumably *I* was the one who'd put that pouch there.

Emma plunged her index finger inside the pouch and touched cold metal. It was a tiny, tarnished silver key. She held it up to the light. It looked like the kind of key that could open a journal or a jewelry box.

A knock sounded and Sutton's door swung open. Laurel stood in the doorway in a cloud of tuberose per-fume, her hands on her hips. There was a sour look on her face. "Mom wants you downstairs for breakfast." Then she glanced around at the clutter strewn across the floor. "What in the world are you doing in here?"

Emma looked around at the mess. "Um, nothing. Just looking for an earring." She held up a silver star stud she'd just found under the bed. "Found it."

"What's that?" Laurel pointed accusingly at the key in Emma's palm.

Emma stared at it, too, cursing herself. If only she'd thought to hide it before Laurel saw it. "Oh, just some old thing," she said vaguely, dropping the key on Sutton's bedside table like she didn't have a care in the world. Only when Laurel turned away did she scoop it back up again and shove it into the pocket of Sutton's jeans. If the key had been important enough to hide, maybe it led to some huge secret. And Emma wasn't going to rest until she found out what it was.

Which meant, no doubt, that I wouldn't rest either.

15

PROJECT: RUN AWAY

Thursday afternoon, Emma sat in Fashion Design, Sutton's last class of the day. Headless mannequins covered in draped muslin bordered the room. A makeshift runway shot through the center. Students sat at worktables, fabric, scissors, buttons, zippers, and thread strewn around them. Hollier's one and only fashion design teacher, Mr. Salinas, paced the room, wearing slim-cut trousers and a pale blue scarf tied around his neck. He looked like Tim Gunn's younger brother.

"Today's presentation will push the boundaries of form versus function," he announced in a pinched voice. He tapped a long, skinny finger on the glossy cover of French

Vogue, which he had more than once called his "Bible." "It's the question on the tip of every editor's tongue," he mused. "How does fashion translate from the runway to real life?"

Emma glanced at her mannequin. Her creation wasn't exactly translating, per se. Plaid flannel crossed the midsection, pinned awkwardly at the waist where Emma had attempted to make the outfit A-line. A black chiffon top hung crookedly with ruffles that sagged at the collar. The worst part was the pin: Emma had tried to make a flower-shaped brooch out of the excess plaid fabric. Add that to the red pen marks that dotted the mannequin's bare arms, and the whole thing looked like a drunken schoolgirl-gone-goth with a bad case of the chicken pox. Although Emma loved fashion—she scoured thrift stores and made a lot of on-the-cheap outfits look expensive—sewing clothes wasn't really her thing. She suspected Sutton took this class for the same reason she took a lot of the electives in her schedule—because they were fairly easy As and didn't require much reading.

"What does the artist within have to say?" Mr. Salinas blathered on. "This is what we must ask ourselves."

Emma ducked down, hoping Mr. Salinas didn't call on her—she hadn't exactly been trying to *say* anything. She had bigger things to worry about than *pushing the boundaries of form versus function*, like figuring out if Thayer had killed her sister before he got out of jail and came after her again.

"*Ma*deline?" Mr. Salinas called out, dramatically emphasizing the first syllable of her name. "Tell us what you've created here with your avant-garde ballerina."

Madeline stood and smoothed down her black leather miniskirt. She was the best in the class and she knew it. "Well, Edgar," she started. She was also the only student who called Mr. Salinas by his first name. "The look I've created is called the Dark Dance. It's sort of ballet-meets-street. It's the dancer after hours. Where does she go? What does she do?" She gestured toward her mannequin, which wore a blazer over a black dress and tights. "It's the dark, deviant part of all of us that lies under the façade of perfection."

Mr. Salinas clapped his hands together. "Brilliant! Absolutely divine. Everyone, *this* is the kind of work I expect you *all* to be doing."

Madeline sat back down, looking satisfied with herself. Emma tapped her knee. "Your dress looks amazing. I'm super-impressed."

Madeline nodded curtly, but Emma could tell by the way her features softened that Madeline was touched. Emma's—or, rather, *Sutton's*—opinion really mattered to her.

While Mr. Salinas called on a few more students—their

responses clearly boring him compared to Madeline's—Emma's thoughts wandered. She'd practically memorized her sister's notes to Thayer, and phrases like *Someday we can be together when the time is right* and *We'll sort out all our problems* flitted through her mind. Even though Sutton had written almost thirty pages to Thayer, she hadn't been particularly specific. Why couldn't they be together? Why wasn't the time right? What were the problems that needed sorting out?

I tried my hardest to think about what I might have meant. But nothing came.

Then Emma thought about the key tucked safely into her pocket. She'd tried it in every possible place today—a jewelry box in Sutton's closet, a toolbox in the Mercers' garage, and a little door to a room on the second floor of the house that she'd never been in before. She'd even run to the nearby post office at lunch in case the key was to a PO Box there, but the proprietor said Emma's key was much too small for any mailbox. Maybe it, too, was a dead end.

Emma resisted the urge to rest her head on the desk and fall asleep. This was getting exhausting. Sure, she wanted to be an investigative journalist when she grew up, and uncover corporate scandal and horrific crimes, but it was different when her life was on the line.

"Earth to Sutton!" Polished fingernails snapped in front of Emma's face. Charlotte's green eyes bored into her.

"Are you okay?" Charlotte asked, looking concerned. "You went kind of comatose for a second."

"I'm fine," Emma murmured. "Just sort of . . . bored."

Charlotte raised an eyebrow. "If you remember, *you* were the one who convinced both of us to take Fashion Design." She crossed her arms over her chest. "I keep saying this, but you've seemed so weird lately. You know you can talk to me, right?"

Emma ran her fingers along the fabric of her dress, considering. If only she could tell Charlotte about Thayer. But it would be a mistake—if she let on that Sutton and Thayer had been romantically linked, Charlotte would immediately accuse her of cheating on Garrett. Garrett was always a touchy subject with Charlotte—he'd broken up with Charlotte to be with Sutton, and Emma suspected she'd never gotten over it.

I was almost positive that was true.

But then Emma got an idea. She reached into her pocket and unearthed the small silver key. "I found this in my room this morning and can't for the life of me remember what it unlocks. Do you know?"

Charlotte plucked the key from Emma's palm and turned it over in her hands. It glinted in the harsh overhead light. Emma noticed Madeline peering at her out of the corner of her eye, but then she quickly turned and faced front.

"It looks like it unlocks a padlock, maybe," Charlotte said.

"A locker?" Emma guessed eagerly. Maybe Charlotte had seen Sutton open a secret locker Emma didn't know about.

"Maybe a filing cabinet." Charlotte handed it back to her. "What does a key have to do with your bizarre attitude lately? Does it unlock your sanity?"

"I don't have a bizarre attitude," Emma said defensively, slipping the key back in her pocket. "You're imagining things."

"Are you *sure*?" Charlotte tried.

Emma pursed her lips. "I'm positive."

Charlotte stared at her for a beat, then picked up her drawing pencil. "Fine." She furiously doodled swirls and stars across her fashion sketchbook. "Be secretive. I don't care."

The bell rang, and Charlotte jumped up. "Char!" Emma called after her, sensing that Charlotte was more irritated than she let on. But Charlotte didn't turn. She sidled up to Madeline and disappeared into the hall. Emma remained at her desk, feeling drained. When she trudged into the hall, she endured yet more stares from random students whose names she didn't yet know.

"Did you hear that a soccer scout from Stanford came here asking about Thayer?" a girl in a denim jacket whispered to her dark-haired friend, who was wearing an eighties-style off-the-shoulder striped shirt.

"Totally," her friend murmured back. "But because Thayer's in jail, there's no shot of him getting in there."

"Oh, please." The girl in the denim jacket waved a hand. "His lawyer is getting him out. He'll be free by next week."

Please, no, Emma thought.

"But even so, what about that limp?" Eighties Stripes asked. "I heard it was really, really bad. How do you think he got it, anyway?"

The answer, to them, was obvious. The two girls whipped around and looked at Emma as she passed, their eyes blazing.

It felt like everyone was whispering about her, even the teachers. Frau Fenstermacher, her German professor, nudged Madame Ives, one of the French teachers. Two cafeteria workers stopped their conversation and stared. Freshman, seniors, *everyone* looked at her as if they knew all of her business. *Would you just leave me alone?* Emma wanted to scream. It was ironic: When she school-hopped as a foster kid, she'd been a nobody, a ghost in the hallways. She'd longed to be someone everyone knew. But notoriety came with a price.

Didn't I know it.

As Emma rounded the corner into a windowed hallway

and looked out onto a courtyard dotted with cacti and potted ferns, she caught a glimpse of Ethan's dark hair a few inches above the other students. Her heart pounded against her chest as she maneuvered her way through the swarming crowd.

"Hey," she said, taking his elbow.

A smile lit up Ethan's face. "Hey, yourself." Then he noticed Emma's gloomy expression. "Are you okay? What happened?"

She shrugged. "It's one of those days where it's a little hard to be Sutton Mercer. I would give anything to get out of here. Get a break from being Sutton for a while."

A wrinkle formed on Ethan's brow, and then he held up one finger in an *aha* gesture. "Absolutely. And I know exactly where I can take you."

Three hours later, Ethan angled his car off of Route 10 at an exit marked PHOENIX. Emma frowned. "Can't you tell me *something* about where we're going?"

"Nope," Ethan said, a sly smile playing across his lips. "Just that it's somewhere no one has ever heard of Sutton Mercer, Emma Paxton, or Thayer Vega."

I wanted to laugh. When I was alive, I had the notion that everyone had heard of me—*everywhere*. And it was sweet that Ethan had driven my twin all the way to Phoenix to get her away from the madness.

Once off the highway, Ethan turned down a dilapi-
dated downtown Phoenix street lined with big Dumpsters
overflowing with drywall scraps, broken glass, and empty
paint cans. An unfinished apartment building loomed over
the street, boasting a sign that said units would be available
for rent starting in November. Taking in the windowless
façade, Emma seriously doubted that claim was true.

"Okay, now will you tell me?" Emma begged when
Ethan pulled off the creepy back alley and into a parking
lot, coming to a stop in front of an old Art Deco–style
hotel.

"Patience, patience!" Ethan teased, undoing his seat
belt. He slammed his car door shut and stretched languor-
ously, making a show of taking his time.

Emma tapped her foot. "I'm waiting."

He made his way around the car and put his arms
around her. "Waiting for what?" he asked. "This?" He
lowered his lips to hers, and she kissed him back, relaxing
into his embrace.

She smiled when they broke apart, her entire body tin-
gling. Then she burst out laughing. "Wait a minute. Did
you drive me all the way to Phoenix just so we could
make out in public?"

"No, that's just an added bonus." Ethan turned and
gestured to the Art Deco hotel. "We're here to see a show
by my favorite band, the No Names."

"The No Names?" Emma echoed. "Never heard of them."

"They're awesome—punk rock but with a bluesy edge. You'll love them."

He took her hand, lacing his fingers through hers, and led her inside the hotel, which was seemingly stuck in a fifties time warp. There were kitschy turquoise- and salmon-colored tribal designs on the walls, deco light fixtures, and even an old cash register behind the concierge desk instead of a sleek flat-screen computer. A metal sign pointed to the club at the back of the lobby, though it wasn't particularly necessary—Emma could hear the thudding bass and amplifier feedback as soon as they swept through the revolving doors. The air had an odor of cigarettes, cheap beer, and sweaty dancing bodies. A bunch of too-cool-for-the-show kids hung out in the lobby, smoking and checking out the newcomers.

After they paid the ten-dollar cover, Emma and Ethan made their way into the club. The room was large, square, and dark except for the lights on the stage and a bunch of Christmas lights around the bar area, which was on a raised platform at the back. There were bodies everywhere—guys who refused to move, girls who swayed with their eyes closed, caught in their own musical dreams, lines of kids six deep, all with arms entwined. A few of them glanced at Emma with boredom. Any other time, she would have been intimidated by their aloofness, but today it was deliciously welcome. No one recognized her. She didn't have baggage here. She was just a random No Names fan, like everyone else.

Emma edged toward the bar, tapping what felt like hundreds of shoulders and murmuring millions of *'scuse me*s and *sorry*s. The noise on stage was so loud that Emma's ears immediately began to feel muffled and full.

Ethan and Emma reached the bar, crumpling against the counters as if they'd just braved a hurricane. The bartender set coasters in front of them and they both ordered beers. Emma spied the last empty table, threw her bag over the back of the chair, and peered at the stage. A three-piece band was in the middle of a fast, growling song. The drummer writhed, octopuslike. The bass player rocked back and forth from one foot to the other, his long hair obscuring his face. The lead singer, who had shocking pink hair, stood in the middle of the stage, strumming violently on the guitar and singing seductively into the microphone.

Emma stared at her, transfixed. She had piled her hair on top of her head in a fifties-style beehive, and she was wearing a sleek black dress, black boots, fishnet stockings, and long, black silk gloves. If only she could be as uninhibited and cool.

"You're right! This band is awesome," Emma yelled to Ethan.

He smiled and clinked his beer with hers, bobbing his head to the beat. Emma peered into the crowd some more. The light created halos around the tops of people's heads. A lot of kids were dancing. Others were taking photos with their phones. A bunch of fans were crammed against the stage—a lot of them were guys, probably hoping for a look up the lead singer's dress.

"My friend Alex from Henderson would be all over this scene," Emma said sadly. "She loved going to shows like this. She was the one who introduced me to every cool band I listen to."

The disco ball flashed over Ethan's face, illuminating his blue eyes. "Maybe I can meet her when all this is over with."

"I'd like that," Emma said. Alex and Ethan would love each other—they were both into poetry and didn't care at all what other people thought of them.

Once they finished their drinks, Emma pulled Ethan from his stool and dragged him onto the dance floor. Ethan cleared his throat uncomfortably. "I'm not exactly a great dancer."

"Neither am I," Emma shouted over the music. "But no one here knows us, so who cares?"

She grabbed his hand and spun him around. He spun her back with a laugh, and they began dancing together, jumping and shimmying to the music.

When the No Names finished their set, Emma was exhausted and covered in sweat, but she felt light as a silk dress.

"There's something else I want to show you," Ethan said, pointing to an emergency-exit door and directing her through a dark, dripping hallway beyond it. A heavy metal door off to the side said OBSERVATION DECK. Ethan nudged it open and they climbed up a narrow stairwell.

"Are you sure we're allowed in here?" Emma asked nervously, her shoes echoing on the metal risers.

"Yep," Ethan said. "Almost there."

At the top, they pushed through another heavy door and emerged into the open air. The observation deck wasn't much more than a flat roof with a couple of ratty teak chaises and end tables, a trash can overflowing with empty bottles of Corona Light, and a large potted fern that looked half dead, but the city of Phoenix surrounded her, full of lights and sparkle and noise.

"It's beautiful!" Emma breathed. "How did you know this was up here?"

Ethan walked over to the railing and tipped his face up to the night sky. "My mom was sick for a while. She had a lot of doctor's appointments around here. I got to know the city pretty well."

"Is she . . . okay?" Emma asked softly. Ethan had never told her about his mom being sick.

Ethan shrugged, seeming a little closed off. "I guess so. As good as she can be." He stared out at the twinkling lights. "She had cancer. But she's okay now, I think."

"I'm sorry," Emma breathed.

"It's cool," Ethan said. "I was the one who helped her through it, though. You know how I told you my dad practically lives in San Diego? Well, he never came back for any of her chemo treatments. It blew."

"Maybe he couldn't deal with her being sick," Emma said. "Some people don't handle that stuff very well."

"Yeah, well, he *should* have," Ethan snapped, his eyes flashing.

Emma backed off. "I'm sorry," she whispered.

Ethan shut his eyes. "*I'm* sorry." He sighed. "I've never really told anyone about my mom. But, well, I want us to be totally honest with each other. I want us to share everything. Even if it's bad. I hope you share everything with me, too."

Emma breathed in, feeling both touched and horribly guilty. There was something *huge* she wasn't sharing with Ethan: the prank against him. Should she say something? Would he be angry that she'd let it go on for so long without telling him? Maybe it was better just to say nothing and figure out a way to thwart the prank before it happened. What Ethan didn't know wouldn't hurt him.

Way to be totally honest, Sis. But I understood the predicament she was in.

Emma wrapped her arms around Ethan's waist and leaned her cheek against his back. He turned around and hugged her to him, kissing her forehead. "Can we stay here forever?" she asked with a sigh. "It's so wonderful not being Sutton for once. Just being . . . *me*."

"We can stay as long as you'd like," Ethan promised. "Or, well, at least until we have to go to school tomorrow."

Cars honked on the streets below. A helicopter zoomed overhead, sending a single white beam to a source near the mountains. A car alarm blared, cycling through a series of irritating beeps and whoops and buzzes until someone shut it off.

But as she stood warm and safe in Ethan's arms, Emma decided this was the most romantic date she'd ever been on.

16

THE MAKEUP

On Sunday afternoon, Emma, Madeline, Charlotte, Laurel, and the Twitter Twins waited in line at Pam's Pretzels, a shoddy stand propped in a corner of La Encantada on the outskirts of Tucson. Even though Sutton's friends had sworn off carbs, the pretzels were worth breaking their diets for. They were covered in Mexican *queso* and contained a spice combination that was, as Madeline put it, "better than sex." The smell of baked bread and mustard infused the air. Customers swooned as they took big, doughy bites. One woman looked like she was actually going to faint with pleasure as she chewed.

The line was long, and a bunch of college-age boys in

band T-shirts and long, grungy hair stood in front of them. Madeline was inching away from them as though they had fleas. Charlotte, whose flaming red hair was tied back in a severe bun, elbowed Laurel, who was busy texting something to Caleb. "Does that bring back fond memories?" she said, gesturing to a four-by-four-foot raised garden box covered with felt.

Laurel giggled at what Charlotte was pointing at. "That Christmas tree was *so* much heavier than it looked. And I had tinsel in my hair for days." She shook her hair around for effect.

Madeline covered her mouth and let out a snort. "That was priceless."

"Seriously," Emma said, even though she had no idea what the girls were talking about—probably an old Lying Game prank.

The line moved quickly, and soon it was the Twitter Twins' turn. "One pretzel with queso, extra dipping sauce." Lili shifted her weight from one black knee-high stiletto boot to the other. The other girls ordered more or less the same thing, and once the pretzels were ready they carried them to a courtyard table and sat down. Only Emma and Madeline lingered at the fixin's bar, slowly salting their treats.

Emma looked around. The outdoor mall was bustling today with girls in short shorts, batwing-sleeved blouses, and high wedge heels. Everyone toted carrier bags from

Tiffany, Anthropologie, and Tory Burch. She craned her neck and noticed the vintage store on the second level. Not long ago, she and Madeline had gone to that vintage store and had a great time. She'd felt like *Emma* that day, not The Girl Who Was Supposed to Be Sutton.

Madeline breathed in. When Emma turned, she noticed that Madeline was looking up at the vintage store, too. Then she faced Emma, her expression contemplative and a little awkward. "Listen, I don't want to be pissed at you anymore," she said.

"I don't want you to be pissed at me either!" Emma exclaimed gratefully.

Madeline lifted a hand to shade her eyes. "No matter how upset I am about Thayer, I know him disappearing isn't your fault. I'm really sorry I've been so awful to you."

Relief coursed through Emma. "I'm sorry, too. I can't imagine what this has been like for you and your family, and I'm sorry if I made things worse in any way."

Madeline opened a packet of mustard with her teeth. "You do have a way of causing drama, Sutton. But you have to tell me the truth. You really don't know why my brother showed up in your room?"

"I really don't. I promise."

A long beat went by. Madeline inspected Emma carefully, as though trying to read her mind. "Okay," she said finally. "I believe you."

Emma let out a breath. "Good, because I've missed you," she said.

"I missed you, too."

They hugged fiercely. Emma squeezed her eyes shut, but suddenly she got the distinct feeling someone was staring at her. She opened her eyes and looked into the dark parking garage next to the pretzel kiosk. She thought she saw someone crouch behind a car. But when she squinted harder, she didn't see anyone.

Madeline linked her arms through Emma's as they rejoined the girls. Charlotte grinned, looking relieved, too.

"I have exciting news, ladies," Madeline announced. "We're throwing a party on Friday night."

"We are?" the Twitter Twins asked in unison, whipping out their iPhones, excited to break the news to their rabid followers. "Where?"

"You'll know when you know," Madeline said cryptically. "I'm only telling Sutton, Char, and Laurel." She narrowed her eyes on Gabby and Lili. "It's super private so we don't get caught, and you guys aren't exactly good at keeping secrets."

Gabby's plump lips popped into their trademark pout.

"*Fine*," Lili said with an overdramatic sigh.

Laurel tossed the remnants of her pretzel into a garbage bin wrapped in a bright green poster that read, CAN IT FOR A BETTER PLANET! She adjusted the buckle closure on the strap of her bag. "What can we do to help? And what's the dress code? Sundresses?"

Madeline took a long swig of lemon-lime seltzer. "It'll start at ten, but we'll have to get there early to set up. Leave the catering and drinks to me and Char. You handle the guest list, Laurel, and Sutton, you put together a playlist. And as for dress code, maybe shorts, heels, and a dressy top? Definitely something new. C'mon. Let's get shopping."

She grabbed Emma's hand and pulled her up. Emma smiled, appreciating Madeline's olive branch. The girls walked to a boutique called Castor and Pollux. As soon as they passed through the front doors, the smell of new clothes and sugary perfume swirled in their nostrils. Glassy-eyed mannequins dressed in pleated chiffon skirts and herringbone jackets posed with their hands on their narrow hips. Stiletto heels much higher than anything Emma had ever worn lined the perimeter of the store.

"These would look awesome on you, Sutton," Charlotte said, holding up a silver wedge.

Emma took it from her and discreetly checked the price. *Four hundred seventy-five dollars?* She tried not to swallow her tongue as she set it back down. Even though she'd been here for a month, she still wasn't used to the way Sutton's friends shopped with abandon. The cost of each individual item in Sutton's closet was close to what Emma normally spent on an entire year's wardrobe. And that was a *good* year—when she was fourteen, she didn't have money for *any* new clothes. Her foster mother, Gwen, who lived in a tiny town thirty miles from Vegas, insisted on sewing all of her foster kids' back-to-school outfits on a 1960s Singer sewing machine—she considered herself something of a fashion designer. Worse, Gwen was into gothic romance, which meant Emma started eighth grade wearing long, flowing velvet skirts, cream blouses that resembled corsets, and hand-me-down Birkenstocks. Needless to say, Emma wasn't the most popular girl at Cactus Needles Middle School. After that, she'd always made sure to have a job, so she could at least buy the basics.

Lili gravitated to a table stacked with paper-thin tees and tanks, while Gabby made a beeline for a rack of polo shirts. Charlotte steered Emma to a row of minidresses, pointing one out. "That lavender one would look amazing with your eyes," she offered.

The girls convened in the curtained-off open-air dressing room surrounded by four three-way mirrors. When they tried on matching short skirts and flowing tops, it was as though a dozen Xerox copies were reflected back at them.

"That's gorgeous, Mads," Emma offered, eyeing the lime green cotton skirt Madeline had pulled on. It showed off her long, lithe, ballet-dancer legs.

"You should totally get it," Charlotte said.

"I can't," Madeline mumbled.

"Why not?" A wrinkle formed on Charlotte's brow. "Do you not have money? I'll buy it for you."

Madeline kicked it off. "It looks lame on me."

"It does not!" Charlotte scooped the skirt off the ground. "I'm totally buying this."

"Char, don't bother," Madeline snapped, an edge to her voice. "My dad will never let me wear it. He'll say it's too short."

Charlotte let the skirt slip between her fingers, her mouth flattening into a straight line.

The dressing room fell silent. The girls turned away, busying themselves with their piles of clothing and looking anywhere but at Mads. The mention of Mr. Vega had that effect.

Emma pulled a lavender dress over her head, carefully sliding the spaghetti straps over her shoulders. The silk was soft against her skin, and the waist nipped perfectly, making Emma's rail-thin body look a little curvier than usual.

"Ooh, Sutton!" Charlotte whistled.

"Hello, gorgeous," Laurel trilled, seemingly forgetting her sibling jealousy.

Emma tried not to stare at herself too hard in the mirror, but she couldn't help it. The dress made her look amazing.

Sutton would have been used to trying on expensive clothing that made her look like a million bucks, but Emma had always settled for good-enough pieces from Goodwill or hand-me-downs from other foster kids. It felt so special to be in something that fit her like a glove.

Laurel placed her hand on Emma's shoulder. "You know who would love you in that? Ethan."

Emma flinched. "Excuse me?"

"I've seen him talking to you at school," Laurel said. "It's obvious he has a crush on you."

Emma widened her eyes at Laurel, hoping she could telepathically tell her to shut up. But Laurel continued, winding a tendril of blonde hair around her fingers. "You know what you should do? Get him to invite you back to his place so you can steal his poems."

"Ooh, you mean for the prank?" Lili said.

"Uh-huh," Laurel said. "We need poems to publish online to make him look like a plagiarist. You're the perfect person for it, Sutton, since he's already got it bad for you. *And* you're awfully good at stealing, that little slip-up at Clique aside." Laurel bumped her hip.

Emma stared at her hard, anger boiling beneath her skin. Apparently, Laurel was still furious at her. Then again, she hadn't said anything to get Thayer out of jail, which meant Laurel wasn't letting up on the Ethan prank.

She straightened up, deciding not to let Laurel get the

best of her. "If he notices his poems went missing, he'll know it was me who took them."

"Oh, you'll figure out a way to go unnoticed," Laurel trilled.

"C'mon, Sutton. This plan rocks." Madeline grinned. "Maybe you should even invite him to come help us set up before the party, really make him think you're friends. Besides, we'll need the man power."

Now everyone was staring at Emma. Beads of sweat pricked the back of her neck. In the mirror, she could see a bloom of red spreading across her cheeks.

They were interrupted by an ice-blonde salesgirl who popped her head around the dark velvet curtain and asked if they were buying anything. Charlotte handed her several shirts, a dress, and a pair of jeans. Madeline shoved the green skirt at her, saying she didn't want it. The Twitter Twins both bought leggings. Emma stared down at her pile of clothes, her brain racing. *How* was she going to get out of this Ethan prank? She thought about what Ethan had said on the roof: *I want us to be totally honest with each other.* She wasn't exactly holding up her end of the bargain.

"Sutton, you coming?"

Emma jumped and looked up. The dressing area was empty. Charlotte had poked her head back through the curtain, a strange look on her face. All of the other girls were standing at the register, clothes in their hands.

"Uh, sure," Emma mumbled, scooping up the lavender dress and Sutton's bag. As she sauntered toward the register, she felt Laurel staring at her, a smirk on her face. But then, she felt a second pair of eyes boring into her from the esplanade. She whipped around and squinted. This time, the figure wasn't quick enough to hide. The hair on the back of her neck bristled. The person was definitely male. He stepped into full view and met Emma's gaze. Emma gasped.

And so did I. It was Garrett, and he looked pissed. After a beat, he stormed away.

17

THE FALSE BOTTOM

On Tuesday afternoon, the Hollier High tennis team was on the courts for a doubles scrimmage. The sky was blessedly cloudy, meaning it was actually bearable to play. The sounds of a pop XM radio station filled the air—Coach Maggie always liked to have upbeat music to get the girls moving. A giant tub of Gatorade sat on the sidelines, tubes of extra balls were tipped over by the trash can, and Maggie, who was wearing her ubiquitous Hollier Tennis polo and khaki parachute pants, strutted up and down the courts, surveying ground strokes and serves.

"Out!" Nisha Banerjee's shrill voice sounded across the net from Emma. She pointed her shiny black racket at the white line and shot Emma a look that said *Too bad, bitch.* "And that's the match!"

Laurel, who stood on the baseline at Nisha's side, laughed mirthfully. "Not even Sutton Mercer could return that power serve!" She raised her hand and slapped Nisha's in a high five.

"Looks like the best women won!" Nisha tossed her black ponytail over her shoulder.

Emma rolled her eyes as Nisha and Laurel pranced across the court with their rackets held high. Maggie had emailed the team the previous night with a list of who would be matched with whom for the scrimmage, and Laurel and Nisha had preplanned matching hot pink workout shorts, tight white tank tops, and green wristlet sweatbands.

The whole thing made me bristle. Since when was my sister allying with Nisha, my biggest rival? Obviously this whole Thayer thing was making her go to extremes.

Emma turned to Clara, the sophomore who'd been assigned as her doubles partner for the day. "Sorry. I was not playing well today."

"No, Sutton, you were great!" Clara's voice rose hopefully. She was pretty enough, with jet black hair, a perky, upturned nose, and startling blue eyes, but she had such a desperate look on her face. She'd been deferential to Emma all afternoon, complimenting her sucky serves, contesting calls against Emma's shots even though it was clear they were out, telling Emma repeatedly how pretty her sparkly hairband was. It was ridiculous how scared of Sutton people were, tiptoeing around her like she had the run of the school.

Or maybe, I thought, *they were tiptoeing around me to make sure I didn't play a Lying Game prank on them.*

After watching a few more matches, Emma headed to the locker room. Coach Maggie caught Emma's attention from the next court over and raised her fingers in a sympathetic wave. She tapped the base of her chin and mouthed *Keep your head up.*

The locker room was cool and smelled like freshly scoured tile. The brightly colored food-pyramid poster had come unpinned on one side and hung lopsided. A gaggle of girls in bathing suits pushed through the swinging doors that led into the locker room from the pool. The thick stench of chlorine filled the air as they made their way to the showers.

Emma turned in to a row of blue-gray lockers and found Laurel had made it there first. She had already changed out of her tennis gear into snug-fitting sweat shorts and a white tee and was sitting cross-legged on the long wooden bench, her back turned. Her iPhone was poised at her ear, and she was saying something in a hushed voice. It sounded like *If she's truly loyal, she'll go along with it.*

"Excuse me," she interrupted, resting Sutton's racket against the bench.

Laurel jumped an inch and dropped her phone. "Oh. Hey." Her face turned bright red, and Emma realized with a jolt that Laurel must have been talking about her. But what had the words meant?

Emma twirled the combination lock to Sutton's sports locker between her fingers. The door popped open with a *clank*. She stuffed Sutton's sneakers into the locker and checked her reflection in the small magnetic mirror.

"Nice effort today," Laurel said sarcastically. "I guess you can't win them all, huh?"

"Whatever," Emma shot back. She was too tired to get into a bitchy fight with Laurel right now.

"Seriously, though," Laurel said. "When was the last time you lost to me or Nisha? No offense, Sutton, but Clara was playing well. It was *you* who wasn't."

Nerves jumped in Emma's stomach. Talk about an understatement. She hadn't been playing well since she'd taken over Sutton's life. "I guess I'm just off my game lately," she said, trying to sound nonchalant.

Laurel adjusted the strap of her gold sandal and rose from the bench. "I'll say." She gave Emma a knowing look. "Maybe someone's just distracted because she has to prank her secret boyfriend."

Emma bit her lip and stared into Sutton's locker.

"Lili texted me. She set up the website our fake poet is going to post Ethan's work to," Laurel announced.

"She did?" Emma asked weakly.

"Yep! But you can still call it off. You know what you have to do to make that happen!" Laurel trilled. Then she jingled her car keys. "I'm taking Drake to the groomer's at six. Don't let Mom start dinner without me." She turned and waltzed from the locker room.

Emma listened as the door slammed, then let out a sigh. Slowly, she kicked off her tennis sneakers and slid on Sutton's espadrilles. A figure sidled up beside her, and when Emma turned, she saw Clara standing at the end of the aisle, an apologetic smile on her face.

"Is it okay if I grab my stuff?" she asked.

"Of course," Emma said, laughing.

Clara scuttled to her locker. Emma glanced inside, noting how precisely her extra T-shirts were folded, and how she kept her deodorant, shampoo, and body wash in a line at the bottom. Then, her breath caught in her chest. The metal bottom of Clara's locker was a full two inches lower than Sutton's.

Clara noticed her looking and flinched. "Oh, God. I usually keep my locker much neater than this."

Emma stared at her. Did Clara think she was going to punish her or something? "Don't be silly. I was actually admiring how organized it was."

"Really?" Clara's eyes lit up. And then she bit her lip nervously. "Hey, Sutton, I heard there was going to be a top-secret party this Friday. Maybe at an abandoned house or something?"

"That's right," Emma said. Madeline had told her the details about the party, saying that it was in a house that had been foreclosed upon months ago. She took in Clara's eager expression, then stepped forward. "Do you want to come? I can text you the details."

"Really?" Clara looked like she was going to keel over with delight. "That would be amazing!"

Clara thanked Emma at least six more times before she finished up, grabbed her stuff, and disappeared. Emma looked around the locker room. It was full of kids on the tennis and swim teams. There was no way she could investigate Sutton's locker right now. She'd have to wait in a quiet corner until the school emptied out . . . and then make her move.

By seven, the school was completely silent. The lights flickered off, shrouding Emma in darkness where she sat outside the library. A few teachers passed by on the way to their cars, but no one asked why she was there. Finally, she made her way back down the hallway and reentered the girls' locker room. The door shut behind her, leaving her blind in the pitch-black darkness. The smell of bleach barely masked the dull stench of sweaty gym clothes. Water dripped in the showers, and a sighlike sound echoed in the air.

Emma groped for the light switch, and ugly fluorescent light filled the locker room. She made her way to Sutton's locker, her fingers trembling as she turned the lock. She emptied out sneakers, pink-trimmed tennis socks, a box of Band-Aids, and spray-on sunscreen, tossing them all onto the bench. She stuck her fingers into the corner of the locker and pried open the base, flinching at the metal scraping noise that reverberated through the empty room.

Just below where the locker bottom used to be was a narrow, dirty space. Nestled among dust bunnies and rusted bobby pins was a long, thin silver lockbox. Heart pounding, Emma rifled through her wallet and found the small key she'd uncovered in Sutton's room. Slowly, she inserted it into the lock.

It fit.

Emma turned the key and opened the box. Inside was a mess of papers. She pulled out the paper on top and looked at the tight, neat handwriting. It was a letter, signed with Charlotte's name at the bottom. *I'm so sorry about everything, Sutton,* Charlotte wrote. She'd underlined *everything* three times. *Not only about Garrett, but about how unsupportive I've been while you're having a hard time with you-know-who.*

I stared at the note. What did it mean? What kind

of hard time was I having, and with whom? A moment slipped through my mind as I remembered Charlotte and me standing outside Hollier with bags slung over our shoulders, hunching toward each other and speaking in whispers. *She knows, Sutton, she does*, Charlotte whispered. *She's not a fool.* And then she added, *You need to think about where your loyalties lie.* I tried hard to hold onto the memory for longer, but it slipped away faster than it came.

Emma refolded Charlotte's message and dug deeper into the box. There was a list from Gabby and Lili of reasons why they should be allowed in the Lying Game, most having to do with their "awesome style and flair for drama." Next was a German test; all of the answers were filled in and it read TEACHER'S COPY in the top right corner. Emma dropped it as though it were on fire, paranoid Frau Fenstermacher might barge into the locker room and catch her red-handed.

The dripping noise from the shower slowed to a trickle. A vent clicked on, and a cough echoed somewhere in the distance. Emma shook off her nerves and kept digging through the notes. She flipped through an old detention slip, a pop quiz with a fat red *F* on it, and then she came across a dog-eared note written in a slanted, boyish scrawl:

Dear Sutton, I'm sorry. I don't want to be this way with you—this angry. It's like something inside me is making me. But I'm worried that unless things with us change, I'm going to snap. —T

A chill ran down Emma's spine. This was from Thayer. It had to be.

She didn't know what he was apologizing for, but the letter sounded like a threat and showed just how unstable Thayer was. A lump formed in Emma's throat as she reread Thayer's note. She was tired of wondering and guessing. There was only one way to know exactly what the hell was going on.

She had to see Thayer.

18

VISITOR FOR VEGA

The lockup was connected to the police station, though the entrance to the jail was through a separate door, with a different set of guards. Emma hesitated in front of the steel gate, taking heaving breaths. Finally, an overweight, bald guard in a navy uniform and carrying a paperback book strutted up to the door and peered at her. "Help you?" he asked, jingling a set of long, silver keys on his belt. "Visiting hours are almost over," he continued gruffly.

Emma checked the Cartier watch she'd found in Sutton's jewelry box. 7:42 P.M. "I'll just be a few minutes," she said, forcing her face into the sweetest smile she could muster.

The guard glowered at her. Emma got a glimpse of his book. The cover showed an overly muscled man with a sword strapped to his back, kissing a lithe blonde woman. When Emma was little, she'd read Harlequin romances like that—they were usually the only types of books on her foster mothers' shelves. For a while, she'd pretended that a brunette dressed as a pirate on the cover of *Shipwrecked and Heartbroken* was Becky.

Finally, the guard buzzed her in. He pulled out a clip-board with a sign-in sheet attached. Emma tried to keep her hand steady as she signed SUTTON MERCER under the column marked VISITOR and THAYER VEGA under INMATE. She knew what she was doing was risky, but she had found out as much as she was going to on her own. Now she needed to hear it from Thayer. And face-to-face in a jail, where they'd be separated by bulletproof glass, was about as safe as this conversation was going to get.

The guard glanced at the name Emma had written, then nodded. "Come with me." He led her through a heavy steel door and down a long hallway.

A second guard, this one wearing a matching navy uniform with STANBRIDGE printed on a nameplate on his burly chest, waited for Emma in a small, square room separated in the middle by a sheet of thick glass. Emma was happy to see it wasn't Quinlan—she didn't feel like dealing with him today. "You'll sit here," Stanbridge said, gesturing to a cubicle that faced the glass and was lined up evenly with a cubicle on the other side.

Emma sat on a hard, orange, plastic chair. The two wooden panels that squared her off must have been for privacy, not that Emma needed it in the empty room. Graffiti splashed across the panels in colored marker and ink: CP LUVS SN. HEARTS 4 EVER. Dates as far back as 5/4/82 were carved into the wood.

A door swung open on the other side of the glass, and Emma flinched, her heart leaping to her throat. There, sweeping through the door, escorted by a pudgy guard with a bowl cut, was Thayer. His skin looked pale and taut against his bones. When he saw Emma, he stopped short. His mouth tightened at the edges. For a moment, Emma felt sure he'd turn back and retreat through the door. But then the guard put a hand between Thayer's shoulder blades and gave him a small shove toward her.

Thayer reluctantly stepped forward and settled in the seat opposite Emma. When he picked up the phone receiver on the opposite side of the glass, the orange sleeve of his jumpsuit fell back to reveal a tattoo Emma hadn't noticed at the precinct. An eagle emblem was inked on the underside of his wrist with the initials SPH printed in tiny letters beneath it. Was this the strange tattoo Madeline had spoken about?

I examined Thayer carefully, taking in every inch

of him. I tried to imagine loving him. Having a secret relationship. Risking friendships just to be with him. Even dead, even memory-less, I could feel something stirring inside me for him, a magnetic pull that made me want to get as close to him as possible. At the same time, as I took in his dark eyes and menacing expression, I felt afraid. I knew there was something huge in my memories that I hadn't seen yet, a horrible moment I had blocked out.

Emma picked up the receiver and took a deep breath. "We need to talk," she said in the strongest voice she could find. "I have some questions for you about that night," she went on, meaning the night Sutton died. "About everything," she added.

Thayer raised his eyes to hers. Dark, bluish half-moons stamped the area beneath them; it looked as though he hadn't slept in days. "You got my messages. You shouldn't have any questions. But instead you acted like a complete psycho and ruined everything."

Messages? A cold, clammy feeling washed over Emma. He had to be talking about the SUTTON'S DEAD, PLAY ALONG OR YOU'RE NEXT note. And what he'd written on the chalkboard at the Homecoming rally after nearly killing Emma with that falling light.

Emma opened her mouth to speak, but no words came out. Thayer leaned back and gave her a cold, calculating stare. "Or is this just a game? Haven't you heard? I'm not one to play games with. Not when I'm the only one who knows who you really are."

Emma's body went weak from her feet to her throat. Her fingers tingled around the base of the phone and she struggled to hold it against her ear. It was glaringly obvious. Thayer knew who Emma was . . . and who she wasn't. He had done it. He had killed Sutton. She was sitting across from her sister's murderer.

"Thayer, what did you do?" Her voice was a whisper.

I was dying to know, too. Thayer's words, his posture, his entire being seemed to radiate anger. How could he have said he loved me, then hurt me?

"Wouldn't you love to know?" Thayer grinned, flashing white teeth. "Anyway, did you hear the good news? We got the hearing moved up to next week. I'll be out of here soon."

"You're getting out next week?" Emma repeated, beginning to tremble. That meant she was only safe for eight more days.

"Yep. My lawyer is trying to get the case dismissed. I'm a minor, and they've got me on trumped-up charges as an adult, but my lawyer's going to prove it's bullshit. This is Quinlan's idea of revenge—that guy hates me. He hates you too, Sutton." He gave her a long look. "And when I'm out, we'll finally be able to talk one-on-one. Just like old times."

The words Thayer was saying were innocent enough, but his voice dripped with sarcasm and hatred. He arched forward, inches from Emma's face. He bent so close to the glass that Emma could see the outlines of his breath against the pane. His pupils widened into black spheres. Emma clenched the phone tighter, feeling sweat between her fingers and the beige plastic. Then he slammed the phone into its cradle. A dull tone buzzed in Emma's ear.

A hand clapped around Emma's shoulder, and she jumped and twisted around. Stanbridge gazed at her sternly. "Visiting hours are over now, miss."

Emma nodded numbly and followed him out of the room. I trailed behind her, electrical impulses snapping and flashing inside me. Something about seeing Thayer—and that guard clapping a hand on Emma's shoulder—made a few doors unlock in my mind. I smelled the dust and desert flowers of Sabino Canyon. I felt the cool air on my bare skin. I felt that hand clap around my shoulder—maybe Thayer's hand. Maybe right before he killed me.

Once again, I was zooming backward into my past . . .

19

CATCH ME IF YOU CAN

I twist around and see Thayer's face. It is his hand on my shoulder, and he doesn't look happy. He clamps down hard, his fingers gripping the soft skin above my collarbone.

"You're hurting me!" I scream, but his other hand claps over my mouth before I can call for help. He yanks me back from the edge of the cliff, jerking my body against his chest. My fingers claw at his arms and my feet kick frantically against the ground. My elbows stab at his ribs. I'm fighting like a wild animal, but I can't get away from him. He's too strong.

"What are you—" My voice is muffled beneath his hand. I finally manage to free myself from his grip and spin across the hardscrabble path away from him. But he advances toward me

again, arms outstretched. My mind spins. I rack my brain for anything I can say to calm him down. What have I done to make him so angry? Is it because of what I said about Garrett? Or how hard I pushed him to tell me where he's been the last few months?

"Thayer, please," I start. "Can't we just talk about this?"

There is fury in Thayer's eyes. "Be quiet, Sutton."

And then he lunges at me again. I try to scream, but it comes out like a strangled yelp as his hand smacks over my mouth again. His sneakers scratch against the dried leaves below our feet and his muscles flex as he pulls me against him. His breath is hot on my ear. Blood pools in my feet, and a sense of dread crawls across my body.

Suddenly, a scream sounds loud and clear in the distance. It's hard to tell whether it's human or animal. Thayer turns in the direction of the shriek, momentarily distracted. His grip loosens just enough for me to bite the inside of his palm. I taste his salty sweat as I sink my teeth into his skin.

"Jesus!" Thayer screeches. He rips his hand away, trying to catch his balance. I take off, my legs hot with adrenaline. Dirt crunches beneath me and leaves crack as I pound the earth. I fly across the trail, my hair wild and my arms pumping. A branch slices across my cheek, thin as paper and just as sharp. I can feel wetness on my skin. I'm not sure if it's tears . . . or blood.

Things have been tense between Thayer and me before, but I've never seen him like this.

A rush of cold air slaps my body as I push forward. I hear

Thayer's footsteps, and I can tell he's gaining ground. I've traveled this path so many times, though, and the darkness gives me an advantage. I press on through the brambly mesquite trees and brush. Behind me, there's a crash of Thayer's body colliding with a tree or a rock. I hear him swear under his breath, cursing me.

I cut a sharp right around the boulder where my father and I used to stop for water breaks. "Sutton!" It's a man's voice, but the rocks must distort it, because it doesn't quite sound like Thayer's. I continue forward, my lungs burning, the tears running down my face, my heart thudding with fear.

I dart around a massive tree branch that blocks the path and scramble down the steep incline, heading for the trickle of water that passes for a creek—the only body of water in the canyon. I press my heels into the dirt to steady myself as I slip farther into the ditch. My hands reach for something—anything—to grab hold of, and land on a gnarled root along the creek bed. I reach the bottom and spring to my feet, taking off in the direction of the parking lot. I'm close. I just need to make it to my car.

I sprint down the trail toward the lot. I nearly wipe out when my feet slam the gravel. I don't think I've ever been so happy to see my beloved car. Skidding across the lot, I fumble inside my purse for the keys. My fingers close around the heavy, round Volvo keychain, but I'm shaking so badly that it flies out of my hands, landing with a jingle near the front tire. "Shit," I whisper.

"Sutton!" a voice booms.

I turn to see Thayer emerge from the clearing. He's barreling toward me, his hands clenched into fists, his shoulders rigid. I shriek. Time stands still. My limbs won't move. I scramble for my keys on the ground, but there isn't time. I turn to bolt just as his arms wrap around me. His fingers dig into my flesh.

"No, no!" I scream. His skin burns against mine. "Thayer, please!"

"Believe me," Thayer whispers in my ear. "This is hurting me more than it's hurting you."

I feel him dragging me toward the thick woods next to the parking lot. But before I can see what happens next—my last moment, surely—the memory explodes like a bomb, leaving me with nothingness.

20

BLOOD DOESN'T LIE

Thirty minutes later, Emma got out of a cab in front of Ethan's house. It had begun to pour, a bizarre phenomenon for Tucson. It made the air smell like ozone and wet asphalt. The gravel in his front yard glinted under the moon.

Emma dashed across the grass, avoiding raindrops, and rapped on the white door. She leaned her ear close to the wood until she heard footsteps pad down the hallway inside. The door swung open to reveal the foyer. Ethan's pale blue eyes widened at the sight of her. His dark hair was disheveled, like he'd been sleeping.

"Emma?" he asked, carefully stepping forward and touching her shoulders. "What happened?"

"I needed to see you." Emma glanced over her shoulder. "Can I come in?"

Ethan stepped aside. "Of course."

Emma shut the door behind her and collapsed into Ethan's arms. The weight of everything that happened with Thayer pressed down on her until her head fell into her hands. She sobbed for a good five minutes, her nose stuffing up, tears burning her eyes. Ethan rubbed her back the whole time.

I was happy my sister had someone to comfort her. If only I had someone like that. I was the one who'd just seen that horrible memory, after all—*I* was the one who'd been brutally murdered by someone I loved. It felt like my insides had been hollowed out. The Thayer I'd picked up at the bus station seemed nothing like the madman he'd become by the end. How could I have been so stupid as to have gotten mixed up with him?

After Emma's sobs turned to whimpers, Ethan led her through the kitchen and curved around the breakfast bar. A cluster of take-out menus covered the sand-colored granite. Two cans of Coke sat on the long wooden table next to an empty pizza box. The stilted dialogue of a true-crime show sounded from the living room. He kicked open his bedroom door and flipped on the light. "Here, sit," he said to Emma, gesturing to the bed. "Tell me what's going on."

Emma's legs felt numb as she sank onto the dark blue

comforter. She grabbed a quilted pillow and hugged it to her chest. "I saw Thayer," she started, glancing at Ethan nervously.

Predictably, Ethan's face clouded. "In jail? I told you not to!"

"I know, but I—"

"Why didn't you listen?"

Tears flooded Emma's eyes again. She didn't need a lecture right now. "I didn't know what else to do," she said defensively. "I needed answers. And he gave them to me. He told me he was the only one who knew who I really was."

"He *said* that?" Ethan's eyes widened.

"Uh-huh." Emma nodded. "He talked about the letters he sent me, too. He must have meant the note that was on Laurel's car, the message on the chalkboard at the pep rally. He did it, Ethan. I know it."

Ethan placed his head in his hands. "I'm so sorry."

Then Emma pulled Thayer's note to Sutton from her pocket and unfolded it. "I found this today," she said, passing the paper to Ethan.

He grimaced as he read the letter. When he finished, he folded it neatly and handed it back to her. "Whoa. It's like he basically confessed that he might hurt her unless things changed between them."

"I know. And then . . . he *did* hurt her."

I shivered at Emma's words, the memory once again spiraling in my mind. But where had Thayer taken me? It had to have something to do with my car, right? There was blood on it, after all—surely *my* blood. If only I could have seen the rest of the memory. I felt like the puzzle was almost complete, save for that missing piece.

"Every time I've seen him, he's looked at me like he knows I'm not Sutton," Emma whispered. "Thayer must have killed Sutton and lured me here," she said softly. "And think about it. Since he was missing, he never had to be anywhere at any given time. He would have been able to slip around Tucson easily, spying on me, leaving me notes, threatening me."

"You're right," Ethan said softly. "It would have been easy for him."

"He's got me where he wants me. If I say one word against him, he'll tell the cops who I am. And then they'll blame me for Sutton's death. This is playing out exactly as you said it would." She shut her eyes and started to sob again. "He told me that his lawyer is working hard to get him out of jail by next week. That could be in a matter of days! What am I going to do?"

"*Shhh,*" Ethan whispered. He took Emma's hand and rested it against his jeans. "It's okay," he whispered. "Thayer is still locked up. You're still safe. There's still time to prove what he did. I'm here with you, okay? I'm not going to let you go through this alone. I'll keep you safe."

Emma laid her head on his shoulder. "I don't know what I'd do without you."

"And I don't know what I'd do without *you*. If something happened to you . . ." Ethan broke off, his voice cracking. "I couldn't bear it."

It was such a relief just to hear those words. Emma swallowed a sob and smiled gratefully at Ethan. Her lips were about to touch his when she noticed a leather journal next to the bed. It was open to a page near the back and neat letters formed short verses, like a poem. Suddenly, the guilt flooded back. The prank. Laurel had asked her to steal his work. She winced, then pulled away from him.

"I need to tell you something else," she said. "Something you're not going to like."

Ethan cocked his head. "Of course. You can tell me anything."

Emma stared at Ethan's hands entwined with hers, hating what she had to do next. But she had to warn him. She took a deep breath. "Sutton's friends are planning this prank on you. It has to do with your poetry reading."

Ethan shrank back. "*What?*"

"I tried to stop them. But they really—"

Ethan waved his hands, cutting her off. He blinked at her hard, as though Emma had just hit him over the head with a shovel. "How long have you known about this?"

Emma lowered her eyes. "Um, a few days," she said in a small voice.

"A few *days*?"

"I'm sorry!" Emma cried. "I tried to stop it! It wasn't my idea!"

Slowly, Ethan's expression turned from hurt to disappointment to disgust. "I think you should go," he said numbly.

"Ethan, I—" Emma tried to reach for his hand, but he was already making his way to the door. "Ethan!" she called after him, running into the hall. They were almost to the foyer when she caught his arm and swung him around. "Please! You told me we could be honest about everything! And I thought—"

"You thought wrong," Ethan interrupted, wrenching his arm away. "You could have called this off instantly. They think you're the all-powerful Sutton Mercer. One word from you and the prank's off. Why didn't you do that? Is it because you don't want them to know about me? Are you"—his voice caught, and he cleared his throat roughly—"*ashamed* of me?"

"Of course not!" Emma cried, but maybe Ethan had a point. Why hadn't she tried harder to nip it in the bud? How had she let it get so out of control?

Ethan's hand turned the doorknob. "Just go, okay?

Don't bother talking to me until you remember who you are—Emma Paxton, the nice twin."

"Ethan!" Emma cried, but he'd already pushed her outside and slammed the door in her face. It was raining harder now, and the drops mixed with the tears that streamed down her cheeks. It felt like she'd just lost the only good thing she had in the world. She cupped her hands against the glass of the side window and stared into the house, watching as Ethan stormed back down the hall, knocking over a stack of books on the living room table as he went.

It was a scene I hated to watch. Once again, I cursed the Lying Game. If my friends and I hadn't started that stupid club, Emma wouldn't be heartbroken right now. Her one and only ally wouldn't hate her.

Emma rang the doorbell a few times, but Ethan didn't answer. She texted him to please talk to her, but he didn't reply. After a while, there was no use in lingering—Ethan had made his feelings clear. She trudged across the front lawn, instantly getting soaked, wondering how she was going to get back to the Mercers. As she was pulling out Sutton's cell phone to call the cab service again, the phone lit up in her hands. Emma frowned. The number was from the Tucson police station. A horrible thought came to her: What if the cops were calling about Thayer? What if he was being set free?

"Uh, hello?" Emma yelled over the rainstorm, trying to quell the nerves in her voice.

Detective Quinlan's voice boomed on the other end. "Evening, Miss Mercer. We got the blood results back from your car."

Emma tensed. "W-what are they?" She braced herself, sure he was going to say the blood was Sutton's.

"The blood is a perfect match for Thayer Vega," Quinlan's low voice pronounced.

Emma stopped short in the middle of the street, certain she'd heard him wrong. "*Thayer?*"

"That's right," Quinlan said. "Any idea how it got there? Mr. Vega certainly isn't talking."

"I . . ." Emma trailed off, not having a single thing to say. She paused next to a spindly mesquite tree, trying to catch her breath. She felt completely blindsided.

"Sutton?" Quinlan prompted. "Is there something you need to tell me?"

Emma huddled under the tree, not that it provided much shelter from the storm. There was so much she needed to tell him. Did she dare? Could she somehow convince him this time that she was Sutton's twin, but that she hadn't wanted to steal Sutton's life? Would he believe her if she told him Thayer had been sending her threatening messages—*and* that Thayer had killed Sutton? She doubted it. Sure, she had Thayer's note from Sutton's locker, the one that said he was going to snap, but while it was proof enough for her, it was unlikely the police would consider it definitive evidence.

"I-I'm sorry. I have no idea how it got there," Emma answered finally. She shut her eyes, thinking. "Were there any other fingerprints on the car?"

Quinlan sighed. "Just yours and your father's. He was a co-owner of the vehicle, correct?"

"Uh-huh," Emma said distantly. She recalled Mr. Mercer talking about how he and Sutton had restored the Volvo together.

There was a cough on the other end. "Well, since there's no longer any reason for us to hold your car, you can come pick it up," Quinlan said gruffly.

"Thanks," Emma said, but Quinlan had already disconnected. She held the phone outstretched, staring at it as though it were an alien life form. Wind tossed a cold, wet leaf against her ankle. An engine whined in the distance. The world was still turning as usual, but Emma felt utterly changed. *Thayer's* blood. But . . . *how?*

I was as stunned as she was. I thought back over the memory I'd just regained. It didn't make sense—Thayer was the lunatic after *me*, not the other way around. There was only one answer: I must have somehow managed to get into my car and hit Thayer before he killed me. I was glad for that—Thayer may have taken my life, but at least I got a piece of him on my way out.

21

MOTHER KNOWS BEST

That night, Emma rolled over in bed and looked at the bright neon green digits of Sutton's alarm clock. It was 2:12 A.M. She'd been crying since a cab dropped her off at home, and her throat was so parched she could barely swallow. In all her life, she'd never felt so confused and alone. Not when she had to move out of Henderson and say good-bye to Alex. Not when she'd had to stay in the state home for an entire month when social services couldn't find her a foster family. And not even when Becky had left her at her neighbor's and had never come back to get her.

All those times were hard and sad, but when she left Henderson, she could still call Alex. When she was at the state home, she could play with the girl who shared her bunk bed. And when Becky left, she could cry to her friend's mom and say she missed her.

But now she was living with a secret so big she was sure the weight of it would crush her. And with Ethan mad at her—so mad that he might never speak to her again—she had *no one* to turn to. She couldn't tell anyone else who she really was. She couldn't make a list of *Things I Hate About Being Sutton* or *Things I Miss About Being Emma* or even keep a journal, for fear that someone might find it and discover her true identity.

And the news about Thayer's blood terrified her. Did that mean Sutton had hit him? What if that caused his limp? Madeline's voice echoed through Emma's mind: *He'll never be able to play soccer again. It was his biggest love—the thing he was best at—and now his future is ruined.* Maybe there was a motive here. What if Thayer was so furious at Sutton for hurting him that he got her back . . . by killing her?

Emma flopped back into Sutton's down pillow, the soft feathers molding perfectly to the shape of her head. Everything felt so impossible. Why was she doing all this? What was the point? Maybe she should take off again and leave it all behind. If she wanted to run, now was the time. With Thayer behind bars, he couldn't track her every movement. She could finally be free. She was eighteen.

She could get her GED, declare residency somewhere, and apply for in-state tuition . . .

But even as she thought it, Emma knew she wouldn't leave. She was living the life of someone she wanted so desperately to know, trying to get justice for her sister. She would never be able to forgive herself if she just gave up, because giving up meant that the person who had murdered Sutton, who had robbed Emma of the chance to get to know her twin sister, would walk free.

It was unimaginable that my murderer would get away with it. I couldn't accept that, and I hoped Emma would have the strength to stick around—even though I also knew it was getting more and more dangerous for her to be here.

Emma flung the covers off her legs and padded across the bedroom. She unlocked the door and tiptoed down the dark hallway, descending the stairs and narrowly avoiding the stack of magazines Laurel had left on the bottom step. A scraggly aloe plant cast long shadows across the tile. A dripping noise sounded from outside the living room window and Emma watched rain fall in slow drops from the drainpipe. In the hallway, moonlight cast an eerie glow across the family photographs. Emma caught her reflection in a scalloped, gold-framed mirror at the end of the hall. Her dark hair hung long and loose, and her oval face looked like a white sheet against the darkness.

She rounded the corner into the kitchen and felt the cold tile beneath her bare feet. She was about to open a cabinet when a shadowy figure moved in the corner. She jumped backward, her hip slamming against a chrome dial on the stove.

"Sutton?"

Emma's eyes focused on Mrs. Mercer, her body hunched forward as she held Drake by the collar. The dog let out a low bark.

"What are you doing up so late?" Mrs. Mercer straightened and let Drake go. He came over and sniffed Emma's hand before curling into a ball at the foot of the fridge.

Emma tied her messy hair back into a ponytail. "I couldn't sleep so I came down to get a glass of water."

Mrs. Mercer put her hand on Emma's forehead. "Hmmm. Are you feeling okay? Laurel says you came home soaked from the rain."

Emma forced a weak laugh. "Well, I didn't have an umbrella. Last time I checked, we lived in Arizona." She took in Mrs. Mercer's rumpled hair and robe. "What are *you* doing up?"

Mrs. Mercer waved her hand dismissively. "Oh, Drake was whining, so I got up to let him out." She went to the sink and filled a glass, dropping two ice cubes in it. The cubes cracked loudly in the water. She sat at the counter and pushed it toward Emma, who took a grateful sip.

"So . . ." Mrs. Mercer propped her chin in her hand. "Why can't you sleep? Anything you want to talk about?"

Emma put her head down on the counter and sighed. There was *so much* she wanted to talk about. She couldn't talk about Sutton's murder, but maybe she could get some advice on Ethan. "I hurt a guy I care about and I don't know how to fix it," she blurted.

Mrs. Mercer looked sympathetic. "Did you try apologizing?"

There was a soft rumbling noise as the ice machine deposited a new batch in the freezer. "I tried . . . but he didn't want to hear it," Emma said.

"Well, maybe you need to try again. Figure out exactly what you did wrong and exactly how you can fix it, then make it happen."

"How am I supposed to do that?" Emma asked.

Mrs. Mercer leaned back in her chair and ran her fingers along a pineapple-printed dish towel. "Sometimes, actions speak louder than words. Show him that you're sorry, and hopefully everything will fall back in place. Just be the best Sutton you can be. He's got to understand that people make mistakes sometimes. And if he can't forgive you, he's not worth keeping around."

Emma thought about this for a moment. Sutton's mom was right: She'd just made a mistake, nothing more. And maybe she couldn't be the best Sutton she could be, but she could definitely be the best Emma. Ethan had said Emma had forgotten who she was—the nice twin. With so much going on, it was hard to maintain her identity—and know what she wanted. Emma's needs felt so secondary in comparison to what happened to Sutton. Wanting anything beyond staying alive and solving her sister's murder seemed like such a luxury.

She sat up straighter, a firm sense of resolve settling over her. She just needed to stick to her plan. She was going to prove that Thayer murdered her sister. That way, she could go back to being Emma Paxton. But in the meantime, she was going to behave in a way she could be proud of, even if her actions weren't one hundred percent Sutton-like.

Emma stood up and hugged Mrs. Mercer. "Thanks, Mom. That was just what I needed to hear."

Mrs. Mercer hugged her for a moment, then leaned back and looked at the girl she thought was her daughter with surprise. "That's the first time you've ever thanked me for giving you advice."

"Well, maybe I should have thanked you a long time ago."

As my mom corralled Drake and led him back up the stairs, I felt a guilty pang. Given what my mother had just said, and what I'd already gleaned about my relationship with my parents, I doubted my mom and I had ever had late-night heart-to-hearts when I was alive. I didn't value my parents' opinions at all, and maybe that was a mistake—yet another in a long list of regrets I couldn't rectify.

I turned my attention back to Emma, who was sitting with her chin cupped in her hand, a distant smile on her face. Even though I knew it was wrong, a bitter edge of resentment flowed through me. Emma was having trouble remembering who she was, but at least she still had a body, an identity. Actually, she had *two* identities—hers and mine. And now she had to live for the both of us.

22

SEEK AND YE SHALL FIND

For the next two days, Emma tried to stick with her decision, keep her head up, and do random acts of Emma Kindness, even if they weren't completely Sutton-esque. She retweeted the Twitter Twins' latest posts about the difficulty of finding clothes worthy of their hotness with an LOL. She complimented Charlotte's backhand during tennis practice. She even told Nisha Banerjee that her hair tie was cute. Nisha had looked astonished—and a little suspicious—but thanked Emma.

Emma hadn't had any success with Ethan or Laurel, though. On Wednesday she'd let Laurel have the last pomegranate-flavored yogurt in the fridge compartment in the cafeteria line, knowing it was Laurel's favorite, but Laurel just grunted and greedily took it. When Emma caught sight of Ethan in the hall, he'd yanked his backpack higher on his shoulder and darted across the hall to avoid her.

On Thursday after tennis practice she scanned the cars in the parking lot and realized that a certain VW wasn't in its regular parking space. She let out a long groan.

"Laurel ditch you again?" Madeline appeared behind Emma, carrying a stack of books. Her blue eyes were bright and feather earrings grazed her shoulders.

"Yep," Emma said, unable to hide her irritation. "She's being a real bitch this week."

Madeline let out the first real laugh Emma had heard from her in weeks. "She sure is." She touched Emma's elbow. "Don't worry. She'll get over it. I did."

Two freshman boys passed behind her, clutching Roller-blades and elbowing each other. One caught Emma's eye and his face broke into a massive grin. He nodded in her direction and picked up his hand in a slow wave. Emma smiled back in another act of Emma Kindness.

Madeline pulled her car keys out of her leather purse. "Want a ride home?"

Emma eyed Madeline's keychain. "Actually I'm just going to the police station. I'm going to finally get my car."

Madeline flinched a little at the words *police station*, then frowned. "Isn't it at the impound?"

SARA SHEPARD

A dart of nerves shot through Emma's stomach. Sutton's friends thought that her car had been impounded because she racked up too many tickets and she simply hadn't picked it up yet. They didn't know Sutton had retrieved her car the day she died. Or used it to pick up Thayer. *Or* perhaps hit Thayer with it.

"Uh, the impound was full, so they moved it to the lot behind the police station," Emma fudged, crossing her fingers that Madeline would buy it. She hated lying, but she wasn't about to say that Sutton's car was actually in evidence with Madeline's brother's blood on it. Luckily, Madeline just shrugged and unlocked her SUV with two loud *bleep*s.

"Get in. I'll save you the two-block walk."

Emma climbed in, resting her bag on her lap.

"So, excited for Charlotte's tomorrow?" Madeline asked as she turned the ignition. "It's been a while since we've had a dinner at the Chamberlains'. I've missed Cornelia's cooking. Wouldn't it be amazing to have a personal chef?"

Emma made an *mm* of agreement, remembering that the girls had arranged to spend the evening at Charlotte's for dinner. She wasn't surprised the Chamberlains had a personal chef—their house was enormous.

"Of course, I shouldn't say that." Madeline made a wry face. "If my dad heard me talking about how much

I wanted a personal chef, he'd probably say I was acting spoiled and greedy." She rolled her eyes and tried to laugh lightly, but her face kind of crumpled.

Emma pulled her bottom lip into her mouth, sensing Madeline's pain. "You know, if you want to talk more about your dad, I'm here."

"Thanks," Madeline said softly. She reached into her hot pink metallic Not Rational handbag, yanked her sunglasses from their case, and slipped them over her eyes.

"Is everything going okay? Is it getting better?" Emma pressed.

Madeline waited until she left the parking lot before she spoke again. "It's pretty much the same, I guess. I hate going home. My dad stomps around everywhere and he and my mom aren't talking right now. I don't think they're even sleeping in the same room." Her glossy lips tightened into a straight line.

"You're always welcome at my house, you know," Emma offered.

Madeline looked at her gratefully. "Thank you," she breathed. Then she touched Emma's arm. "You've never offered that before."

I felt a zing of annoyance. I would have offered if I would have known Madeline needed it.

A minute later they pulled up to the precinct, and Madeline dropped Emma off at the curb. "Sutton?" she said, leaning out the window. "I'm really glad we made up. I probably don't say it enough, but you're my best friend."

"I'm so glad, too," Emma said, her heart warming.

When she went inside, the same receptionist who had been there the last time looked up from her tabloid and considered Emma. "You again?" she asked in a bored voice.

How professional. "I'm here to pick up my car from evidence," Emma said crisply.

The receptionist turned and picked up the receiver of her phone. "One moment."

Emma pivoted and stared at the bulletin board. The MISSING poster of Thayer had been taken down and replaced with an advertisement for HECTOR, THE HONEST MECHANIC YOU TELL YOUR FRIENDS ABOUT.

After a moment, the receptionist pointed outside where a squat guard stood in front of a chain-link fence. "Officer Moriarty will help you," she said, twisting her tongue to blow a purple bubble. A sugary grape smell wafted through the air of the waiting room.

Emma walked back outside, met up with Officer Moriarty, and signed the paperwork for Sutton's car. Officer Moriarty unlocked the fence and led her down a dusty row of vehicles. BMWs and Range Rovers sat proudly next to broken-down clunkers that looked like they wouldn't make it another five miles.

"Here we are," Officer Moriarty said, gesturing to a green vintage car with brightly polished chrome. Emma took in the car, impressed. It had sleek lines and a retro feel, the kind of car she might have chosen herself if she could've afforded one. It was beyond cool.

Of *course* it was cool. I squealed as I saw my car again. But the feeling was bittersweet. I couldn't feel the soft leather against my thighs as I sat in the driver's seat. I couldn't shift gears and feel the car respond. I couldn't feel the wind in my hair as I drove down Route 10 with the windows down.

Emma took the keys from the cop. She inspected the exterior of the car, looking for the telltale blood the cops had found, but she saw nothing beyond a slight dent where Sutton had probably made contact with Thayer's leg. Perhaps they'd cleaned it off. Then she opened the driver's door and plopped down on the leather seat. A strange sensation came over her. Something about this car felt so distinctly Sutton, as though her twin were suddenly present. She shut her eyes and could almost picture her twin behind the wheel, tossing her hair, and laughing at something Charlotte or Madeline said. Emma toyed with a silver guardian angel charm that hung on the rearview mirror, swearing she could smell a trace of Sutton's perfume lingering in the air. She knew how much it would've annoyed her twin for the car to be in the police department's probing hands.

I'll take good care of her for you, Emma thought as she tapped her fingers on the leather-wrapped steering wheel.

I smiled. She'd better.

Knuckles rapped the glass. Emma flinched and looked up to see Officer Moriarty. She slowly rolled down the window.

"Can I help you with anything else, Miss Mercer?" he asked gruffly.

"No, officer, I'm fine," Emma said, forcing an innocent, trust-me tone into her voice. "Thanks so much for your help."

"Then it's best if you left the premises," the officer said, his thumb hooked through a belt loop.

Emma nodded and rolled up the window, then eased the key into the ignition. She didn't need to adjust the mirror or the seats—they fit her perfectly, just like they'd fit Sutton. As she was pulling out of the lot, something on the seat next to her caught her eye. There was something lodged in the leather crease where the back of the seat met the bottom. It looked like a tiny piece of paper.

She drove down the road until the police station was out of view, then pulled over at the curb and put the car in park. Her attention turned to the paper wedged in the seat. She pulled at it, her brow wrinkled. Finally, it broke free. It was a tiny scrap of paper with the words DR. SHELDON ROSE scrawled across it. She recognized the angular writing immediately from the letter she'd found at the bottom of Sutton's sports locker. It was Thayer's.

Her heart pounded. She glanced over her shoulder just as a police car turned out of the parking lot, its sirens blazing. For a few agonizing seconds, she was sure the cops were coming for her—maybe planting this important piece of evidence in the car was a test, and she was in trouble for not volunteering it. But then the car zipped past her, the officer at the wheel staring straight ahead. She let out a long breath. The cops weren't after her. They didn't even know what she'd found.

I only hoped it led to an answer.

23

THE PSYCHOPATH TEST

Emma drove exactly one and a half miles before she pulled over again, this time in the parking lot of the Tucson Botanical Gardens. Brightly colored blooms could be seen behind the gates. Hummingbirds flitted to feeders. But the gardens were closed for the afternoon, and the lot was almost empty. It seemed like the perfect place to sit and think. There was no way she could wait to look up Dr. Sheldon Rose until she got home. She had to investigate this *now*.

Grabbing Sutton's iPhone from the passenger's seat, Emma typed DR. SHELDON ROSE into the search engine. In seconds, the results appeared, listing dozens of doctors across the country. Gastroenterologists. Cardiologists. Some guy who did "Chakra Cleansing." There were client testimonials, locations, and telephone numbers. Papers authored by various doctors named Sheldon Rose popped up with titles like "The Brain in Motion" and "Healthy Liver, Healthy Life." And then there were PhD doctors— a Sheldon Rose who taught Victorian literature at the University of Virginia, a Sheldon Rose who worked on smoking cessation therapy in New Hampshire, and one who headed up the MIT computer science department.

Emma clicked on the link to a primary care doctor; maybe Thayer had caught some kind of flu or infection while he was in hiding. The website showed six doctors who worked in a white brick medical facility called Wyoming Health. Dr. Sheldon Rose of Casper, Wyoming, stared back at her with a smug look on his pockmarked face. It didn't seem like the right answer.

A car honked on the street. A bunch of kids rode by on BMX bikes. A shadow around the side of a gas station across the street caught Emma's eye, but when she looked closer, she didn't see anyone there. *Calm down,* she thought. *No one followed you. No one knows you're here.*

She scrolled through the next page of search results. She wasn't sure exactly what she was looking for—or how long it would take to find it—but there had to be *something,* and she'd know it when she saw it. She clicked on link after link, dead end after dead end. After ten minutes, she was about to give up, when suddenly she came upon a website for a Dr. Sheldon Rose in Seattle, Washington. When she opened it, her breath caught in her throat. The home page featured an emblem of an eagle with its wings stretched wide and its head tipped up and to the left. There were tiny initials below its talons that read SPH. It looked like the very same eagle in Thayer's tattoo.

Her pulse raced as she clicked on the links. A photo of Dr. Sheldon Rose gazed back at her with black eyes nearly hidden behind thick, red-framed glasses. His shaved head and wide jaw made him look more like a bouncer at a motorcycle bar than a doctor. A sick feeling slivered through Emma's stomach as she scanned his bio: DR. SHELDON ROSE IS A PSYCHIATRIST WHO SPECIALIZES IN PSYCHOPATHIC BEHAVIOR AND OTHER EXTREME MENTAL DISORDERS. He treated his patients at Seattle Psychiatric Hospital—SPH. A *mental* hospital. The words on the tiny screen blurred before Emma's eyes. Had Thayer been admitted to a mental hospital? Is that why he had a tattoo of an eagle on his arm? And what did that say about the state he'd been in on the night of Sutton's disappearance?

I thought again about how furious Thayer had been when he'd chased me down the trail. It was like something in him had truly snapped. Or maybe like he'd gone off his medication.

Emma picked up Sutton's cell with shaking fingers and dialed the main number listed for the hospital. A ring sounded in her ear before a woman picked up and announced, "Seattle Psychiatric."

"I'm calling to see if you've treated a patient there," Emma said. "His name is—"

"I'm sorry, ma'am. That's confidential. We can't give out patients' names." An annoyed *click* sounded from the other end.

Duh. Of course they weren't going to give out that kind of information. Emma ran a hand through her hair, wondering how she was going to find this out. A garbage truck rumbled past. The wind kicked up, bringing with it the mingled scents of rotting trash and flowers from the gardens. Emma peered at the gas station across the street again, searching for the phantom shadow. When she was certain no one was there, she cleared her throat and redialed the same number.

"Seattle Psychiatric." This time it was a man's voice.

"I'm calling to speak to Dr. Sheldon Rose," Emma said, assuming a professional tone.

"Can I tell him who's calling?" The voice sounded bored, as though he wanted to be anywhere in the world other than a reception desk.

"Dr. Carole Sweeney," Emma said, pulling a doctor's name out of thin air. It was the name of her favorite pediatrician—and she'd had at least a dozen of them. During the ten months she'd lived with a foster family in northern Nevada, Dr. Sweeney treated Emma and the six other children in the foster home. Their foster mom couldn't afford a babysitter, so every time one of the six got sick, she lugged them all to her office. Dr. Sweeney's waiting room was full of rainbow-colored building blocks, tattered stuffed animals, and coloring books scattered across a red plastic table in the center. When Emma and her foster siblings used to chase each other around the table, making tons of noise, Dr. Sweeney never yelled at them.

"Please hold," said the male voice.

Emma's heart pounded. Piano music tinkled through the phone as she waited.

"Dr. Rose's office," a woman's voice said.

"Is the doctor available?" Emma tried to sound rushed and important.

"No, he's not in, can I take a message?"

"Who am I speaking with?" Emma asked.

There was a sharp intake of breath on the other line. "This is Penny, Dr. Rose's nurse," the voice finally said.

"This is Dr. Carole Sweeney from Tucson Medical," Emma blurted. She kept her voice urgent, as though she was in the middle of a life-or-death situation. "I've just admitted a patient by the name of Thayer Vega. He's in bad shape."

"Bad shape? What do you mean?"

Emma felt a twinge of guilt. She hated lying like this.

But I was impressed. Was this the same girl who used to question the morality of the Lying Game and the pranks we pulled? And here she was impersonating a doctor—which *had* to be illegal—while trying to learn confidential medical information. My, my, how playing Sutton Mercer had changed her.

"He's, um, unconscious," Emma went on. "I just need to know the date he was released from your care."

The nurse let out an aggravated breath. "One moment." Her fingers clicked across computer keys. "Aha. Thayer Vega was in and out of treatment and was released for good on September twenty-first of this year—against doctor's orders. Now, what did you say your name was? What hospital are you at?"

Emma quickly hit end. She was suddenly trembling so badly that the phone tumbled from her hands and into the foot well. Disbelief and fear mingled in her mind. It was true. Thayer had been in a psychiatric hospital . . . and he'd been in and out of treatment, and then left *against doctor's orders*. Uncured. On the loose. He might have been—he might *be*—a psychopath.

And I might have picked the wrong guy to mess with.

24

WHO DO YOU THINK YOU ARE?

"Tonight is going to be awesome," Charlotte said on Friday morning as she and Emma walked down the Hollier science wing. The air smelled like charred chemicals and gas from Bunsen burners. "Cornelia is planning an awesome meal for us. We'll meet at my place, eat and get ready, and then head over to set up for the secret party. Sound good?"

"Sure," Emma said cautiously, staring down at her bare knee poking through Sutton's carefully distressed jeans. She'd never understood buying three-hundred-dollar jeans that were *made* to look old—why couldn't you just go to Goodwill and get a genuinely worn-in pair?

Uh, because stuff from Goodwill isn't cool? I didn't care how savvy Emma was with making cheap stuff look stylish. Brand names were always king in my world.

"See you later!" Charlotte trilled as they turned to the foreign language wing, peeling off for Spanish class while Emma entered the German room. Faded white chalk marking verb conjugations lingered on the blackboard, and someone had drawn a frowning stick figure with a dream bubble that read I'D RATHER BE ANYWHERE BUT HERE. The faint smell of glue wafted through the air. Emma spotted Ethan slumped in a seat in the corner of the classroom. He glanced up at her and quickly averted his eyes. Her stomach twisted.

Frau Fenstermacher wasn't in class yet, so Emma stalked over to the chair where Ethan sat. She stood there for almost ten seconds, but he pointedly didn't look her way.

"We need to talk," she finally said, her voice determined.

"I don't think so," Ethan said, his head still turned toward the window.

"*I* do." Emma grabbed Ethan's arm until he stood, and pulled him out of the classroom. A couple of kids stopped and stared, probably wondering why Sutton Mercer was taking Ethan Landry by the hand. But Emma didn't care who looked. She needed to sort this out with Ethan—*now*.

A smattering of students filtered through the hall,

hustling in the final moments before the bell. Emma glanced to her left and saw Frau Fenstermacher's shape-less form approaching. Emma steered Ethan toward the next corridor, praying they'd gone unseen. They pushed through two glass doors that emptied onto a long stretch of lawn abutting the track.

Ethan shoved his hands deep into the pockets of his mud-colored cargo shorts. "We should go back inside."

"There are a few things I need to say," Emma inter-rupted, walking toward the track. "And you need to listen."

She opened the gate and they crossed the patch of lawn that stretched before the white starting line. Silver hurdles were assembled in straight columns. A water bottle lay tipped over next to a forgotten clipboard. They climbed the bleachers slowly, their shoes making tinny clanking noises on the metal planks. Emma wandered down a row halfway to the top. She sat on the hard metal and Ethan followed suit. The wind whipped across Emma's face. She pulled her long hair into a ponytail and turned to face Ethan.

"I don't want to prank you," she said. "I never did, and I'm not going to let them go through with it. It's just hard, with everything going on, to know how to best derail it without giving myself away."

Ethan pretended to be fascinated with the stitching on

his pockets. Two students from Fashion Design class sped by on bicycles, apparently also skipping class.

"Ethan," Emma said, her voice full of frustration. "Talk to me! I'm sorry! I don't know what else to say. Please don't be mad anymore."

Finally, Ethan let out a breath and stared into his open palms. "Okay. I'm sorry, too. I guess when you said Sutton's friends were going to prank me . . . I freaked."

"But why didn't you believe me when I said *I* wasn't going to?"

Ethan shook his head. When he finally spoke, his words were slow and strained. "You just look *so much* like her. You're wearing her clothes. You're hanging around with her friends. You've even got on her locket."

"So?"

A muscle in Ethan's neck tensed. As he looked away, Emma realized there was something else, something he wasn't telling her. His gaze met hers and she saw a flicker of hurt pass over his light eyes.

"I never told you this," he finally said. "But during freshman year, just after Sutton and her friends started the Lying Game, they pulled a prank on me. It was awful and it ruined my chances for a science scholarship in this program that I wanted more than anything. My family didn't have the money to send me themselves. I was almost guaranteed the spot, but after the prank . . . I wasn't." There was a clanging sound as he tapped his sneaker against the bleachers. "I thought I was over it, but I guess maybe I'm not."

I hovered close, feeling terrible. It was yet another example of how my pranks had really hurt people. I tried to remember pranking Ethan, but I couldn't see a thing. The only memory I had of Ethan was when he'd interrupted my friends fake-strangling me in the desert. For a split second, I'd felt pure gratitude that he'd saved me . . . but then I'd gotten annoyed because he'd seen how scared I'd been.

"What did they do, exactly?" Emma asked.

Ethan shrugged. "It doesn't matter. Suffice to say they blew my chances."

Emma took Ethan's hand and squeezed it tight. "Listen, I'm not Sutton, okay? Maybe we're alike in certain ways, but I would never hurt you. You have to know that."

Ethan nodded slowly, linking his fingers through hers and returning her squeeze. "I do know that. I swear. And I'm sorry I've been so distant. I should have believed you."

There was a long pause. The two of them watched a bunch of blackbirds land in the center of the track and then take off again. "You know what we should do?" Emma said slowly, unable to stop the smile spreading across her face. "Let's figure out a plan to double-cross them."

"Sutton's friends?" Ethan gave her an incredulous look. "Are you sure?"

"Positive. I care about them, but it sounds like they need a taste of their own medicine. I'm sick of pranking people—and maybe if we can outsmart them, the whole Lying Game will lose its luster." She turned on the bleacher so she was facing Ethan. "As of now, Sutton's friends are planning on stealing your poems before your poetry slam and putting them online under someone else's name. They want it to look like you plagiarized them."

Ethan let out a whistle. "Wow. That's low." His light eyes darkened and he looked out onto the track. "Why would they do that to me?"

A cloud passed over the sun and Emma watched her shadow disappear. "Laurel's furious at me right now for getting Thayer in trouble. This is her idea of revenge. She knows that I . . ."—she swallowed awkwardly—"*like* you, and she's hitting me where it hurts."

A small smile played at the edge of Ethan's lips. "I see. Maybe we can meet at our usual spot and bat around ideas?"

"Well, I think we have to find a new spot, given that Laurel now knows that we meet there," Emma pointed out. Her insides felt warm and settled. Thank God Ethan was back on her side. "Now that *that's* out of the way," she said, "there's more I need to fill you in on." She scanned the track, making sure they were still alone.

Ethan's eyebrows spiked. "More about the case?"

When Emma told him that the blood on the car matched Thayer's, not Sutton's, Ethan stared at her incredulously.

"That's not all," Emma went on. "I went to pick up Sutton's car from the evidence lot, and I found something weird." She explained the slip of paper with Dr. Sheldon Rose's name, and how she traced it to a psychiatric hospital in Seattle. "Dr. Rose's nurse said Thayer checked out on September twenty-first. *Against doctor's orders.*"

Ethan stared at her, his face pale. "Thayer was in a mental institution?" he said, shaking his head. He pressed his palms over Emma's. "It's him. It has to be. He snapped and killed Sutton. What's to stop him doing the same thing to *you*?" He gripped her hands with his. "How am I going to protect you?"

Emma took a breath, feeling the smallest bit safer now that she had Ethan on her side again. "You can't," she said, watching Ethan's face fall at her words. She squeezed his hands and went on, "We need to find proof that he did it. The only way I'll ever be safe again is when Thayer is behind bars—permanently."

A door to the school slammed loudly, and they both looked up. The bell sounded, indicating that the period was over. Emma had skipped a whole class. In her old life, she'd never even been late to school. But making up with Ethan was worth it. "We should go back in," she said softly.

"Do we have to?" Ethan asked. "I'd rather spend the whole day together."

"Me, too," Emma murmured. Then she turned to Ethan, getting an idea. "Sutton's friends are planning a secret party, and I have to be there early to help set up. Do you want to come? I know parties aren't your thing, but maybe it's time we did something to take our minds off of me being stalked by a psychopath."

"Not funny," Ethan said, pushing a hand through his hair. "But . . ." He looked down at his sneakers. "Are you sure? Your friends will be there. Being out with me is not something Sutton would do. And it will ruin our counter-prank."

Emma thought for a moment. "Well, then we forget the counter-prank. The best way to call off the poetry prank is for us to show up together at the party. And even if it's not something Sutton would do, it's what *I* want to do," Emma said bravely. Now that she had decided to go public, she didn't want to spend any time apart.

25

SOUND THE ALARM

That night, Emma angled the Volvo into Charlotte's circular driveway and turned off the ignition. The Chamberlains lived in a six-bedroom stone home with two balconies that protruded from the second floor. Its grandeur still took Emma's breath away, even though she'd been there several times. She'd never known anyone with this kind of money.

Laurel unlocked her car door and slid out, not bothering to thank Emma for the ride. They'd come together because they didn't want to bring too many cars to the party and tip off the cops. Emma had considered ditching Laurel at home to pay her back for abandoning her at tennis so many times, but she figured that wouldn't help to repair their rift.

Before either of them could ring the bell, the door swung open and Madeline smiled back at them, dressed in a bright red ruched dress that stopped at mid-thigh. "Hello, *dah*-lings!" she cried dramatically. "Welcome to dinner! You both look smashing!"

"Thanks," Emma said bashfully, looking down at the emerald green one-shouldered number she'd found in Sutton's closet. She'd agonized over choosing an outfit, trying on at least six dresses before settling on this one. She'd wanted something especially pretty to go with her newly styled hair and carefully applied makeup. This was the first time she and Ethan would be seen together in public, and nosy gossip-hounds would no doubt be taking tons of pictures for Facebook and Twitter. It was ironic: At her old schools, Emma secretly longed to be part of the popular crowds whose personal lives were splashed across the pages of social media sites. But now that she *was* one of those girls, she just wanted to be left alone.

The grass is always greener, I suppose.

Laurel and Emma followed Madeline down a long hallway that led to the Chamberlains' massive kitchen. It looked just like the display kitchens in *House Beautiful* that Glenda, Alex's mom, was always tearing pages from and stuffing into a folder she marked DREAM HOUSE. The air smelled of pot roast, fresh bread, and—of course—Charlotte's Chanel Chance perfume. For a moment, Emma's gaze flickered to the kitchen island where the unknown assailant had come up behind her and held Sutton's locket to her throat.

Except that the assailant *wasn't* unknown anymore. It was Thayer. Emma glanced at Madeline, feeling an awkward twinge. What would Mads do when she found out her beloved brother was a murderer? She'd be doubly shattered: Not only would she discover that her best friend was dead, but she'd lose Thayer, too.

"Sodas, girls?" Charlotte appeared from behind the refrigerator door. She was wearing a tight black dress with leather triangles that crisscrossed her slightly ample midsection. It was a dress Emma wasn't one hundred percent sure looked good on her, but she didn't dare say anything.

"Too bad it can't be champagne!" a voice trilled. Mrs. Chamberlain appeared from the dining room and placed a hand on Charlotte's shoulder. "If you girls skipped that party and hung out here for the night, I'd crack open a bottle of Veuve Clicquot for you. But I can't have you drinking and driving!"

"That's okay, Mom," Charlotte said, looking a little embarrassed. If there were a *Real Housewives of Tucson*, Charlotte's mom would be a shoo-in for a cast member. She looked ten years younger than her age—which Charlotte claimed was the result of monthly Botox injections and hours spent on the elliptical machine—and she wore outfits far more fashionable than most of the kids at Hollier. She was currently cloaked in a tight black dress that showed off her surgically enhanced cleavage. She also, it seemed to Emma, was dying to be Charlotte's best friend instead of her mother. It was a far cry from foster mothers who only spoke to their foster kids when they were yelling at them or needed them to lie to the social workers so they'd get their monthly checks.

"Well, I'm thrilled you could make it for dinner," Mrs. Chamberlain went on, leading the girls into the dining room. There were five seats at the table, and each place had a place card in front of it, as though they were at a wedding. Emma was next to Charlotte and across from Madeline.

When Mrs. Chamberlain ducked into the kitchen to get everyone drinking glasses, Emma leaned forward. "Where are the Twitter Twins?" She'd suddenly noticed a lack of texting taking place at the table.

Laurel glanced briefly at Madeline and Charlotte, then shrugged. "Didn't you hear? They're at the hair salon. I swear, getting invited to their first super-secret house party as real Lying Game members is totally going to their heads."

Charlotte studied the place cards, then looked up at her mother, who'd just returned to the dining room. "Don't we need another glass for Dad?"

A strained look passed over Mrs. Chamberlain's face. "He's not coming," she said quickly. "He got stuck at work."

"Again?" An edge sharpened Charlotte's voice.

"Will you get the bottle of Sancerre for me please, Charlotte?" Mrs. Chamberlain suggested tensely. A long pause ensued. Emma recalled how she'd seen Mr. Chamberlain at Sabino Canyon the day she arrived in Tucson, when he was supposed to be out of town. Perhaps he was hiding something—and perhaps Charlotte and her mother had their suspicions about what it was.

Charlotte yanked a pinkish-colored bottle from a wine fridge that was built into a cabinet next to the sink, clapped a bottle opener over the cork, and poured a glass for her mother. She then lifted her own glass of Perrier by the stem and held it high in the air. Mrs. Chamberlain, Madeline, Emma, and Laurel followed suit.

"To a fabulous dinner party," Mrs. Chamberlain said.

The five of them clinked glasses and took sips. Cornelia, the personal chef, who had stiff gray hair and a round, pie-like face, carried in a roast, red potatoes, a big chopped salad, and warm garlic bread.

"So tell me about this party you girls planned," Mrs.

Chamberlain said after taking a delicate bite of meat. "Where is it again?"

"Uh, a country club across town," Charlotte lied smoothly. It wasn't as if they were going to tell Mrs. Chamberlain they were going to a foreclosed house.

"It's going to be sick," Madeline said. "Everyone from Hollier is going to be there."

"We invited people from a couple of the prep schools, too," Charlotte added.

"What she means is, we invited *guys* from the prep schools." Laurel adjusted a feather barrette in her hair.

Charlotte gave her a playful punch. "You better be grateful we're letting *you* come."

Emma looked back and forth at them, amazed they were talking about this in front of Mrs. Chamberlain—weren't parents supposed to frown at the idea of parties? But Charlotte's mom was smiling and nodding like she thought it was all great.

I remembered being so jealous of Charlotte's mom, wishing that my mom was more like her. But watching from afar, seeing how sweet my mom was with Emma, I wondered. Did Char's mom give her advice in the middle of the night, or just beauty tips and pointers on plastic surgery? It made me realize once more how much I'd taken my mom for granted.

Sutton's iPhone vibrated in Emma's lap. She pulled it

out of her clutch and gazed at the screen under the table. ANY CHANCE YOU CAN PICK ME UP? asked a text from Ethan. MY CAR WON'T START.

Emma's nerves buzzed. This was really happening. They were really going to a party . . . together. SURE THING, she wrote back. BE THERE IN AN HOUR. She hit send.

"Who are you writing to, Sutton?" Laurel asked, peering at Emma across the table.

Emma clenched her fists in her lap. "That's for me to know and you to find out," she said breezily. The girls would know soon enough when she and Ethan arrived at the party; she didn't need it to dominate the dinner discussion now.

As the meal progressed, Mrs. Chamberlain regaled them with some of her favorite high school memories, many of which involved becoming Homecoming Queen two years in a row. After the girls carried their plates to the sink and got dishes out for dessert, Emma excused herself to the powder room in the hall. Just as her hand grazed the doorknob, she noticed a glowing greenish light down the hall, right near the foyer. The Chamberlains' alarm system.

She looked around. The girls were in the dining room, chattering on about Laurel's most recent date with Caleb. Mrs. Chamberlain was out on the back porch, smoking a cigarette. No one was watching.

She tiptoed down the hall and peered at the security system. It was a simple setup with an LCD touchscreen, like an iPad, with numbered buttons for entering a code. Whoever had disabled the alarm would have had to use their fingers. If Thayer hadn't wiped down the screen after letting himself in, maybe his prints were still on it.

"Sutton?" Madeline's voice called. Emma looked up to see her standing in the hall, peering at her. "What are you doing?"

"Just checking out this photo," Emma lied, pointing to a framed black-and-white photograph of a young Paul McCartney that hung next to the alarm.

She scuttled back to the dining table just as Mrs. Chamberlain brought out chocolate mousses in individual goblets. "Cornelia's specialty!" she exclaimed. "It's going to be *soooo* good!"

The girls made appreciative coos and dug in. When Mrs. Chamberlain returned to the kitchen, Laurel leaned across the table, a hint of chocolate on her lips. "You know what else is going to be good? Our prank on Ethan Landry." She glanced at Emma, raising her eyebrows. "I hope you asked him to come help us set up tonight."

"Seriously." Charlotte clapped her hands together. "The prank's going to be *amazing!*"

Madeline cackled with delight. Only Emma stared at her plate, a queasy feeling trickling through her stomach.

Laurel pouted at her from across the table. "What's wrong, Sutton? Don't you think it's a perfect prank?"

Emma swallowed a sip of Perrier, its bubbling tartness tickling her nose. The way she saw it, she had two options: buckle to Laurel's whims and go along with this, or stand up for herself and make Old Emma proud. She took a deep breath.

"Actually, I think it's a horrible idea," she said. "We already got Ethan once, remember? I've decided. I'm not being part of the prank. You girls will have to go it alone."

Madeline's face fell. Charlotte wrinkled her nose. Laurel's cheeks reddened. "You *what*?" she snapped.

Emma knew she was doing a little bit of damage to Sutton's reputation, but she didn't care. She stood, placing her spoon to the side of her untouched mousse. "Charlotte, please tell your mom thanks for the delicious dinner. There's someplace I need to be right now. I'll see you ladies at the party." She glanced at Laurel. "I assume you can get a ride with one of them?"

Laurel stared back at Emma, her mouth hanging open. She didn't say a word as Emma sailed from the room and out the front door, her head held high. Sutton's friends watched her the whole way. No one said a word.

And that, I thought, *was how you make a dramatic exit.*

26

FORECLOSED BUT NOT FORGOTTEN

When Emma pulled up to Ethan's driveway, she was still flying high from finally standing up to the girls about the prank. She had a big smile on her face as she exited the car, but her expression quickly shifted when Ethan slunk out his front door and slammed it shut, his stealthy, guilty posture that of someone sneaking out.

"Everything okay?" Emma asked as Ethan jogged across the lawn.

"Sure." Ethan ran a hand over his close-cropped hair. "My mom was just giving me shit about chores. That's all."

"Been there," Emma said. "Should I go in and say hi? I'd like to meet her."

There was a miniscule pause. "Another time," Ethan
finally said. Then he leaned forward and kissed her cheek.
"You look gorgeous. Love that dress."

You noticed, Emma thought, butterflies sweeping
through her stomach. She smoothed down the skirt of
the emerald green dress. "You look pretty good yourself."
Ethan was wearing dark-wash Levi's and a fitted, olive
green button-down that showed off his trim waist and
broad shoulders.

Emma gestured to Sutton's car, and Ethan let out a low,
appreciative whistle and got into the passenger seat. "I've
only seen this ride from afar—Sutton used to freak if anyone but her friends got near it in the parking lot. I never
thought I'd actually get to sit in it."

"Well, there's a new Sutton in town," Emma giggled.

That didn't mean the new Sutton could mess up my car, I
thought in annoyance. Emma better maintain it.

"So the party's in a foreclosed mansion in the foothills,
apparently somewhere called Legends Road," Emma said.
"Do you know where that is?"

"I'll show you the way." A grin spread across Ethan's
face. "An abandoned house. It's crazy. Sounds much more
interesting than the usual Hollier parties."

Emma smirked. "How many Hollier parties have you
actually been to, loner boy?"

"You got me." Ethan ducked his head. "Not many."

There was a long pause. Something pulsed in the air between them. Maybe it was that tonight was their first appearance as an actual couple. As Emma shifted gears and sped down Ethan's street, she realized that her stomach was humming with nerves. She peeked at Ethan, noticing how he was repeatedly licking his lips. Maybe he was nervous, too.

"So what's wrong with your car?" Emma asked.

Ethan shrugged. "It probably just needs to be jumped. I'll deal with it tomorrow."

They turned onto the main road and passed Sabino Canyon. Emma felt a twinge of dread—it was the spot where she'd first arranged to meet Sutton, *and* where the cops had found Sutton's car.

And maybe, I thought, *where I hit Thayer . . . and he killed me.*

Emma drove higher into the foothills, the Catalina Mountains shimmering red in the setting sun. The road twisted, and Emma gripped the steering wheel to navigate the turns. The farther north they went, the bigger and grander the houses became. The sky darkened as they passed a luxury strip mall consisting of a wine shop, a Pilates studio, and a bunch of real-estate agencies, another marker for a trailhead, and dozens of Southwest-style mansions tucked into the rocks.

"Hey, is that the street?" Emma interrupted, pointing

to a yellow-and-green painted sign marked LEGENDS ROAD.

"Looks like it," Ethan said, squinting into the semi-darkness.

Emma turned onto the road and almost hit a road-runner that darted across the lane. Desert brush lined the side of the pavement and Emma steered the car around a rock that must have fallen from the bordering cliffs.

"We have to find somewhere secluded to park," she explained, looking for a good spot on the shoulder. "Mads says we can't park in front of the house—that'll tip off the police that we're throwing a party there." But she didn't want to park just anywhere, either—Sutton's car had been impounded, partly, for unpaid traffic violations. All she needed was Detective Quinlan finding yet another reason to drag her down to the station.

The road zigged and zagged, the land barren on either side of them. "There aren't any other houses here?" Emma said aloud.

"Strange." Ethan glanced out the window at a tangled tree branch that reached like fingers toward the windshield. "Maybe whoever had this place owned the surrounding land, too. It's one way to guarantee the view."

Emma drove another half mile before a towering white stone mansion came into sight. Oval arches shot high into the evening sky, and immaculate black shutters framed wide, illuminated windows. A massive balcony jutted from the side of the house and soared over a cliff that dropped at least one hundred feet to a rocky bottom. A FOR SALE sign was tipped over in the front lawn, long abandoned. The circular driveway was empty. So was the road around it.

"It's gorgeous," Emma breathed, pulling over. "But where are the other girls' cars? They should have been here by now to set up." She checked her watch. She was late—it was almost 9:30.

"Maybe there's another route around the back? Or maybe they parked even farther away to avoid suspicion." Ethan unbuckled his seat belt and they both got out of the car.

A silver slice of moon hung high in the sky. A gust of wind whistled between the rocks and tossed Emma's hair across her shoulders. She followed Ethan along crooked stone steps embedded into a small hill that led to the house.

They climbed along the final yards of the path and onto a smooth porch made of solid granite. Ethan's knuckles pounded the front door. He glanced at Emma while they waited and angled his ear close to the door. "Weird. I don't hear anyone inside," he said, narrowing his eyes. "No music, no nothing."

Emma knocked again. "Hello?" she called. When no one answered, she tried the golden knob and pushed against the oak. The door swung open, revealing a double staircase that circled upstairs to an open-air second level.

An unlit crystal chandelier hung in the foyer. Bright stars were visible through massive skylights. A grandfather clock in the far right corner of the entranceway was the only visible fixture—otherwise, the house was completely empty.

"Hello?" Emma called again. The girls should have been here already. Her voice echoed through the empty house. In the dim moonlight, she could see cobwebs glistening in the corners. She turned to glance at Ethan. "Maybe they're not here yet?"

"Maybe?" Ethan stepped back and gazed up the stairs.

Thwap.

Emma and Ethan wheeled around. The front door had slammed behind them.

Emma ran to the door and tried the knob. It wouldn't budge. "Who's there?" she cried. Something electric snapped along her body. There was no window facing out onto the front porch, so she couldn't tell who'd just shut them inside.

Ethan yanked Emma closer to him. *Scraaaaatch.* A sound like fingernails down a windowpane echoed through the air. "What is that?" Emma screeched.

"Someone's outside," Ethan said. He pulled at the doorknob again, but it still wouldn't give. "Who's there?" he boomed. "Let us out!"

"Oh my God," Emma whispered into Ethan's chest, gripping the sides of his shirt. "What if it's Thayer? What if he got out of jail early and followed us?"

A sinister feeling passed through my weightless form as a horrible idea occurred to me. Maybe it *was* Thayer. What if he'd found out that Emma had called his old hospital and was coming to shut her up for good?

"I won't let him hurt you," Ethan said, hugging Emma tight. "I promise."

Another groan sounded from outside. Then there were scraping sounds, like someone was trying to get in. "We have to hide, Ethan!" Emma screamed, looking around at the bare rooms, the blank walls. She grabbed his hand and started up the stairs, but her heel caught on the first riser. She tumbled into Ethan, and he caught her around the waist. Another *thud* sounded from outside. More horrible scratches. A shadow passed across the back wall. And then, a scream.

Emma answered with a shriek, but when a second scream came, she stood up straighter. That wasn't a guy's voice, but the high-pitched wail of a girl. Giggles sounded from outside. And suddenly, Emma smelled the distinct fragrance of Chanel Chance.

Suddenly everything clicked into place. *Of course.*

Emma grabbed Ethan's hand. "This is a prank. *We're* the prank. Sutton's friends are messing with us."

Confusion settled across Ethan's fingers. "You're sure?"

"Positive."

Ethan's shoulders dropped with relief. He stepped closer to Emma and slipped his hands along Emma's dress onto the smooth skin of her back. He pulled her close. "Well, then this is the best prank ever. I wouldn't mind spending all night locked up alone with you in here."

Emma felt her nerves spike for an entirely new reason. Her body was so close to Ethan's she wondered if he could feel her heart beating through the thin silk of her dress. She looked up into Ethan's face just as he tilted his chin to kiss her. She felt herself come alive as his lips met hers. She wrapped her arms around Ethan's neck and returned his kiss, wishing the moment never had to end.

The door flew open with a *creak* and a swell of cool night air pushed against Emma's back. Madeline stomped into the house, flanked by Charlotte, Laurel, and the Twitter Twins, who were dressed in head-to-toe black and snapping pictures rapid-fire on their iPhones.

"Gotcha!" Madeline cried.

Charlotte clapped her hands together and the Twitter Twins let out excited squeals. "You were so scared!" Gabby cried.

"I was not," Emma said quickly.

"Were too." Laurel smirked. "Your new guy didn't make you feel safe?" Her eyes flickered to Ethan.

"At least this explains why you didn't want to pull a prank on him," Madeline said, shaking her head. "Are you going to introduce us, Sutton?"

Emma looked at Sutton's friends. They didn't look

particularly annoyed or disgusted that they'd just caught her kissing Ethan—just left out of the loop. She grabbed Ethan's hand. "This is Ethan Landry. My . . . *boyfriend*." Her voice rose at the end, a tiny question mark. She glanced at Ethan to make sure this title was okay. Ethan nodded as a slow grin spread across his face.

"So, are you two, like, in love?" Lili asked. Her raccoon-ish eyeliner was even more dramatic than usual, making the whites of her eyes glow bright. Gabby made kissing noises with her pouty lips and Laurel and Charlotte giggled.

Emma laughed despite herself. "How long have you guys been planning this?" she asked.

"Ever since Laurel explained a few days ago why you weren't totally up for the Ethan prank." Charlotte curled a red tendril around her finger. "We've been teasing you all week. As soon as you left dinner, we flew into action. Lili and Gabby stood at the base of the road to make sure no one got here early. We wanted you to get here when the house was empty—and super-scary."

"And we disconnected Ethan's car cables so you'd have to give him a ride," Lili said proudly.

"You did what?" Ethan gaped.

Gabby waved her hand dismissively. "Don't worry. You just need to reconnect the cables. I saw a YouTube video on it."

Ethan shook his head but laughed.

"So the real party is still here?" Emma asked.

"Yep!" Laurel chirped. She pointed to two plastic bags hidden in the corner of the dining room Emma hadn't noticed before. And then, as if on cue, the door swung open, and a bunch of kids spilled inside. The entire boys' baseball team. Nisha and her tennis cronies. A bunch of kids who always said hello to Emma in the halls, and a lot of people Emma didn't recognize. Last but not least, Garrett stepped through the door, carrying a massive keg. When he set eyes on Ethan and Emma, who were still holding hands, his expression soured.

"Hi, Garrett," Emma tried, knowing just how futile her attempt at friendliness was.

Garrett's muscled arms tensed as he adjusted his grip on the keg. "So now you're with Ethan?" he growled.

"I am," Emma answered proudly, ignoring Garrett's hateful gaze. She wasn't going to let anything bother her tonight. Things suddenly felt perfect.

A techno song suddenly blared over a portable stereo someone had brought. Plastic cups were passed around, and drinks were poured. "Whoooo!" Charlotte cried, waving her hands over her head to dance. Emma pulled Ethan into the circle and started to dance, too.

The party had begun.

27

ONE FLEW THE COOP

The mansion filled to capacity in no time. Warm bodies mingled and flirted, red plastic cups in hand. Emma snaked through the crowd with Ethan on her arm, feeling happier than she had in ages.

"I'm going to get a beer," Ethan said, glancing at his phone before shoving it into his pocket. "Want one?"

Emma shot him a smile. "I still have to drive us home, remember? Unless you want to camp out tonight in the middle of nowhere . . ." She gestured outside to the rocky cliffs surrounding the mansion.

Ethan grinned and leaned forward. His lips brushed her cheek as he whispered, "What exactly are you suggesting?"

Her cheeks flushed at what she'd implied—a sleepover with Ethan. "Some of us have a curfew," she whispered.

"Too bad," Ethan whispered back. His lips touched hers. A bunch of kids whistled. Emma sensed a flash of a phone camera. That Sutton Mercer was dating Ethan Landry was a huge deal. But no one was laughing at them—instead everyone was staring at Ethan, like they'd suddenly realized just how cute he was.

As a bunch of boys did shots in the corner and a crowd of kids danced to vintage Michael Jackson on the make-shift dance floor, Emma felt Sutton's clutch vibrate. She dropped Ethan's hand and asked him to grab her a Sprite. Then, she stepped away from the stream of partygoers and pulled Sutton's iPhone from her clutch: ONE MISSED CALL.

There was a number she didn't recognize in the call log along with a voicemail alert. Emma caught Ethan's eye across the room and motioned that she'd be right back. Then she negotiated her way through the sweaty crowd toward the back of the house, where it was hopefully quieter.

She rounded a corner into the kitchen, where liquor bottles lined the counter along with half-eaten bags of Fritos and abandoned plastic cups. A girl with short black hair poured tequila and margarita mix into a blender and pressed a button, sending the contents whirling. The shrill buzz of the blender and the sweet smell of lime filled the kitchen and followed Emma down a dark hallway. She trailed her fingertips along the wall to get her bearings and ducked into a back room. Moonlight spilled through an open window to illuminate dark wooden floors and long windows. There were only two objects in the room: a long, cracked mirror propped up in the corner and a small doll with marble eyes sitting on the windowsill. Emma turned away from the doll, an eerie feeling washing over her.

Pressing the voicemail icon, she lifted Sutton's phone to her ear. A loud voice boomed through the speaker. "Hello. This message is for Sutton Mercer. It's Detective Quinlan. I need to speak to you. Please call me at this number—it's my cell. I'll have it on me all night. It's urgent, so call me as soon as you get this."

An emergency? Emma's fingertips prickled. She gripped the phone, ready to dial the number, when a loud crash sounded outside the room. She jumped and turned around. Bass reverberated through the house. Laughter echoed off the walls. Even though she was alone, it was still too loud for her to have a real conversation. She let herself out of the room, glancing once more at the eerie, glassy-eyed doll, and headed for the back door.

The back of the house boasted a patio that butted up to the mountains. There was a small trail at the edge of the property; Emma walked toward it, wanting to put as much distance as possible between herself and the loud party. Twigs and dried leaves cracked beneath her feet. She scrolled through Sutton's phone and selected the most recent missed call.

Quinlan answered on the first ring.

"This is Sutton," Emma said shakily.

"Hello, Miss Mercer." Quinlan's voice was tight. "I thought you should know that Thayer posted bail. We had no choice but to release him."

"*What?*" Emma gasped. "When?"

"A few hours ago."

Her heart was pounding so fast she was sure it was going to explode from her chest. Thayer had been on the loose for a few *hours*? "Did Mr. Vega change his mind?" Did Madeline know? Why wouldn't she have said anything?

"It wasn't Mr. Vega," Quinlan said.

"Who was it?" Emma demanded, passing the wooden sign that marked the beginning of the trail.

There was a long pause. Emma listened to breathing on the other end. "Look," Quinlan finally said. "I noticed how freaked out you were about Thayer in the station the other day. If there's anything you want to tell me about him, any reason you might be afraid of him, you should speak up now. Normally I don't believe a word you're saying, but I know you're either hiding something or are truly scared of something. Which is it, Sutton?"

Emma ran her tongue over her teeth. If only she could tell Quinlan the truth. If only he'd believe her.

"After months of hiding, he resurfaced in your bedroom, Sutton," Quinlan went on. "If there's any reason he might want to hurt you, we can protect you."

Emma shut her eyes. Protection was what she wanted most in the whole world. But Quinlan *wouldn't* believe her if she told him the truth. He would think she was making it up. Or, worse, if he bought the story that she was Sutton's twin, he'd think she was the murderer. "I'll be fine," she mumbled.

Quinlan's breath caught on the other end. "Okay," he said after a pause. "Well, you know where to find me if you change your mind." The line went dead.

Somewhere in the distance, a coyote howled. Emma's fingers trembled as she stuffed the phone into Sutton's clutch. Had she just made a huge mistake? Should she have told Quinlan the truth, now that Thayer was on the loose?

Snap.

Emma whipped around, suddenly on alert. She'd wandered so far onto the trail during her talk with Quinlan that she was surrounded by darkness. She couldn't see the house anymore. She spun in every direction, trying to make sense of which way she needed to walk to get back to the party. The wind whistled through the desert brush.

"Hello?" she called out. Silence. She took a step in one

direction, then another. "Hello?" All sound had fallen away. It was like she was in the middle of nowhere.

A hand landed on the back of her shoulder. Emma froze, her body going cold. All at once, she realized her mistake in wandering out there alone in the darkness. It was Thayer. It had to be. He'd come back to hurt her, just like he'd hurt her sister. She hadn't been listening to his messages carefully enough. She hadn't been playing along.

"*Sutton*," a voice whispered.

The hiss of my name echoed over and over in my head. All at once, I felt the same bright, snapping sensation and familiar tingle. Another memory was coming, maybe the final piece to what happened to me that terrible night. I surrendered to the vision, letting it take me away.

28

WE ALL FALL DOWN

"Sutton!"

Thayer's fingers dig into my upper arm as he yanks me into the thick brush. I kick and scream as he clamps a hand over my mouth again and drags me farther from the parking lot. The brush thickens and attacks my skin in sharp scrapes. Tears sting my eyes and blur my vision, but I can't wipe them away—he's got my arms pinned against my sides as he heaves my body over the dirt.

"Thayer, stop!" My voice is muffled against his grip. My feet kick out and send leaves and soil flying.

Thayer drops me carefully to the ground and angles my body against the scratchy bark of a tree's thick trunk. "Jesus, Sutton, stop screaming for one freaking second."

I pry his hand from my mouth and take gulping breaths. I'm ready to let out another yell when I see Thayer's shoulders relax. He drops his arms and plants his hands on his knees, out of breath. "You're faster than I thought," he says. His eyes scan the brush over his shoulder. "I'm trying to protect you. I think we got away in time."

"Wait, what?" I ask, blinking hard. It takes a moment for my thoughts to recalibrate as Thayer cuts through the brush onto the main road. I trail after him. "Was someone chasing us? Who?"

Thayer shakes his head. "Trust me, you don't want to know," he pants.

"Thayer, tell me what you—"

Tires screech behind us, and I turn just in time to see a car careening out of the Sabino Canyon lot. Off-yellow, perfectly round headlights rapidly advance on us, and with a jolt I realize it's my Volvo—my father and I restored the vintage headlights, which look different from modern-day Xenons.

My insides whirl with fear and surprise. I dart off the path, nearly impaling myself on a prickly pear. Then I turn to Thayer next to me. "Someone's in my car!"

"H-how?" Thayer asks slowly, still breathing hard.

But there's no time to explain about how I'd dropped my keys by the door. The car barrels straight at us, the tires squealing. I can't make out the driver's face, but whoever it is has straight, determined arms locked on the steering wheel. Thayer freezes in the middle of the road, right in the car's path.

"Thayer!" I scream. "Get out of the way!"

But it's too late. The car strikes him with a sickening thud. Time slows as Thayer's body flies into the air, crumpling against the windshield with a loud crack.

"Thayer!" I wail again.

With the scream of rubber on pavement, the car reverses. Thayer rolls off the hood and the car speeds away. The headlights click off and the car vanishes, leaving us in eerie silence.

I can barely feel my legs as I stumble to where Thayer's body lies limp on the ground. His leg is twisted awkwardly. There's blood on his head. He looks at me weakly, letting out a low moan. "Oh my God," I whisper. "We have to get you to the hospital." My thinking is suddenly crystal clear. I reach into my pocket for my phone. "I'll call 911."

"No," Thayer moans, grabbing my hand with what strength he has left. "I don't want my parents to know I'm here. They can't know I'm back in town." His breathing heaves. "I need to go to a different hospital. Somewhere out of town."

"That's impossible. I can't drive you anywhere. Some maniac has my car," I protest.

"Laurel." Thayer reaches a hand into the pocket of his shorts and pulls out his own cell phone. "She'll do it. I'll call her."

A twinge of jealousy spikes my insides. I don't want Laurel doing this for him. I don't want my sister sharing in the secret that he's back. But this isn't time to get territorial. I sit back on my haunches, feeling helpless. "Okay. Call her."

Thayer dials, and I hear ringing. "Laurel?" he says when she answers. "It's . . . me."

There is a sharp gasp on the other end; surely Laurel is incredulous. She has every right to be. As far as I know, Thayer hasn't contacted anyone since June. Except me.

"I'm hurt," Thayer goes on. "I need you to come and get me."

Thayer holds up a hand. "I can't explain, okay? I just need you to go with me on this. I'm at Sabino Canyon."

He gives her the rest of the details, and I can tell by his relieved expression that Laurel said she'd do it. When he hangs up, I rest my hand on the stubble lining Thayer's jaw. He feels too cold and his eyes are wild like an animal's. Blood seeps from the wound on his head. Whenever he moves he winces; his leg is bent horribly.

"I'm so sorry," I say softly, trying hard not to cry again. "I don't understand what happened. I don't know who could have been following us. I should have never suggested we come here."

"Sutton." Thayer's eyebrows narrow in concentration. "This isn't your fault."

But I can't help feeling that it is. I freaked out and ran away from Thayer. I dropped my keys at my car. I bend my face close to Thayer's and rest my head on his chest. All of my fears about him seem so unfounded. I'd let myself get caught up in the rumors about him instead of trusting that he loved me.

Before I know it, headlights appear on the road, almost as if Laurel's been waiting around the corner. I stand up and Thayer glances at me with surprise. "Where are you going?"

"I have to hide," I tell him. "No one should know we've been talking. Laurel will keep the secret that you're back in town, but not if she knows I'm involved."

Thayer looks shocked, maybe even a little scared. "But . . ."

"Believe me," I interrupt. "This is the best way." I press my lips to his. I can barely make myself pull away, but when I do, I tell him, "I'll be in touch as soon as I can—look for my note."

I clamber up the side of a small hill packed with desert sand and hide behind a cluster of thick bushes. The headlights grow brighter and bounce along the trail, illuminating rocks and slick mud. Laurel's car skids to a halt, and her door flies open. She explodes from the car and runs to Thayer's side, her blonde hair flying.

"Thayer!" she cries, dropping to a crouch and putting a hand on his arm. "What happened? Are you okay?"

"I will be." Thayer's face tightens into a grimace. "I think my leg's broken. I need you to get me to a hospital . . . somewhere out of town."

"But we have amazing doctors here! You could—"

"No arguments, Laurel. Please."

Laurel nods, staring at the odd angle of Thayer's leg and looking freaked. "I'll do whatever you need me to," she says. I can tell she's trying to sound tough.

My sister helps Thayer into the backseat of the car so he can sit with his legs stretched out. He moans as he pulls his body across the cushions. I try to catch a glimpse of him, but I can only see his white soccer sneakers dangling over the edge of the seat. Something inside me breaks open. I have a horrible premonition: This will be the last time I ever see him. That tiny peck on the lips was our final kiss good-bye.

Just after Laurel shuts Thayer's door, she glances around the brush surrounding the clearing. Her hands shake slightly at her side. I watch, helplessly, as her eyes squint and stare. She's looking through each bush and thorny branch, one by one.

I start to duck, but it's too late. Her eyes lock with mine. She blinks and takes a sharp breath before running to the driver's side and slamming the door.

A sharp gust of wind whistles through the branches above my head. My legs feel shaky and I dig my fingers into the wet dirt to steady myself.

Laurel reverses and pivots the car over mud and rocks. She flicks on her brights to illuminate the treacherous path ahead. Then she speeds away into the night. I watch the red taillights disappear into the distance, trying not to think about Thayer. But I can't help it. I think of him wincing every time the car hits a bump. I think about when I'm going to see him again—if I'm going to see him again. And I think about how someone used my car to run down the boy I'm in love with . . .

But . . . who?

29

LIKE POISON

Emma whipped around, ready to find herself face-to-face with Thayer, ready to defend herself against someone twice her size in the middle of the desert with no witnesses. But instead, Laurel's piercing blue eyes stared back at her.

"What are you doing out here?" Laurel snapped, retracting her hand from Emma's shoulder.

Emma took a breath, her body still tensed. "Just taking a walk," she said, unclenching her fists and resting them at her side.

Laurel put a finger to her lips. "Wait, let me *guess*," she said, her words singed with annoyance. "I'll bet you're out here calling Thayer now that he's out of jail."

Emma flinched. "You know he's out?"

"What, did you think you were the only one?" Laurel's face dropped into a scowl. "I wish you'd leave him alone. He doesn't need more of *you*, Sutton. You've done enough already."

Emma stared at her. "What are you talking about?" Did Laurel mean how Sutton had hit Thayer with her car? How could she know about that?

Laurel crossed her arms over her chest and rolled her eyes. "I'm so sick of this. I *know*. I know what you're hiding."

Emma blinked at her. The night air hung heavy and silent between them. Panic gripped her limbs. *Hiding?* Was she talking about Emma's real identity? Had she figured it out? Had Thayer told her?

"You're going to stand there and pretend you have no idea what I'm talking about, aren't you?" Laurel asked, her eyes widening.

Tiny scratching noises sounded in the underbrush as some animal scurried among the cacti. A shiver ran along the back of Emma's legs and she tried to keep her glare even. The last thing she wanted was to give away how afraid she was.

"I was the one who saved him, after all," Laurel spat. She yanked her honey blonde hair into a ponytail and stared at Emma like she was waiting for her to defend herself.

A low buzzing noise sounded. Emma couldn't be sure whether it was music from the party or desert bugs swarming in the distance. Who had Laurel saved him from? From Sutton?

"I have *no* idea what you're talking about, Laurel," she said finally, making her voice sound as condescending as possible.

Laurel cocked her head to the side and dug her heels into the dirt. "I saw you hiding in the bushes after Thayer got hit by that car at Sabino Canyon. He denied it, but I know you were with him." She shifted her weight and crossed her arms over her chest. "Why were you hiding? Why did you pawn him off on me? So I could take him to the hospital to be treated? Was that too much for you to handle?" She dropped her chin and shook her head. "Or was it just your usual MO?" She stared at Emma a long moment before lowering her voice to say, "You created too big of a mess to pick up yourself."

"No!" I yelled at my sister. "I hid because I was afraid you wouldn't get Thayer what he needed if you knew I was involved! I was trying to do the best thing for him!" But of course she didn't hear me. I thought again about the memory I'd just seen. I felt foolish for being so convinced Thayer was my cold-blooded killer when I now realized that he was just looking to protect me. The anguish of seeing him lying there, twisted and hurt, felt fresh and raw.

Who could have hit him with my car and just sped away like that? Maybe whoever had been chasing us. Which meant Thayer might know who my killer is without even knowing I'm dead.

Emma, meanwhile, blinked at Laurel's words. She tried to understand what they meant. Part of this made sense— Thayer was hit by a car that caused his limp. But she had no idea Laurel had been involved that night. And the way Laurel was talking, it sounded like Sutton *hadn't* been the one to hit Thayer.

"What else do you know?" she asked slowly. "What else did you see?" If Laurel had seen Sutton hiding, maybe she'd seen someone else there, too. Sutton's true killer.

A coyote howl pealed over the rocks. Laurel glanced in its direction and sighed. "If you mean did I see the two of you making out, I didn't. And I don't know who hit him, either. He wouldn't tell me anything that happened. Do *you* know who hit him? Are you making him keep quiet about something?"

"I don't know anything," Emma said. It was the truth.

Laurel's silk dress billowed in the wind. She ran the palms of her hands over her bare arms. "All you've done for the past month is pester me about the night of August thirty-first, trying to get me to spill that I was with Thayer. Thinking I didn't know you were there, too. That *is* why you asked me over and over what I was doing that night, isn't it? Because you wanted to know if I saw you? Well, I *did*. I saw you, hiding in the bushes and abandoning Thayer when he needed you the most." She scrunched up her face with disgust. "How could you have done that? And how could you have screamed when he came into your bedroom? Are you *trying* to ruin his life?"

"I'm sorry," Emma blurted.

"Sorry's not good enough," Laurel snarled. "You need to stay away from him. He told me as much. Every time you're around him, something terrible happens."

"Wait, he *told* you that?" Emma asked, rewinding. "When did you talk to him?"

Laurel dropped her hands to her hips. "On the way to the hospital. I'm the one who cares about him, Sutton. I'm the one who took him to the hospital, where he was in surgery all night. And I'm the one who posted his bail, in case you haven't figured that one out yet, while you were running around, hooking up with your new boyfriend."

"You posted his bail? *How?*"

Laurel crossed her arms over her chest. "If you must know, I've been saving. And with the bond Grandma gave me years ago and all the money people contributed to the Free Thayer campaign, it was enough. But why do you care? Thayer obviously doesn't matter to you. So just leave him alone, okay?" With that, she spun around and marched back to the party.

Emma ran her hands along her face, replaying everything Laurel had said over and over in her mind. The tables had just turned again. So . . . Thayer *hadn't* killed Sutton? He'd left Sutton alive, then Laurel had taken him to the hospital. But there were so many unanswered questions. It had to have been Sutton's car that hit Thayer, but who had been driving? Was someone else with them that night, someone who didn't want them to be together? Or had someone stolen Sutton's car?

If only I knew who Thayer was protecting me from. Who we were running from. Who was sitting behind the wheel when the car rammed straight into him.

But I didn't know a thing. All I saw after that moment when Laurel and Thayer sped away was darkness. And with that darkness came a horrible realization: Emma and I were back to square one.

30

CHEESE, MILK, AND EX-CONS

On Saturday morning, Emma pulled into the parking lot of Trader Joe's and eased Sutton's Volvo into a prime spot in front of the store. After she turned off the ignition, she unfolded the shopping list Mrs. Mercer had given her that morning. It included things like tahini butter, kimchee juice, and unsweetened almond milk. "You know how particular Grandma is," Sutton's mother had warned as she went down the list, explaining each item. "Get this stuff *exactly* as I've described it, or I'll have a very cranky mother-in-law on my hands." The whole family was preparing for Grandma Mercer's arrival early next week for her son's birthday party. Apparently, Grandma was a bit of a handful.

Emma watched customers emerge from the grocery store, smiling and clutching brown paper bags, and sighed. They all looked so happy and carefree. She was pretty certain she'd be the only Trader Joe's patron who'd spent the previous evening crossing a murder suspect off her list.

As she got out of the car, warm Tucson air stuck to the back of her neck. She pulled her chestnut brown hair into a ponytail and checked her reflection in the car's window. She was about to head toward the front doors when she noticed a familiar figure climbing out of a navy blue BMW across the lot. She felt her insides twist and heat rise to her cheeks.

Thayer.

He hadn't seen her. Emma could turn and run in the other direction, but now that she knew he was innocent, she owed him an apology. Her legs felt unsteady as she crossed the parking lot toward the car. She forced herself forward until she stood a few feet from him. "Thayer?" Her voice came out shaky. Something about him still made her so nervous.

Thayer turned and squinted. His white T-shirt was wrinkled, and his army green cargo shorts hung low, like they were too big for him. His jaw tightened and he ran a hand through his hair. "Oh. Hey."

"You're out of jail," Emma said, immediately feeling stupid.

"Is that a problem?" Thayer leaned on the BMW's

hood, examining Emma carefully. Almost like he knew she wasn't the girl he fell in love with. But Emma was being paranoid. She knew now that Thayer had no idea about the twin switch. He wasn't Sutton's killer.

"Look, I'm sorry about the way things worked out," she said softly. "With . . . you know. That night. The hospital." She held Thayer's gaze, wanting him to believe her, wanting him to know Sutton didn't mean to hurt him.

I wanted Thayer to know it, too.

Thayer's face softened slightly. He fidgeted with the strap of the black backpack slung over his shoulder. "Look, Sutton. I'm actually not supposed to be around you."

"I know," Emma said quickly, suddenly nervous. She lifted a hand to shade her eyes and shifted her weight in Sutton's flip-flops. "Laurel told me. I ruin your life every time I'm near you."

A confused look passed over Thayer's features. "Uh, no. I can't be around you because your dad said so. I got a call from him this morning." His expression darkened at the mention of Mr. Mercer. "He said that if he caught me hanging around with you or Laurel, he'd figure out how to throw me back in jail."

Emma frowned. "Why does he hate you so much?"

Thayer tilted his chin and gave Emma a weighted glance that made her feel like she'd asked a question Sutton would've known the answer to.

"I mean . . ." Emma went on, leaving a heavy pause between them, hoping Thayer would let her in on whatever he wasn't saying. But he just looked at her meaningfully, his eyes small slits.

"I should go," he mumbled finally, and turned toward the store. But a few paces away, he turned and looked back, running a tanned hand over the back of his neck. "Actually, there's something I've been wanting to ask you."

Emma swallowed hard. A few rows over, a car alarm went off. An old man shoved an empty shopping cart into the corral. She stared at Thayer and waited for his question. She hoped she knew the answer.

Thayer looked down at his beat-up Converse. "Why didn't you respond to my notes?"

Emma scrambled to think. When he'd referenced his notes, she'd assumed he meant the note someone had stuck on Laurel's car, warning Emma that Sutton was dead and she needed to play along. But now she realized he must have meant something else.

"I emailed you and emailed you," Thayer continued. "But you never wrote back. Was it because of the accident? Because I broke my leg and wouldn't be Mr. Athlete anymore?"

"It's not like that at all," Emma said softly.

"Of course it's not," I whispered along.

Emma's mind raced, putting together the pieces of

what Thayer was saying. Sutton and Thayer did have some sort of secret email correspondence. Of course Sutton wouldn't have written to him after the last night they saw each other—she was dead. And naturally, when Emma took Sutton's place, she wouldn't have known what that covert email address was. "I'm sorry I didn't contact you," Emma said. "I would have, if . . ."

"Save it," Thayer interrupted. He shrugged a shoulder and raised his glance to give her a long stare. "I missed you, Sutton. And I was so angry when you cut me out of your life. You were the only person who understood me. But now you're acting like you don't know who I am. I came to your room that night because I wanted to tell you the truth about where I've been. I emailed you I was coming, but I guess you didn't get it. But then you acted all afraid of me. Like I was going to hurt you."

"I know and I'm sorry," Emma said, her eyes lowered. "I was confused and surprised. And stupid. It was a mistake."

"I just wanted you to listen," Thayer said. He looked so forlorn that Emma reached out and touched his arm. He didn't pull away, so she moved a little closer and folded her arms around his shoulders, squeezing tight. At first, Thayer remained stiff and closed-off, but soon he melted into her, burying his head into her neck and running his hands up and down her arms. The movement was so passionate and real. It was glaringly clear to Emma just how much he cared for Sutton.

And the ache I felt inside made it glaringly clear just how much I'd cared for him. And how stupid I'd been to let him go. If only I had gone with Laurel to the hospital. If only we had all ridden together, maybe I wouldn't be dead now.

Thayer traced a line from Emma's shoulder to her wrist before pulling his hand away and looking sheepish. "I shouldn't be pissed, really," he said. "You had your reasons for not reading my messages, not writing back. I know I come on strong. I know I get too passionate, blow hot and cold. And I wasn't telling you everything. You wanted to know what happened to me, and I never told you. But it wasn't because I didn't trust you. It was because . . . well, I was embarrassed." A sad smile crossed his face. "I went to rehab, Sutton. For alcohol abuse. It was just something I had to do on my own. I was just so angry, all the time. I drank to numb it all, but it just made everything worse."

"Rehab?" Emma blinked. "Are you . . . okay?"

Thayer nodded. "I had an amazing doctor, and it was such a meaningful, helpful experience that I got this." He rolled up his sleeve and showed her the tattoo on his arm of the eagle in flight.

Emma stared at him, thinking of her conversation with Dr. Sheldon's nurse. "Did you do the whole program?"

"Well, I was stuck in the hospital with my leg for a while, and then I left a little before my doctor wanted me to, but I was ready to come back to Tucson. To see you," Thayer said earnestly. "I've told my parents where I was, too. My dad was horrified, of course, but he's coming around, especially since I'm clean now. He's even letting me back in the house, though we'll see how that goes."

"That's . . . great," Emma said slowly, taking it all in. She thought about the SPH website. Emma had just *assumed* that Thayer was locked up on the psych ward in the hospital, but of course a rehab center could be part of a mental-health facility.

"And then there's this." Thayer held up the rope bracelet around his wrist, smiling wryly. "Remember how we fought over it because a girl made it? But Sutton, she's fifty-two years old and has a husband and three kids."

I let out a long breath, remembering the fight Thayer and I had had at Sabino Canyon, the one that had kicked off that weird chain of events. I *had* felt jealous, sure that Thayer was somewhere cool and interesting without me. If only he had been honest. If only I hadn't jumped to conclusions.

Thayer let out a breath and rested a large hand on the hood of his car. "You know, Sutton, you seem . . . so different. What's changed?"

Emma licked her bottom lip and tasted Sutton's

watermelon-flavored gloss. No doubt Thayer knew her twin well. A part of her longed to tell him the truth, now that she knew he was innocent. He cared so deeply for her sister that he might help her and Ethan out. But she didn't know him well enough to trust him with her secret—not yet, anyway.

"Nothing's changed," she said sadly. "I'm exactly who I always was. I've just . . . grown up a little."

Thayer nodded, even though it looked like he didn't understand what he was saying. "I guess I've grown up, too," he mumbled. "Rehab and jail will do that to you."

They both stared at each other. Emma wasn't sure what more there was to say. Shrugging, she gave him a little wave and turned toward the store. When she looked over her shoulder, Thayer was still watching her, maybe hoping she'd come back to him. But she didn't. She wasn't Thayer's to have, and she was with Ethan now.

When Emma didn't return to him, Thayer's face fell. He looked crushed.

I was crushed, too. Thayer didn't understand why I no longer loved him back. And unless Emma solved my murder, he would never get the answer.

31

MEET THE MERCERS

That afternoon, Emma sat on the Mercers' front porch and thumbed through Laurel's glossy copy of *Elle*. A faint citrus smell wafted from the neighbor's lemon tree and the sounds of an ice cream truck jingled from the next street over. One of the tennis-team moms jogged by with her golden retriever and gave Emma a wave just as Ethan's beat-up Honda pulled to the curb. The engine coughed and sputtered as Ethan turned off the ignition.

Emma's heart gave a tiny flutter as he stepped from the car. Ethan looked nervous as he raised his hand in a wave. At that moment, Mr. Mercer emerged from the garage clutching a white rag covered in black grease stains.

He looked up with surprise, but then shrugged and shot Emma a weak smile.

Ethan walked up the front steps, noticing Sutton's dad, too. "Is it okay that I'm here?"

"It's more than okay," Emma answered. "I told them about us at breakfast." From now on, there would be no more hiding. They could be friends—and more—out in the open now.

Mr. Mercer's cell phone suddenly bleated loudly. Sutton's dad, who was pretending to be absorbed in polishing his motorcycle but was clearly watching the interaction between Emma and Ethan, glanced at the caller ID. His face darkened, and he swore loudly. He slipped into the cover of the garage to take the call.

"That's weird," Emma said, her eyes on the garage.

"Maybe it's a work call." Ethan forced a grin but Emma could tell he was uncomfortable. "A hospital patient gone haywire."

A car door slammed and an engine growled to life. Mr. Mercer's Audi reversed down the driveway. Emma waved good-bye to him, but Mr. Mercer didn't even notice her. His face was drawn as he backed the car onto the street and hit the gas. He swerved, blasting his horn when two boys zoomed by on skateboards. Emma frowned. Maybe that phone call *had* been a work emergency.

"Remind me not to get on that guy's bad side," Ethan said, running a hand through his dark hair.

He sat next to her, and Emma filled him in on everything she'd found out the night before—it had been too loud and crowded to talk at the party, and they'd had Laurel in the car on the drive home. Ethan's eyebrows went higher and higher as she explained that Thayer couldn't have killed Sutton.

"Let me get this straight," Ethan sounded out after Emma finished. "The night Sutton died, someone *else* hit Thayer with Sutton's car?"

Emma nodded. "It definitely wasn't Sutton who hit him. Someone must have taken her car and dumped it in the desert. Maybe that person came back and killed Sutton, too."

"So who was it?"

"I don't know. I want to ask Thayer, but it might make me look suspicious if I don't know."

A gust of air caught the wind chime, and Ethan flinched at the sudden ringing, making Emma smile. "Scared of a little wind?" she teased.

"Very funny," Ethan said, glancing across the lawn. "I *am* scared that whoever killed Sutton is still out there," he whispered.

"I know," Emma said, shivering despite the heat. "Me, too."

A frown settled on Ethan's face. "If it wasn't Thayer, who could it have been? All signs pointed to him. He made perfect sense. And I *still* think he's dangerous."

Emma shrugged. "Even if he's troubled, he didn't do it. I suppose that it's too much to hope the killer has left town? I haven't heard from him, or her, since the dance."

"Maybe." Ethan folded his ankle over his knee and glanced sideways at Emma. "But something tells me that's too good to be true. Whoever it is could still be out there. I'm up for finding the truth if you are."

"Definitely," Emma whispered. She leaned her cheek on Ethan's shoulder. He kissed the top of her forehead and she tilted her chin to meet his lips. Ethan returned her kiss, wrapping his arms around her waist and pulling her close. His hand reached up to trace the soft hairs that framed her face. He kissed her softly, his lips fitting perfectly with hers, making Emma want to freeze time. She'd never had a real boyfriend, and now she had something—some*one*— more amazing than she could have ever imagined.

A car pulled into the driveway, and Emma and Ethan broke apart. The car door of a blue BMW opened, and Thayer hoisted himself out. Emma felt Ethan stiffen next to her.

"Oh!" Emma said. "Uh, hey, Thayer." What was *he* doing here? Hadn't he just said that morning that Mr. Mercer had warned him away?

"Don't stop on my account," Thayer said in a sarcastic voice, arms crossed over his chest.

He walked slowly across the front yard. Even with his limp, he had that specific kind of confidence that seemed easy. "So. What's up?"

"We're just hanging out," Emma said foolishly, fumbling for words.

"We?" Thayer's pale eyes flickered next to Emma. When Emma turned her head, she saw Ethan stepping quickly off the porch. His sneakers kicked up gravel as he trekked across the driveway toward his car.

"Ethan?" Emma called. "Where are you going?"

Ethan didn't answer as he strode away. It was like he couldn't get away fast enough. His hands fumbled with the keys as he let himself into his car. He hit the gas, and in a flash, he was gone.

Emma stared at the disappearing cloud of exhaust. What the hell was *that* all about? Next to her, Thayer made a *tsk* sound with his tongue. "Why don't you and your friends leave that poor guy alone?"

"What do you mean?" Emma snapped.

Thayer threw his hands up in surrender. "Don't jump all over me!" He put a sneaker on the porch and leaned forward, flexing his calf. "Seriously, Sutton. First it was that prank where the poor kid lost his science scholarship, and now you're faking a relationship with him?"

Emma stared at him, trying to understand. Slowly, it sunk in. Thayer assumed if Sutton was kissing Ethan, it had to be a part of some prank she and her friends were pulling for the Lying Game. Emma opened her mouth, wanting to make it clear that she and Ethan definitely *were* a real item, but she remembered how hurt he'd looked in the parking and didn't want to rub it in.

"So what are you doing here?" Emma said, deciding to change the subject. "I thought you were scared of my dad."

Thayer shrugged. "Laurel gave me the all clear. I came to hang out with her—it's been forever since we talked."

He moved toward Emma to walk in the house and paused briefly by her side, as if he wanted to say more. He was so close that Emma could smell his pine soap and fresh-smelling clothes. His bare legs were long and muscular. His white soccer sneakers were scuffed and caked with dirt, as though he'd just come off the field. He reminded her of all the hot, unattainable jocks Emma had ever gone to school with, the ones who'd never given her the time of day.

She quickly snapped back to reality. Okay, so Thayer was cute. But *Ethan* was her boyfriend.

Suddenly, a prickly feeling danced across the back of Emma's neck. She turned around, sure she was being watched. A breeze rifled through the leaves of a tall weeping willow. Birds shot up in a cluster, calling to each other with tiny squawks. Emma looked all around, finally noticing a face in the window. It was Laurel, staring at her and Thayer from the living room. Emma raised her hand in a wave, but Laurel just kept glaring. Her light eyes sent a chill straight to Emma's bones. She looked furious enough to kill.

EPILOGUE

As I watched Laurel glare at Emma, a flash of my last memory swarmed my vision. I saw myself hiding in the brush after Thayer had been run down. I'd felt so distraught, so overcome with guilt and fear for his safety. And then I saw two eyes lock with mine. Laurel stared at me with burning rage. Everything in her look said that she blamed me for what happened to Thayer. And I had a strange feeling she was going to do more than just glare at me. Her look said she wanted to reach through the brush and teach me a lesson for all the ways I'd ruined everything.

She looked like she wanted to hurt me—and she looked like she wanted to do the same to Emma now.

In moments, Laurel's face disappeared from the window. Thayer slipped inside the house to see her. My twin remained on the porch, reeling from everything that had just happened, too afraid to admit what she'd just seen.

But I couldn't help but mull it over in my mind. Yes, I'd ruled Laurel out as a suspect. She'd been at Nisha's sleepover all night on the night I died. But there was something about that fact that didn't add up. If Laurel had rescued Thayer from Sabino Canyon, then she hadn't been at Nisha's the whole night. Either Nisha was mistaken . . . or lying . . . or Laurel had snuck out without her knowing.

And if Laurel had snuck away from Nisha's, why couldn't she have snuck away from Thayer, too? Dropped him off at the hospital, then returned for me while he was in surgery. She'd looked so mad. I had ruined her beloved's life. I had had a secret tryst with him, a tryst she wanted to have. I had gotten everything she wanted . . . always.

I hated to think my own flesh and blood could have done such a thing. But that was the wrinkle: Laurel wasn't my flesh and blood. Sure, we'd grown up under the same roof, lived by the same rules our parents had imposed, but there was always a big chasm between us. I was adopted; she wasn't. We never let each other forget that. The only real flesh and blood I had was Emma.

And Emma needed answers, fast. Because it looked like my killer could be closer than either of us realized—maybe even under the very same roof.

~ ACKNOWLEDGMENTS ~

Thanks, as always, to the fantastic team at Alloy, namely Lanie Davis, Sara Shandler, Josh Bank, and Les Morgenstein, as well as Kari Sutherland and Farrin Jacobs at Harper—this was a tough book to write because of the circumstances, and we all pulled together to make it work. I'm also grateful to Kristin Marang for her web and cross-promotional genius—I don't know what I'd do without you! Huge kudos to everyone working on *The Lying Game* TV show, including Gina Girolamo, Andrew Wang, Charles Pratt Jr., and all of the other amazing writers, producers, and crew—not to mention the lovely Alexandra Chando, who plays the best Sutton and Emma

I could imagine. I'm so excited to see what twists and turns are next!

Most of all, a big thanks to Katie Sise—without you, this book wouldn't exist. Thank you, thank you, thank you!

Read on for a preview of
THE LYING GAME
book four

HIDE AND SEEK

⁓ **PROLOGUE** ⁓

DEAD LIKE ME

I'd always thought the afterlife would be like an eternal stay at a resort on St. Barts—hot French waiters bringing me fruity drinks until the end of time, the azure Caribbean sky in a permanent sunset, a cool ocean breeze tickling my forever tanned skin. It would be my reward for living a full, fabulous, long life.

I couldn't have been more wrong.

Instead I died days before my eighteenth birthday and what was supposed to be an amazing senior year. And rather than sipping a mojito on a white-sand beach, I woke up in Las Vegas, tethered to a twin sister I never knew I had. I watched as Emma Paxton was forced into my life and had to begin impersonating me. I watched as she sat at my place at the table with my family and giggled with my friends, pretending she'd known them forever. I watched her read my journal, sleep in my bed, and try to figure out who killed me.

And I seemed to be stuck here until further notice. Everywhere Emma went, I went, too. Everything she knew, I knew as well—the problem was, I didn't know much beyond that. My life before I died was a question mark. Certain things have come back to me—like how I wasn't exactly the nicest girl at Hollier High, how I took for granted all the things I'd been given in life, and how I'd made plenty of enemies by playing vicious pranks on people who didn't deserve it. But everything else was a blank, including how I died, and who murdered me.

One thing I did know was that my killer was now watching Emma's every move right along with me, making sure that she plays along. I was a breath away when Emma found a note saying I was dead and warning her that if she didn't pretend to be me, she'd be dead, too. I felt the stars explode behind Emma's eyes when she was nearly strangled during a sleepover at my best friend Charlotte's house. I had a front-row seat when a light fixture in the school's auditorium careened toward her head. They were all warnings. My killer had been so close. And yet, neither of us had seen who it was.

It was up to my twin to catch my killer, and there was nothing I could do to help. It wasn't like I could communicate with her. Emma had cleared my best friends, Charlotte Chamberlain, Madeline Vega, and Gabby and Lili Fiorello, as murder suspects—they each had alibis for the night of my death. But the alibi she'd been counting on to clear my adoptive little sister, Laurel, suddenly wasn't so airtight.

Now I watched as my family sat on chaise lounges at the local country club, shading their eyes from the brutal Tucson sun. Emma settled into a seat next to Laurel and buried her nose in a magazine, but I could tell she was studying my sister as closely as I was.

Laurel pored over a leather-bound beverage menu through the shade of thick black Gucci sunglasses, then casually rubbed a dollop of tanning oil on her shoulders as though she didn't have a care in the world. Fury streaked through me. *I'll* never feel the sun on my skin again and it might be because of her. She had a motive, after all. We shared a secret crush—and I was the one who got Thayer in the end.

My mother pulled her BlackBerry from her straw Kate Spade beach tote. "You won't believe the way the RSVPs are pouring in for Saturday, Ted," she murmured, staring at the screen. "It looks like you'll be turning fifty-five with a bang."

"Mm-hmm," my dad said absently. It was unclear whether he really heard her. He was too busy looking across the pool at a tall, muscular boy running a hand through his dark hair.

Speak of the devil. Thayer Vega himself.

My heart thumped as Emma glanced in Thayer's direction. Laurel's gaze turned, too. No matter how cool my younger sister tried to play it, she couldn't hide the flash of hope that passed over her face. *Not on your life,* I thought angrily. I may be dead, but Thayer belongs to me—and *only* me. We'd had a secret relationship when I was alive, something that I'd only fully remembered a few days before. For a time, it had seemed like Thayer could have been my killer—we'd had a secret rendezvous the night I died. But thankfully, Emma had cleared him—someone had hit him with my Volvo, maybe aiming for me. Laurel had whisked Thayer off to the hospital, where he'd remained all night. I was relieved he wasn't the one who did it . . . until I realized that maybe the person who did was sitting next to Emma right now. Just because Laurel took Thayer to the hospital didn't mean she stayed with him. She could have come back to give me a piece of her mind . . . or to finish me off forever.

We all watched as Thayer climbed the metal steps of the diving board. He stalked to the end of the board, limping slightly, and tested the spring with a few bounces.

His stomach muscles rippled as he gathered momentum. He raised his tanned arms above his head and dived into the water, cutting the still surface with his perfect form. He stayed under for the length of the pool, little bubbles rising to the surface in his wake. I could almost feel the butterflies fluttering in my no-longer-there stomach as I watched him move beneath the water. Something about Thayer Vega still made me feel so *alive* and it took me a moment to realize that I wasn't.

Laurel's lips flattened into a grim line when Thayer surfaced and grinned at Emma, and I realized something else. If Emma's not careful, she'll end up just like me.

1

DON'T FEED THE EARTHLINGS

Emma Paxton leaned in close to the Saturn-shaped mirror in the Tucson Planetarium and pursed her lips as she reapplied a coat of cherry-flavored gloss.

Taking a deep breath, Emma stared at herself in the mirror. "This is your first official date with Ethan," she said to her reflection. She drew the last word out, savoring it. She couldn't remember the last time she'd been this excited about a guy—she'd dated guys before, but she moved around from foster home to foster home too often to ever really fall for someone. But lately, everything in her life had changed. A new home, a new family, and a new hot guy, Ethan Landry.

And a new identity, too, I wanted to add as I floated behind her, watching her in the mirror. As usual, my reflection wasn't anywhere to be seen. It had been that way ever since I popped into Emma's life when she was still living in Las Vegas. For all intents and purposes, Emma wasn't Emma anymore. She was me, Sutton Mercer. Other than my killer, Ethan was the only person who knew her true identity. He was even helping Emma figure out what happened to me.

Emma's phone pinged with a text. It was Ethan. HERE. JUST GOT TICKETS.

BE OUT IN A SECOND! she typed back.

Emma dried her hands, then pushed through the swinging door, fiddling with Sutton's locket. Her heart picked up speed when she spotted Ethan leaning against a curved, carpeted wall across the crowded room.

She loved how broad his shoulders looked in his gray polo and the way his hair fell into his dark blue eyes. His navy blue Chuck Taylors were unlaced, his hunter green T-shirt hugged his well-defined arms, and his jeans were perfectly broken in. She snaked around the line of people waiting to get into the planetarium and tapped him on the shoulder.

He turned around. "Oh, hey."

"Hey," Emma said, feeling suddenly shy. The last time she'd seen Ethan things had ended a little awkwardly. Thayer Vega had shown up at her house, and Emma hadn't introduced Ethan as her boyfriend. It had seemed cruel, somehow, to tell the boy who'd loved Sutton so desperately that she'd moved on. She'd called Ethan later to explain, and he'd seemed to understand. But what if he hadn't?

Before she had a chance to say anything, though, Ethan pulled Emma to him, and their lips met in a kiss. Emma sighed.

Lucky, I thought. What I wouldn't give to kiss someone again, although Thayer would be my top pick. I was happy for Emma, but I hoped all those love chemicals didn't distract her from the real task at hand: figuring out what the hell had happened to me.

"This looks fun," Emma said, lacing her fingers through his when they broke apart. "Thanks for bringing me here."

"Thanks for coming." Ethan pulled two tickets out of his back pocket. "It seemed appropriate for our first official date. It reminds me of how we first met," he said a little bashfully.

Emma blushed. This was *definitely* at least number three or four on the *Top Ten Cutest Ethan Moments* list. The night she'd arrived in Tucson, before he'd even figured out who she was, they'd looked up at the sky together, and Emma had told him how she named stars. Instead of making fun of her, Ethan had found it interesting.

Ethan walked toward the planetarium entrance. "We still have a little while until the comet," he said. "Want to check out the exhibits?"

Emma nodded.

"I wish teachers made space more interesting," Ethan said, strolling to an exhibit. His brow furrowed in concentration as he studied the photograph. His deep-set blue eyes glanced over the words written below it, his lips moving the tiniest bit as he read. "They make it so dry and bland, it's no wonder no one cares."

"I know what you mean," Emma said. "That's why I like *Star Trek: The Next Generation*. They make space so fantastical that you don't even realize when you're learning something."

Ethan's light eyes widened. "*You're* a Trekkie?"

"Guilty." Emma ducked her head, immediately cringing that she'd revealed something so dorky.

I quickly glanced around. Thank God no one *I* knew was in this place to overhear Emma's shameful admission. The last thing I needed to hit the gossip mill was that Sutton Mercer was into the ultimate nerd TV show.

Ethan just grinned. "Wow. You really *are* the perfect girl." He looked down at her. A slight flush passed over his face. "Any chance this Trekkie has a shot at taking you to the Harvest Dance?"

"I think that could be arranged," Emma said coyly. A headline flashed through her mind: *Foster Girl Gets Asked to Harvest Dance: Miracle!* She'd been making up diary headlines for her life ever since she could remember, and this was one for the front page.

A small child darted past Emma and pressed his hands against the glass in front of the comet display, breaking her from her reverie. She focused on the exhibit in front of them, a photograph of a black hole surrounded by a navy sky spotted with blazing stars. *A black hole is a region of space in which nothing, not even light, can escape*, read a placard next to the photo. Emma shivered, suddenly thinking of Sutton. Was this where she was now? Was this what the afterlife looked like?

Uh, not exactly, I thought.

"You okay?" Ethan asked, his brows knit in concern. "You just got really pale."

"Um, I need some air," Emma mumbled, feeling light-headed.

Ethan led her out the door marked EXIT and into a circular courtyard. Hedges opened up into a small alley, and across the road was a homey restaurant called Pedro's. Colorful Mexican pots sat in the windows, and chili-pepper lights were strung from the ceiling.

Emma and Ethan sat on a bench. She took several deep breaths as a wave of guilt crashed over her.

"Thinking about Sutton, aren't you?" Ethan asked, as if reading her mind.

Emma looked up at him. "Maybe I shouldn't be kissing boys and getting excited about going to dances when my sister's dead."

Ethan's fingers curled around hers. "But don't you think she'd want you to be happy, too?"

Emma shut her eyes, hoping that was what Sutton wanted. But just thinking of Sutton reminded Emma she was in her own version of a black hole: Sutton's life. If she tried to escape being Sutton Mercer, she might die. Even if Sutton's killer was found, Emma would be exposed as a fraud—and then what would happen? She dreamed of the Mercer family taking her in and Sutton's friends welcoming her with open arms, but everyone might be furious that she duped them.

"*I* want to be with you," she said to Ethan after a long beat. "Not as Sutton. As *me*. I'm afraid that will never happen."

"Of course it will." Ethan cupped her chin in his hands. "All this will be over some day. Whatever happens, I'll be there for you."

Emma felt such a rush of gratitude that tears came to her eyes. She moved closer to Ethan, her hip pressing against his. She felt fluttery again as she gazed into his lake-blue eyes and smelled his woodsy aftershave. Ethan leaned in until his lips were a breath away from hers. She was about to kiss him when she heard a familiar laugh.

Emma's head snapped up. "Is that . . . ?" Two figures were being seated on Pedro's outdoor patio. One had blond hair and wore a pink sweater, and the other had on baggy pants and walked with a limp.

"Laurel and Thayer," Ethan whispered grimly, then made a face. "Well, there goes my idea for dinner afterward."

Laurel shook back her golden hair and slipped her arm through Thayer's. She did it casually, and for a moment, Emma wondered if Laurel didn't see her. But then Laurel's eyes cut across the street directly to Emma. A tiny hint of a smile appeared on her face. Not only did she know Emma was there, but she was squeezing Thayer's arm for Emma's benefit.

Bitch, I thought. Laurel had resented my secret relationship with Thayer for a long time. I'm sure she'd been waiting for this moment forever.

Thayer turned, too, and lifted his hand in a half-wave. Emma smiled back, but Ethan's hand tightened on Emma's protectively.

Emma turned to him. "Look, I know you don't like him," she said in a low voice. "But he's not dangerous. There's no way he could have killed Sutton. He was in the hospital all night, remember?"

Ethan looked like he had more to say on the topic, but he let out a sigh instead. "Yeah," he said grudgingly. "I guess. So where does that leave us? Is there anyone we suspect right now?"

Emma's gaze shifted to Laurel, who was peering at Emma over the menu. "Remember how I thought Laurel was at Nisha's the night Sutton disappeared?"

"Yeah, for the tennis team sleepover," Ethan said, nodding.

"Well she wasn't. At least not for the whole time."

Ethan's eyebrows shot up. "Are you sure?"

Emma drummed her fingertips on the bench's wrought-iron armrest. "Laurel is the one who picked Thayer up the night he was hit with the car. She's the one who drove him to the hospital. She couldn't be in two places at once. And if she lied about that . . ."

Ethan leaned forward, a light coming on in his eyes. "You think she dropped Thayer off at the hospital, then went back to the canyon to kill Sutton?"

"I hope not. But I can't rule her out if I don't know where she actually was. I need to find out if she went back to Nisha's or if she was out all night." She fidgeted with the hem of Sutton's black cotton miniskirt. "Laurel just seems so angry. She was able to keep a lid on it until Thayer showed up in Sutton's room and Mr. Mercer called the cops on him. But now that he's back, it feels like she'd do anything to keep him away from the girl he thinks is Sutton—the girl Laurel knows he loves."

"What's the saying? That people kill for money, love, or revenge?" Ethan asked, rubbing his hands together as a cool breeze blew through the courtyard. "Maybe she wanted to get rid of the competition."

"Well, she certainly accomplished that. It looks like they're on a date." Emma glanced across the courtyard again. Thayer rested a hand on Laurel's shoulder. She fed him a chip loaded with guacamole, then shot another self-satisfied smirk in Emma's direction.

I followed Emma's gaze back over to my little sister. Thayer was now giving his order to the waitress, his posture easy and natural. Laurel watched him adoringly, hugging the pale pink sweater-wrap that engulfed her tiny frame. I narrowed my eyes. I recognized that sweater. It, like Thayer, was mine.

Maybe Ethan was right—maybe Laurel wanted everything that was mine. And maybe, just maybe, she had killed me to get it all.

Photo by Austin Hodges

SARA SHEPARD is the author of the #1 *New York Times* bestselling series Pretty Little Liars. She graduated from New York University and has an MFA in Creative Writing from Brooklyn College. Sara has lived in New York, Philadelphia, Pittsburgh, and Arizona, where the Lying Game series is set.

FOLLOW SARA SHEPARD ON

For exclusive information
on your favorite authors and artists,
visit www.authortracker.com.

Don't miss a single scandal!

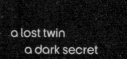

a lost twin
a dark secret
a deadly game

FROM THE CREATOR OF *PRETTY LITTLE LIARS*

THE LYING GAME

© ABC Family

tuesdays at 9/8c